SUNRISE OVER SAPPHIRE BAY

HOLLY MARTIN

CHAPTER ONE

FOURTEEN MONTHS AGO

Aria Philips walked out of her office to find her dad chatting to one of the guests over the reception desk. They were exchanging anecdotes about their golf games and laughing about how bad they were. Her dad had been playing golf as far back as she could remember and he had never seemingly got any better. It never stopped him trekking over to the golf course on the mainland every week to play a round though.

She waited patiently for them to finish talking, although she knew she could be waiting a while. Her dad had all the time in the world for the hotel guests, and most of his day was spent chatting to them. It was no wonder that all those little jobs that needed doing for the smooth running of the hotel never seemed to get done.

The hotel was quiet today. They'd had several guests stay the weekend before for Valentine's Day, but most of them had gone now. Katy, one of the receptionists, was reading a book. There wasn't a lot to do, at least for her. Aria had a list a mile long of things to do; maybe she should delegate some of it.

She glanced around the lobby area, which was filled with

battered leather sofas. There was a young couple sitting on one and giggling over some photos on their phones. Mrs O'Hare, an elderly guest of theirs who had first come a few months before and seemingly spent a lot of time in her room watching porn, was on another sofa. When she wasn't watching porn, Mrs O'Hare swept around the island in a purple cloak and a bright yellow fedora hat with a peacock feather sticking out from the rim. To say she was eccentric was an understatement.

Aria's eyes rested on Noah Campbell tapping away on his laptop and her heart leapt in her chest, which was ridiculous because he was a guest, he'd stay for a few nights, two or three times a year, and then he'd leave. She'd learned many years ago not to get attached to guests. As a kid she'd made friends with the children who stayed in the hotel, playing with them in the gardens and on the beach, and then they would leave at the end of their holiday and she'd never see them again. When she had been in her late teens, early twenties, she'd dated a few men who stayed there, but of course it always had come to an end before even getting started. So she'd learned to be professional, be polite, even be friendly, but to remain detached.

But Noah was different, at least it had started to feel that way. He had got under Aria's skin and made her feel things she'd promised herself she would never feel about a guest. As if he felt her watching him, he glanced up and a beautiful smile crossed his face.

The guest her dad was talking to finally moved away and her dad turned to her, a huge smile on his face.

'How's my beautiful girl this morning?' He opened up his arms. She smiled and stepped up as he enveloped her in a big bear hug. There really was nothing professional about Thomas Philips. He didn't care that there were hotel guests nearby, if he wanted to hug his daughter then he would.

'What are you doing here?' Aria said, smiling against his chest. 'You're supposed to be retired, enjoying more golf, relaxing.'

Her father had asked her to take over as hotel manager the week before, although she'd been doing the job unofficially for years. He'd said he was going to enjoy himself, paint, take up pottery, maybe travel a bit, but it seemed he was having trouble stepping back completely and had been here every day ever since. Thomas still lived upstairs in the same apartment he'd shared with her mum; the same place Aria had grown up in with her twin sisters. Her sisters had left the island many years before and she herself now lived in one of the hotel's cottages out in the grounds. She had talked about swapping with her dad so she could be closer to the hotel if anything happened, and so he could enjoy the peace and quiet a bit more, but her dad didn't really do change.

'Oh you know, just catching up on a bit of paperwork before I leave on my world cruise.'

There was no world cruise, they didn't have any money for that kind of thing, but her father liked to talk about it nonetheless. She imagined him on a cruise, flirting with all the women, doing ballroom dancing, seeing the sights. He would fit right in. Maybe next year they would have enough money to send him on a small cruise, something in Europe perhaps. It certainly wasn't going to happen this year. She'd seen the finances and they weren't good. The hotel wasn't in great shape and that had started to show in the number of guests. Things needed to change and, now she was in charge, she was going to be the one to do it.

Aria stepped back. 'While you're here, I was thinking of doing a bit of redecorating...'

He was already shaking his head. 'When I'm dead and buried you can make as many changes as you want, but this

3

place…' he looked around wistfully. 'Your mum and I had so much fun decorating this place when we first bought it. We would argue over colours and wallpaper patterns and she always won. We had no guests here, no staff, just us for six months, and we made use of that privacy in every room, believe me.'

Aria cringed at that image. When her mum had been alive she and Thomas had never been able to keep their hands off each other. They were always hugging and kissing or holding hands. She had never seen a couple as in love as her parents were. When her mum died about fourteen years before, when Aria had been sixteen and the twins were ten, her dad had been utterly heartbroken. He hadn't painted or changed anything in the hotel since, as if clinging onto the old paint and wallpaper was holding onto her memory. Aria had so many ideas of things she wanted to change around here but Thomas wouldn't budge and they'd had the same argument many times before. Maybe now he had tentatively retired she could get things done, at least in the guest bedrooms where he wouldn't notice them.

She wanted to push it but her dad sat down with a heavy sigh and she noticed how tired he looked. He had been looking quite pale lately, though when she'd asked him about it he'd simply dismissed it as getting over a cold – or man flu as he liked to call it. He'd had several appointments at the hospital but he'd told her that it was because they were trialling some new things for his diabetes. She hoped it wasn't something more. Maybe she should go with him next time.

'I can't wait to see Clover and Skye tomorrow,' her dad said, grabbing a piece of paper and folding it into a perfect paper plane.

'It's been too long since they were both here,' Aria said.

She loved her sisters, and she knew they loved her, but

there was this disconnect between them. Clover and Skye shared this twinnie bond that she wasn't a part of. When they'd been growing up, the twins had been completely inseparable and, even though life had taken them in different directions since then, Aria knew they spoke to each other on the phone every single day. The three of them had a WhatsApp group where they chatted to each other but she knew that Clover and Skye also had a separate chat just for the two of them. Maybe it was the fact that Aria was six years older, or maybe it was that she hadn't shared a womb with them, but whatever it was she wasn't as close to them as she would like.

She ignored the tiny seed of doubt in her mind that said it was because she was adopted and not their real sister, because she knew that was more about her own issues than anything they had ever said or done.

'I'm looking forward to seeing them,' Aria said, honestly. It was always nice to have the whole team back together again. Minus their mum, of course.

Her dad tweaked the aeroplane and then launched it across the lobby. It soared through the air in a perfect arc and landed expertly on top of Noah's laptop. Her dad let out a giggle like a schoolboy caught doing something he shouldn't have been.

Noah looked up and laughed. He picked up the plane. 'I don't think this belongs here.'

Her dad shrugged. 'Or maybe it ended up exactly where it was meant to be.'

Aria suppressed a giggle. 'Dad, he's probably really busy—'

She stopped as a balled-up bit of paper bounced off the side of her face. She looked round at Noah. 'Hey, I didn't throw the plane.'

'Guilty by association. Besides, I was aiming for your dad.'

He stood up, picked up his laptop and walked over to

them. Aria's heart thundered in her chest. God, this man, why did he affect her so much?

'It was probably time I stopped working anyway. I am supposed to be on holiday, after all.' Noah's eyes fell on Aria. 'Would you like to join me for a walk?'

Aria wanted to say no, she had so much work to do, but she was already nodding and her dad was taking the papers from her hand and Noah's laptop from him and shooing them off. She rolled her eyes at the complete lack of discretion. Thomas adored Noah and probably harboured hopes that one day she would get married to him and provide her dad with lots of grandchildren. Aria had never admitted that she secretly hoped for that too.

They stepped outside. The day was warm for February but there was still a nip in the air. Daffodils and tulips were starting to bud and bloom, adding colour to the gardens.

'How's your dad?' Noah asked, shrugging out of his jacket and draping it around her shoulders. She slipped her arms into the sleeves and inhaled his wonderful tangy citrusy scent that lingered on the material.

'He's fine, I think,' she sighed. 'He doesn't look right though, does he?'

'No, I thought that as soon as I arrived. He's lost weight.'

'I thought that too, but I see him every day so it's hard to notice it. He said he's just getting over a cold, so maybe it's that. He's certainly not told me if it's anything else.'

'Well, I'm having lunch with him later, I'll see if he'll tell me anything.'

'And report back.'

'Of course.'

She paused as she picked a tulip from one of the beds, fingering the soft wet petals. 'Thank you for asking after him.'

'Thomas has always been a good friend. You both have,' Noah said.

Friend. She tried to push away the feeling of disappointment that settled in her stomach with that label.

She sniffed the tulip, which smelt divine. Noah was watching her and she held it up for him to smell. As he bent his head down, she thrust the flower over his nose, soaking his face. She burst out laughing at his shocked expression and ran away from him. She heard him laughing as he chased after her.

'Oh, you're going to pay for that, Aria Philips.'

He caught up with her, looping an arm around her stomach and pulling her against him. Desire slammed into her at the feel of his hard body against hers.

'Get off,' Aria laughed, trying to wiggle from his grasp, but not trying too hard. To her surprise, he pulled a felt-tip pen from his pocket, yanked off the lid with his teeth and started trying to draw on her face. 'No! What are you doing?' Aria shrieked.

'It's called revenge.'

'No, I have to speak to guests, I can't have a black moustache or whatever else you plan to draw on me. It's not professional.'

'OK, not your face,' Noah said, scooping her long dark hair away from her neck.

'No!' Aria laughed.

'Keep still, or you'll ruin my beautiful drawing.'

She didn't know why but she allowed him to draw something on her. Actually she did know why, because his fingers on her skin, his warm breath on the back of her neck, was one of the most wonderful feelings in the world and she wanted to prolong that experience for as long as possible, at whatever cost.

'What are you drawing?'

'Something which sums you up perfectly.'

'If you're drawing a pig, then me and you will be having words.'

He laughed. 'There, all done.'

'I'm not sure being branded is a fair exchange for getting you wet with the tulip.'

'Well, I tell you what, you can get me back for it later.'

She smiled and they walked on for a little while.

They stopped at the top of Sapphire Bay. It was a long stretch of white sand that curved round almost the whole western corner of Jewel Island. It was fringed by dunes and long grass and was often the place the locals and many a holiday-maker would go for secret liaisons. She had stumbled across far too many amorous couples in her time on the island so now she gave the dunes a wide berth. The sea was calm here, protected from the elements by the large cliffs that curled out into the bay like a pair of arms hugging the beach. At the end of the beach a natural arch in the cliff led to the secluded Emerald Cove which marked the end of the gardens at Philips Hotel.

They started walking down the steps to the beach, which were wet and a little slippery from the rain the previous night. After a few moments, Noah took her hand to make sure she didn't fall. They reached the bottom but he didn't let go of her hand, a gesture which filled her heart with useless hope.

The sun was glinting on the green waters of the bay, the sky a pale cornflower blue with fluffy white candyfloss clouds gently bobbing by as they made their way along the beach.

'God, I love this place,' Noah said. 'I had no idea when I first came here four years ago for Elsie's ninetieth birthday that I would keep coming back here so often but it draws you in.'

She remembered that first weekend he'd stayed. Noah had started talking to her dad as he worked in the hotel business too, buying and developing hotels, although big shiny city hotels, not quaint old Victorian hotels like their Philips Hotel on a tiny little island off the Cornish coast. Noah and her dad had got on like a house on fire, despite the age gap. The connection between Noah and Aria had been instant too, like two best friends who had known each other for years. He was just so incredibly easy to talk to. He had stayed at the hotel a few months later when he'd popped in to visit Elsie again. He was British but lived in America so didn't get over to the UK as often as he liked. But he was very close to Elsie after she had taken him in when he was younger and so he visited as often as he could.

Then there was the next time he'd stayed...

'It's funny how life works out sometimes, the places you never knew existed that become so important to you,' Noah said. 'I had a crappy childhood...' He paused for a moment as if he was remembering. He'd mentioned that to her before but had never gone into details. 'And that led to me living with Elsie. When she moved here to be closer to her sister, and I ended up moving to America, we stayed in touch and that led me to come here too. I am so grateful that I've found Jewel Island, this little slice of heaven.'

'I'm always happy to have you back here, I miss you when you're not here,' Aria said and then winced inwardly. Was that too much?

They walked on in silence for a while, her hand still in his as they climbed back up the steps at the far end of the beach and into the gardens of Philips Hotel. There was a little shack here, overlooking Emerald Cove. It used to be a beach café but they'd closed it many years before.

9

'Do you remember the weekend of Elsie's funeral?' Noah asked.

She nodded. She remembered it vividly. Mainly because it was that weekend that she'd realised she was falling for this wonderful man. Knowing how close he was to Elsie, Aria had given Noah a hug as soon as he'd walked into the hotel, to say how sorry she was for his loss, but that hug had seemed to change everything between them. He'd held her so tight and for the longest time, as if he'd never been held like that before in his life, and with his arms wrapped around her, his heart pounding against her cheek, she'd felt this feeling of love slam into her, her heart swelling for him so it ached in her chest.

It was also on that visit that she learned he'd just got married, which came as something of a surprise as she hadn't known he was seeing someone. He seemed almost apologetic when he told her about his wife, Georgia. Apparently it had happened very quickly. Aria was pleased for him although he didn't seem that happy and it felt like it was a lot more than grief for Elsie.

She kind of presumed she'd never see him again after that. With Elsie gone, there was nothing on the island for him to return to. Yet he did, taking regular breaks from work. He said he loved the views, the solitude, the slower pace of life, although Aria got the impression it was something more than that. He never came with his wife though. He'd spend time walking round the island and the beaches and sometimes Aria would go with him.

They'd talk and laugh or sometimes just walk in companionable silence. Each time he came she felt like she learned a little bit more. She'd told him about her feelings about being adopted and growing up as the older sister to twins, with their incredibly close twin bond. He'd spoken to her about his job, buying and selling hotels, she knew he had a half-brother, called Charlie, who he wasn't that close to. They'd talked about the difficulties he was having with his wife. Later he'd talked to her about his divorce and how he felt like a failure for not making his marriage work. She'd even been there for him when his dog died. They had become incredibly close but she knew it was silly to have these feelings for him. He would leave after a few days, just as he always did. How could they start something when he was hardly ever here?

'I think it was that weekend that I realised that one day I wanted this place to be my home. I'd never had that before, never even wanted a home. I'd had somewhere I lived but that was a big difference. I thought about it a lot over the last few years, getting a little house overlooking Sapphire Bay, maybe a dog.' He paused. 'I thought a lot about you too. Back then it felt like an impossible dream. But now I'm divorced, it finally feels like I could make a home here one day.' He glanced at her. 'How would you feel if I did move here?'

Her heart filled with hope but then deflated again. His job required him to travel a lot and by all accounts he was very good at what he did. He was not going to give up his glamorous life of staying in exotic locations around the world for a tiny cottage on little Jewel Island. His words echoed in her mind. *I could make a home here one day.* Did he mean he'd retire here in the far-off distant future?

They approached her favourite willow tree, the drooping branches touching the floor. The leaves on the tree were only just starting to bloom but the old branches still provided a wooden screen. Still holding his hand, she pushed the branches to one side and pulled him under.

There was a small area here, sheltered from the outside world, that she'd used as a den when she was a kid. She'd pulled one of the garden benches under here and her dad had even put some shelves up for her to store her things, all those knick-knacks that had been important to her as a child.

'I spent many hours here as a child. It's one of my favourite places because you can see most of the island through here.' She pulled him over to a gap in the branches that overlooked Sapphire Bay and Emerald Cove on one side of the trunk and the little village on the other, the brightly coloured shops and houses, people carrying on with their lives. She pointed out her favourite flower shop and her godmother Kendra's bakery. She paused before she carried on speaking. He knew some of what she was going to tell him but not all of it.

'I was found, wrapped in blankets on a ferry from Spain to England when I was only a few weeks old. I know nothing of my birth parents, nobody does. I can't say if I'm Egyptian or Arabian as I have no idea where I'm from. It was thought I might possibly be from Turkey – the blanket I was wrapped in had a Turkish price tag on. But that doesn't really prove anything. If ever there was something to make me feel like I didn't fit, it's the "Other" box I tick when I have to describe my ethnicity on any government forms, as if I'm something indefinable. I've always struggled with where I belong. I've always kind of felt like a round peg in a square hole, sort of fitting but not quite. Although that was probably due to my own issues than anyone making me feel that way. Being abandoned as a baby has left quite a few residual scars. My parents adored me – there are hundreds of photos of me growing up at the hotel, surrounded by my parents who clearly idolised me, and for a while it was just us, the three musketeers.'

She smiled as she remembered her time exploring the beaches and rockpools with her parents.

'And then Mum fell pregnant with Clover and Skye. When they were born, these blonde-haired, blue-eyed little cherubs, I had never been so aware of my differences before. I stuck out like a sore thumb in the family photos. In a sea of blonde, I looked like some random brown kid who had photobombed their beautiful, perfect family portrait. But this place, Jewel Island, welcomed me with open arms. No one cared that I was the only non-white person on the island, no one cared that I was adopted. And, despite my issues of not feeling like I fitted, like something was missing, this place is my home and I cannot imagine living anywhere else. One day, I will raise a family here, with or without a man to help me. And I'll grow old and grey here.'

She turned to face him. 'Everyone leaves Jewel Island. The children of the guests that I made friends with promised to keep in touch but they never did. The guests, they come and say how beautiful this place is and then they leave. The children I grew up with on the island, most of them have left too. Clover and Skye left the first chance they could. I've come to expect it now. I really really like you, Noah. I love spending time with you and laughing and talking with you, and of course I'd like it to be something more, but I'd really appreciate it if you didn't offer me a bunch of empty promises.'

'My promises are definitely full.'

She laughed and his face grew serious. He rested his hands on her shoulders.

'Whenever I've thought about making a life here, you were always a part of that. I'd like to move here, as soon as I can, and I'd like nothing more than to grow old and grey together.'

She had no words at all. In all her wildest dreams she had never imagined this.

'Aria, I'm going to kiss you now, something I should have done a very long time ago.'

He bent his head at the same time she leaned up and suddenly they were kissing and it was everything she had ever imagined it would be, like two halves connecting. His kiss was gentle as he wrapped his arms around her. She slid her hands around his neck, pressing herself up against him. God, she had wanted this so much for so long. She pulled back briefly to look at him. His eyes were filled with affection and warmth and she leaned up and kissed him again.

Noah's phone beeped in his jacket pocket and she pulled back.

'Crap, sorry,' he said, brushing his hand through his hair. 'I have lunch with your dad now and, as much as I love your dad, I'd much rather stay here with you.'

Aria smiled, shrugging out of his jacket and handing it back to him. 'Go, he said he's got something to ask you.'

'What's that?'

'I have no idea.'

Noah sighed. 'I better go. Would you like to have dinner with me tonight? In my suite, where we have more time and no interruptions.'

She was suddenly unable to find any words as images of what might happen once she arrived in his suite flashed vividly through her mind. God, she wasn't ready for that. They'd had one kiss. Well, that and years of flirting, but still, it seemed a sudden leap. Maybe he just meant dinner and this was all completely innocent.

'I'd like that a lot,' Aria smiled.

'And if you really don't like the tattoo I gave you, then we can wash it off… in the shower.'

Her heart thundered in her chest. There could be no mistaking his intentions now and there wasn't a single part of her that didn't want that.

He gave her another brief kiss and then stepped back, parted the branches and ran back to the hotel.

She smiled as she leaned against the trunk. Her whole life

had been on this tiny island, but right now her world seemed that little bit bigger.

Aria was sitting in reception a while later, giving Katy a fifteen-minute break. She had never been so happy before in her life. She ran her fingers gently over her lips. She could still taste Noah there and she couldn't wait to kiss him again later in his suite. She'd seen him and her dad talking over lunch earlier. Sometimes she would join them in their meetings and they'd talk about hotels or put the world to rights, but her dad had specifically said that lunch today was a private chat. It had looked very serious, whatever it was.

She moved her fingers to where Noah had drawn on the back of her neck. She'd looked at the drawing as soon as she'd got back to the hotel and found a small heart, which had made her smile even more. All of this felt too good to be true, but it was: they had kissed, he had talked about moving here.

Noah suddenly walked into reception and her heart soared at the sight of him. It took her a few seconds to realise he was dragging his suitcase behind him.

She stood up. 'Are you leaving?'

He nodded, looking distraught. 'Something's come up.'

'Are you OK, what's happened?' Aria said.

He shook his head. 'I'm sorry, I really am.'

'For what?'

This wasn't making any sense.

'For… before, in the garden…'

She stared at him in shock. He was back-pedalling, going back on what he'd promised her.

'Wait, you're coming back, right?' Aria said.

15

After the longest time, Noah shook his head. 'I don't think that's a good idea.'

Her eyes widened. She instinctively touched the heart he'd drawn on the back of her neck and his mouth pulled into a tight line.

'I'm so sorry.' He handed her his business card. 'Can you email me my invoice and I'll make sure it gets paid.'

She just stared at him, finding no words at all as he started to walk away. He turned back. 'Aria, I will always be here for you, as a friend. If you need me, if you want to talk, as friends, then my number is on the card.'

'Friends? After what we just shared, that's what you're offering?' Aria said, finding her voice.

'That's all I can offer right now, I'm sorry.'

With that he turned and walked away, taking her heart with him on his way out.

CHAPTER TWO

PRESENT DAY

Aria stared at Noah Campbell's name on the reservation list and sighed. That day they'd kissed had been the last day she had been truly happy and then everything had fallen apart. She had been devastated by Noah's betrayal, hurt that she had trusted him, angry that after what she had told him, he'd still left.

But then everything had got a whole lot worse. A few days after Skye and Clover had got there, her dad told them all that he had only a few weeks to live. By Easter he had gone, and if Aria had thought the pain Noah caused her was bad, it was nothing compared to that of losing her beloved dad.

Noah had called several times after her dad had died, but she'd never taken any of his calls. He'd been at the funeral, of course. There had been people there from all over the world to give her dad the big send-off he deserved. Noah had given her his condolences – he possibly might have squeezed her shoulder, she couldn't remember, the whole day had been a bit of a blur. He'd told her they needed to talk, and to give him a call when she was ready. But she'd never called him. She didn't want to hear how the kiss had been a mistake. After he'd let her down so spectacularly, she didn't want to talk to him at all.

Except today he was coming back and he wasn't staying for a few days as he had on all his previous visits, he was going to be here for a month, and she had no idea why.

She didn't know how she was supposed to react to him when he arrived, but she was damned sure she wasn't going to hide away from him.

She picked up her clipboard so she looked busy and walked out into the reception area.

'Has Mr Campbell arrived yet?' Aria asked Tilly, one of the receptionists.

'Not yet,' Tilly said.

Aria glanced up at the amusement in Tilly's voice and saw she was smirking at her.

'What's that tone for?' Aria said.

'Well, it's the fourth time you've asked today.'

Aria let out a heavy breath, giving up the act. She had known Tilly all her life and there was no point trying to hide anything from her.

'It's not what you think,' Aria said. Well, it had been exactly what Tilly was thinking but not anymore. 'There was... a bit of a bad experience the last time Mr Campbell was here and I'd rather I met him head on.'

Tilly rubbed her oversized belly as she eased back onto the chair. The poor girl probably should have gone on maternity leave a few weeks before but Aria knew that Tilly didn't want to let her down. Tilly hadn't quite reached her due date yet but Aria guessed the baby would arrive any day now.

Tilly fixed her with a look, seemingly not convinced. 'It feels like something more to me. You seem nervous and agitated and I've never seen you like this before for any guest. I can't decide if you're happy about seeing him or angry.'

Aria didn't know the answer to that either because infuriatingly she *had* missed Noah. She picked up the vase of fresh flowers and moved them over to the other side of the reception desk, playing for time. She turned them slightly so they caught the light from the sun streaming in through the door.

Tilly might know everything there was to know about Aria but she hadn't worked in the hotel when Noah Campbell used to stay there on a fairly regular basis, she hadn't seen him flirt with Aria and witnessed the time they'd spent talking to each other. Tilly didn't know that Aria and Noah had actually become good friends and that he always gave her a big hug whenever he arrived. And Tilly didn't know that the last time Noah had stayed in the hotel he had kissed her and it had been the hottest kiss of her life.

She realised Tilly was still waiting for an answer.

'Actually,' Aria lowered her voice conspiratorially. 'I want to get some advice about the hotel. He works in the hotel industry so...'

'Are you still thinking of selling it?' Tilly asked.

Aria sighed and sat down next to Tilly. 'That's the last thing I want but...'

She looked around the reception area, which was deserted. It was the end of the Easter bank holiday weekend, and the start of the school holidays. They were two weeks away from the famous Jewel Island festival of light, one of the biggest events in the island's calendar. The sun had been shining for weeks, the hotel was right on the edge of Sapphire Bay, one of the most beautiful beaches in the world, and, despite all this, Philips Hotel was running less than a quarter full. In fact, she couldn't remember the last time the hotel had been fully booked.

The place was tired, she knew that, but her dad hadn't

wanted to change anything and really there wasn't any money to redecorate anyway.

Aria and her sisters had a meeting with the solicitor tomorrow where any money from her dad's estate would finally be handed over. Aria was hoping there would be enough to start doing the hotel up, although Francis Cole, her dad's solicitor and best friend, had been very vague and evasive about how much money they would actually be getting. Apparently there were... *complications*, although Francis had assured her it was nothing to worry about. Aria had given up trying to get answers from him and been content for him to sort out the estate and let her know when it was all finalised, which apparently it now was.

'But it also depends on what Clover and Skye want as well,' Tilly said, sympathetically. 'Have you spoken to them about it yet?'

Aria shook her head.

She clicked through the reservations for the coming weeks in the vain hope that the hotel had had a sudden influx since the last time she'd looked.

Clover and Skye had never wanted to be responsible for the hotel. As soon as they were both old enough they had left Jewel Island and found their own way in the world. Their parents had instilled in them that they could do anything, be anyone they wanted to be, and both the twins had grabbed hold of that sense of confidence and ran with it. They had pursued lives that didn't include making beds and smiling at every customer even if they were assholes.

When they'd come back and been told the news that their dad was dying, they'd extended their stay, wanting to make the most of every second they could with him. But Aria was surprised they hadn't returned to their lives after Thomas had died. Perhaps it was because the sisters only had each other now both their parents were gone; Aria had the impression they needed this time together to grieve and support each other. She wasn't sure how much longer they'd stay, though, they both had their own lives to return to.

Skye had been working in Canada running her own ice cream and waffle shop. There had been a man, Jesse, her ex-husband, which… was complicated, but Aria knew her sister had been very happy there. She had left that behind to come and work as a chef at a tiny hotel, on a remote island off Cornwall that no one really knew existed. Jesse and a few other staff members were keeping the shop running in her absence but surely that couldn't continue indefinitely.

Clover had been working for a gym in London teaching various fitness classes. Aria knew she hadn't exactly loved working for the gym as her boss was a complete cow, so Clover had quite happily quit to stay at the Philips Hotel. Teaching Pilates, yoga, Zumba and other aerobic classes was something she'd really enjoyed though, and Aria was sure her sister missed that. Clover had done a business and accountancy course with a view to one day opening up her own dance studio and right now she was using some of those business skills to balance the books in the hotel on a daily basis and handle reservations. She was also making a desperate and futile attempt to set the hotel up as a wedding venue. It was obviously not what she wanted to do with her life.

Aria did wonder if, once the estate was finalised, the twins would take their money and go back to their own lives. Because, as beautiful as Jewel Island was, everyone left. If they wanted their share of the hotel, she would have to sell it and there was a tiny part of her that wondered if that might be for the best.

She had been working in the hotel since she was a teen. She knew how to make a reservation on the new-fangled computer system, she was on top of ordering food and other things the hotel needed, and felt she was good at co-ordinating and organising the staff. However, she didn't know the first thing about marketing or what she could do, beyond a lick of paint, to put the hotel back on the map again.

But if she was to sell it what else could she do, where could she go? She had never found her niche in life like her sisters had. She had always been here. The Philips Hotel was her home and it would break her heart if she lost it. But she didn't want her sisters to lose their way of life either.

And it wasn't just her and her sisters who would be affected by the fate of the hotel. There were the staff who worked there, the islanders, too, who all depended on the hotel. So much would change on the island if the hotel was sold and Aria didn't want that. Jewel Island had given her a home.

She really should have spoken to Skye and Clover before now about what they intended to do when their dad's estate was finalised, but if she was honest she was scared of their answer. She had loved having them here over the last year and didn't want them to leave.

She had told Tilly the truth: she did want to speak to Noah about all of this in the hope he might be able to help her with the hotel if she could just put their past and that kiss behind them.

She picked up the phone and rang through to the kitchen. After a few rings, Skye answered.

'Skye, I'm popping into the village. Do you need anything for dinner tonight?'

'Umm, you could get some more bread. The guests seem to go through that like there's no tomorrow. Oh, and could you get some pink food colouring? I might try to make some candyfloss for dessert.'

Aria smiled. There was always something unique and wonderful for dessert since Skye had started working in the kitchen. The guests loved it.

'OK, no problem,' Aria said and hung up, turning back to Tilly. 'I have to go and walk Mrs O'Hare's dog; will you call me when he arrives?' She indicated the walkie-talkie.

'Sure will.'

Aria walked off down the corridor where some of the guest bedrooms were. She knocked on Mrs O'Hare's door and there was the sound of a big deep woof and then scrabbling at the door.

'Snowflake, down,' Mrs O'Hare shouted, which evidently Snowflake ignored as he continued to jump up and scratch at the door.

If ever there was a dog that was inappropriately named it was Snowflake. Snowflake suggested the dog was small and delicate. The bedroom door opened and a monster Pyrenean Mountain Dog barged out and pinned her up against the wall, licking her face affectionately, his whole body wagging with the force of his tail.

'Oh, you are naughty,' Mrs O'Hare giggled as she stared at her dog fondly, making no attempt to remove him from where he stood, front paws on Aria's shoulders, tongue lapping over Aria's face, while she stood there with a fixed smile on her face. She liked dogs, but this was a bit too close for comfort. 'Snowflake likes you.'

Mrs O'Hare was a tiny elderly lady and Snowflake was so huge Mrs O'Hare could probably put a saddle on him and ride him around the island.

'Aria is going to take you for a nice walk,' Mrs O'Hare said in a sing-song voice and impossibly Snowflake's tail wagged even harder.

Snowflake finally leapt down, releasing his prey, and Mrs

O'Hare clicked on the lead, handed Aria the ball thrower and shut the door before Aria could utter a word. A few seconds later the sounds of groaning and gasping could be heard as Mrs O'Hare returned to her porn. It was always the same. Mrs O'Hare had been a few times over the last year or so and every time she would stay in her room and watch porn for almost the entirety of her stay. Then she'd leave with a big grin on her face and a spring in her step. There had been several complaints from guests in the beginning because the volume on the TV or laptop was always turned up so loudly. Aria had resolved it by not putting any other guests near Mrs O'Hare whenever she stayed. Better that than confront Mrs O'Hare about her porn habit.

Snowflake, to his credit, walked fairly slowly down the hall as he sniffed at every doorway, and even when he got outside there was no pulling. A dog his size could very easily dictate the walk, but Snowflake was quite happy to go wherever Aria wanted to go. He was probably just relieved to get away from all the porn.

She walked down the steps onto Sapphire Bay and let Snowflake off the lead. He immediately ran down to the shore and splashed around in the waves.

Snowflake didn't do balls; he didn't really understand the concept of them. He did, however, do stones. Aria had got very good at throwing stones for Snowflake – she was sure that many an Olympic discus or javelin thrower would be jealous of her stone-throwing skills.

She scooped up a stone with the ball thrower and launched it into the sea. Snowflake crashed through the waves after the stone and then returned shortly after to wait for her to throw another. She was happy to oblige as she meandered down the beach.

Once she reached the other end, she put Snowflake back

on the lead and climbed up the steps that led over the headland and down to the village. The Philips Hotel sat on top of a peninsula so some rooms benefitted from the sunrises over Sapphire Bay and some bedrooms were able to enjoy the sunsets over Pearl Beach. From the top of the headland she could see almost the whole of Jewel Island lying out in front of her. There was Jade Harbour at the furthest point from the hotel with all the little sail boats bobbing around in the gentle breeze. The sun sparkled off Crystal Stream, which started at the very top of the island before it joined Moonstone Lake then tumbled down through Ruby Falls, meandered through Amber Fields and ended up in the sea near the village. It was such a pretty little place and had been very popular with the tourists over the years. *Had.*

Aria sighed.

Tourists had stopped coming to the island in their droves many years before and she knew that the hotel was partly responsible for that. The reviews for the hotel in recent years had been far from positive. Many mentioned the faded, outdated décor and the tatty carpets, and this had had a knock-on effect in terms of how many guests wanted to stay. There wasn't a ton of money coming into the island and people had been forced to close the doors on the shops and businesses and seek a living somewhere else. There were still around eight hundred people who lived on the island but Aria remembered when it had been more like two thousand. She wanted to do something to bring the tourists back to the hotel, not just for her benefit but for the people of the island too.

The only problem was she had no idea what.

She took a cobbled path down into Silver Street and walked past the little shops, many of which were closed.

The shops were all arranged perfectly in a bouquet of

bright colours, most of them around the edges of the large village green. The illuminations for the festival of light in a few weeks were already strewn across the green and between the shops, some of them simple strings of lights, some of them suns, moons and stars. Even in the daylight, it looked beautiful.

She waved at Mira, the florist, as she rearranged the tulips in bunches outside her shop.

'Aria, how are you?' Mira said, warmly.

'I'm good.' Aria glanced inside the shop to see how it was decorated today. It always looked like some kind of fairy grotto with lights and great swathes of material hanging from the ceiling and flowers woven between it all. The inside of the shop changed almost weekly with the different seasons and flowers, but it was always a magical dramatic backdrop to sell Mira's flowers.

'I've been thinking about you,' Mira went on. 'I bet you'll be glad when tomorrow is over and your dad's estate is finalised.'

'It'll be nice to finally have it all sorted.'

'Are you worried?'

Aria picked up one of the tulips and smelt it. Mira was really asking if Aria was worried that the rumours were true, that Thomas Philips had left all his money to Clover and Skye, his real children. But her dad had adored her and he'd never treated her any differently to how he treated Skye and Clover. She might not be his flesh and blood but she was his family.

'No, I'm not,' Aria said.

'Death and wills are a funny thing though, aren't they,' Mira said. 'You think you know someone...'

Aria knew Mira was now referring to her own husband who had died two years before. He had left every penny to a woman Mira had never met who he'd apparently been having an affair with for the last thirty years. Death had a way of bringing all the skeletons out of the closet.

'These look beautiful,' Aria said, changing the subject.

'Thank you, I just wish that more of the islanders and tourists felt the same. You've been my only customer for the last few weeks.'

Aria felt horribly guilty about that. 'I think many of the shops just haven't opened for the main season yet and so the owners are either not here or are a bit short of cash. I suppose buying fresh flowers is a bit of a luxury. The guests at the hotel always comment about how beautiful the table arrangements and flowers around the hotel are though.'

'That's nice to hear,' Mira smiled weakly. 'Are you still leaving my cards next to the flowers so the guests can order their own flowers from me?'

'I do, but I guess people are not going to take a bunch of flowers with them when they leave. It's not like they can put it in their suitcase.'

'No, I suppose not,' Mira sighed. 'I think this year will be my last on the island. People are just not buying my flowers anymore and I don't think I can afford to stay when so little money is coming in.'

Aria stared at her in shock.

'No, you can't leave, you've always been here,' she said, desperately. Why did everyone always leave?

'And my grandkids are getting older every day and I never see them. I could buy a little place near them and enjoy my retirement.'

'But what about the flower shop?'

'Maybe someone who loves flowers as much as me will buy it,' Mira said, giving Aria a meaningful look.

Aria smiled and shook her head. 'As lovely as that would be, I have a hotel to run and I'm not exactly making a success out of that. The island needs you and your magic touch, no one else could compete with that. Look, don't make any decisions just yet. I'm sure we can think of something to help you.'

God, what was she promising? The hotel had no money and Aria was already spending money they didn't have in Mira's shop every week. She couldn't afford to pay her any more. But she couldn't help feeling a little bit responsible for the fact that so many shops were closing.

'You've done plenty,' Mira said. 'You don't need to worry about me. You have enough to worry about.'

And the list was getting bigger every day.

'I better go, we'll have some of these tulips in our next order,' Aria said.

Mira nodded and Aria walked on.

Aria spotted Delilah Quinn and her fourteen-year-old daughter, Izzy. Delilah had been the most popular girl in school; pretty, funny, clever. Aria had always admired her even though she was two years younger than Aria. And of course Delilah had dated Blake Jackson, the most popular boy in school. But when Delilah had fallen pregnant when she was only fifteen and Blake had done a runner and left her to raise her daughter alone, Aria found herself admiring Delilah for completely different reasons.

Recently, Delilah had been diagnosed with cancer, and although the doctors were confident she would make a full recovery, the treatment was seemingly taking its toll. She'd had surgery and chemotherapy and was now undertaking radiotherapy just to be completely thorough.

Aria walked over to her. It had been a few weeks since she'd seen her and the brightly coloured headscarf she was wearing made her skin look paler. She had also lost a lot of weight, the chemotherapy she'd recently finished obviously not agreeing with her, but she always had a smile on her face.

'Delilah, how you doing?' Aria said, giving Izzy a warm smile as she made a fuss of Snowflake.

'I'm doing good,' Delilah said. 'I have one more week of radiotherapy, then I'm done. I cannot wait not to have to make that journey every day. The doctors are pleased though, they believe they removed all the cancer cells in surgery, and the chemotherapy and radiotherapy is to make sure it hasn't spread,' she added, glancing over her shoulder at Izzy who was putting her headphones in her ears and fiddling around with her iPod. The mask fell briefly from Delilah's face. 'I lost my job,' she said, quietly.

'What?'

'I get it, I've had so much time off recently.'

'Because you've been sick,' Aria said, incredulously.

'They can't hold my job open indefinitely.'

'Why not, you've worked for that shop for years.'

Delilah shrugged. 'It's fine, well, it's not. I have no idea how I'll pay the bills now but I'm sure something will come up.'

'If you need a job, you've got one,' Aria said. The hotel had no money but she would find a way to pay her somehow.

'That's very kind. And I may take you up on that in a few weeks. I just need to get this radiotherapy finished first and then sleep for a year but, after that, I may come and see you.'

'Anytime, the door is always open. I need a new receptionist anyway. Tilly will be going off on maternity leave soon so I need someone to take over from her. I have Xena and Katy who work part time right now and they're great. But you know what these kids are like – the first chance they get they'll leave the island.'

Delilah grinned. 'They all do.'

'It'd be nice to have someone more permanent,' Aria said.

'I have no experience when it comes to something like that, I'm rubbish with computers.'

Aria shook her head. 'We can train you. If you want it, the job is yours.'

'Thank you.'

Delilah looked around and Aria realised that Izzy might have been listening after all, as she was staring at the two of them.

'The weather is glorious, don't you think,' Delilah said, trying to change the subject. Aria hoped that Izzy was suitably convinced. 'Anyway, must dash, I promised Izzy she could choose some Easter chocolate from the chocolate shop in the village. She's got her eye on one of the white chocolate ducks that are in the sale.'

'Ah Izzy, you must try the praline eggs, they are little bites of heaven,' Aria said.

'Oh, I saw them, they looked good.' Izzy looked at her mum hopefully.

'Let's go and see what we can get for our money,' Delilah said and then waved at Aria. 'See you around.'

Delilah linked arms with her daughter and they walked off down the street.

Aria tied Snowflake up and stepped inside the cosy warmth of The Vanilla Bean, her godmother's bakery. The smell of bread mingled with the sweet scent of custard and cake was comforting and achingly familiar. Kendra was standing in the little kitchen area at the back of the shop and, by the look of it, she was making another batch of cookies. She glanced up as the bell rung above the door and her face lit up to see Aria.

Aria walked into the kitchen and placed a kiss on her godmother's cheek.

'How are you feeling?' Aria asked, stealing a chocolate chip from the countertop. Kendra suffered from terrible hay fever in the spring but her eyes weren't as red as they had been in the last few weeks.

'I'm all good, my lovely,' Kendra said, kneading the dough, 'I'm over the worst of it now. How are you?'

Aria suppressed a smile as Kendra's eyes swept over her, assessing everything with an expert eye. If she had so much as a sniffle, her godmother would know about it and whip out some kind of ancient cure for Aria to take. But Kendra also knew her moods from a very quick glance. Aria could hide nothing from her.

'Ah, Noah Campbell is coming today, isn't he? I forgot,' Kendra said.

How she managed to glean that from just looking at her, Aria would never know.

'Yes, he'll be here this afternoon,' Aria said. She wondered if the whole island was aware of his impending arrival. God, she really hoped she was more discreet than that.

'How are you feeling about it?' Kendra said, spooning out the mixture onto the baking tray in little dollops.

Kendra knew all about Noah's last visit, as did Skye and Clover. Aria had told her dad too, and he had apologised profusely, saying it was all his fault, although Aria didn't understand that.

Aria shrugged. 'I honestly don't know. I'm still angry and hurt, even after all this time, but...'

'Those feelings you had for him don't just disappear because the man was an ass.'

Aria sighed and nodded. She was so confused.

'Maybe this time you'll be able to get some proper answers,' Kendra said. 'He always seemed like such a lovely man, it's hard to believe he didn't have a good reason.'

'I don't think I care about those reasons. He left. I just want to get past that awkward first meeting and then get some professional help with the hotel. It will be strictly business between us, nothing more.'

Aria was aware she was building a wall around her heart; she wouldn't let Noah Campbell hurt her again.

She decided to change the subject. 'Have you heard that Delilah has lost her job?'

'Yes I did. How awful for her – as if she hasn't been through enough. These big companies have a lot to answer for. Where is the compassion?'

'I know. I've offered her a job but it'll be a few weeks before she can take it.'

'That's very kind. I could probably offer her a few hours here too,' Kendra said.

'I'm sure that would help,' Aria said, stealing another chocolate chip as she thought.

'What can I get you, anyway? I'm sure you didn't come down here just to see me and steal my chocolate chips,' Kendra said.

'Of course I did,' Aria said, mock hurt. 'Well, you mainly, the chocolate chips are just an added bonus.'

Kendra rolled her eyes affectionately and moved out into the shop.

'Some of those delicious apple muffins please,' Aria said. 'Also those small crusty baguettes, and do you have any pink food colouring?'

'I can help you with the first two. I might not have pink food colouring though, check the cake-making shelf,' Kendra said, as she started bagging up the bread and cakes.

Aria moved over to the shelf where there were various different cookie cutters, bags of ready-made icing, and various other decorations and cake-making paraphernalia for any of the islanders who wanted to try their own hand at recreating some of the wonderful delights that Kendra sold in her shop.

Aria scanned through the different bottles of food colouring but Kendra was right, there was no pink. She grabbed a bottle of red – she was sure that Skye wouldn't mind. As an afterthought, she grabbed a bottle of blue too; maybe Skye could make Sapphire Bay candyfloss instead.

She brought them back to the counter and grabbed her credit card to pay for everything. She'd argued many times with Kendra over whether she should pay or not – her godmother knew there was no money in the hotel – but Aria refused to let her make all these baked goods for the hotel and then not pay for them.

Kendra gave her the obligatory scowl as she waved her card and started ringing the purchases through the till. 'So you're meeting Francis tomorrow?'

'Yes, it seems to have dragged on and on,' Aria said.

'These things always do.'

'He mentioned there were complications but I just can't imagine what they would be.'

'It's probably just probate stuff,' Kendra said. 'Your dad was not a complicated man.'

Aria smiled. That was true. Thomas Philips was so completely laidback he was practically horizontal.

'There were no secrets or skeletons in closets when it came to your dad.'

'Francis said there was some money in Dad's estate,' Aria said. 'He said it was quite a bit, which surprises me. Dad was always complaining he had no money so I'm not sure where it came from. And how much is *quite a bit*?'

Kendra shrugged. 'I'm not sure, I can't imagine it would be a lot.'

'I have all these plans of what to do with the hotel if there is a decent amount, but knowing my luck it will probably only be a few hundred pounds. It will just be nice to know and to have everything finalised.'

'Do you think Skye and Clover will leave?' Kendra said, tying up the bag.

Aria swiped her card over the card reader. 'I really don't know. I don't think either of them are happy here. Skye has Jesse and—'

'They're divorced.'

'You know it's not as simple as that,' Aria said.

'Yeah, I know. Although Clover might stay, she was never really happy in London, plus after what happened with Marcus I don't think she's in any hurry to go back. And she has the horses to look after now. She's fallen in love with them.'

Kendra might have a point. Aria wasn't sure Clover wanted to leave the horses she had somehow inherited. Ruby Meadow Farm had owned a couple of animals up near Ruby Falls and her sister had taken a bit of a shine to the horses that lived in the field next to her little house. The farmer had asked Clover to keep an eye on the animals while he went on holiday and he'd never come back. He sent money occasionally to help with their food but it seemed that Clover had become the proud owner of three horses, a cow and recently a new addition of a donkey. But would the animals be enough to make her want to stay?

'I think they both have bigger dreams than living out the rest of their lives on Jewel Island.'

Kendra sighed and nodded. 'Do you want these delivered?'

Aria glanced out the window at Neil, Kendra's delivery boy, sitting on the bench curled over his mobile phone as if it was the most precious thing in his life. At fourteen, it probably was. Although, aside from the mobile phone, Neil wasn't a typical teenager. He'd saved a donkey from slaughter a few months before, which was now living with Clover's horses, and he'd been doing odd jobs around the island ever since to raise enough money to keep Sparkle. And although Aria was more than capable of carrying one small bag back to the hotel, she wanted to help. In fact, many of the islanders had suddenly found jobs that needed doing where they hadn't needed anything doing before.

'Yes, I better had, I have Snowflake with me. One whiff of these muffins I think Snowflake will be snaffling the whole bag. Here's a pound for Neil.'

'I'll send them up shortly,' Kendra said.

Aria turned to go but her godmother suddenly came round the counter to talk to her.

'Have you thought any more about the festival of light?'

'Ah well,' Aria said, awkwardly, knowing she had been putting off making any decisions about the spring festival of light for far too long. It was two weeks away and it was kind of expected that the hotel would hold a big party or celebration for all the islanders and guests who were taking part in the festival. Her dad had done it every year as far back as she could remember, with drinks, food and fireworks to mark the end of the light parade. Last year was the first time they hadn't done anything and the islanders had forgiven her as it hadn't been long after her dad had died. The light parade had gone ahead but it hadn't been the same without the big celebration at the end. This year Aria knew she was kind of expected to pick up where her dad had left off, despite the hotel having no money at all. 'I'll make a decision when I know how much money is left in the estate. There's a lot to sort out, a lot to do.'

Kendra nodded sympathetically but they both knew the islanders wouldn't be happy if she didn't do anything.

'Come and see me after you've met with Francis and we can talk about what you're all going to do,' Kendra said.

'OK.'

Aria waved goodbye and left the shop.

'Neil, delivery for you,' Aria called over to him.

Neil unfolded himself from the bench, standing up to his full height, all six foot two of him. He loped over to the shop.

'Thanks Miss Philips,' Neil said, disappearing inside.

She untied Snowflake who sniffed at her hands hopefully.

'Sorry pup, no treats for you today.'

She went back up the steep steps that led to the bottom of the gardens of Philips Hotel. At this time of year the garden was ablaze with colour as flowers bloomed from every corner. The sprinklers were on, casting thousands of tiny rainbows in the air.

As they walked under the shade of a large oak tree, a squirrel suddenly ran out in front of them, spotted Snowflake and, instead of running back up the tree, made a dash for it across the neat manicured lawns. There were a few seconds where Snowflake stood staring after it in shock before the dog took off in hot pursuit – unfortunately with the lead still wrapped round Aria's hand. She tried to plant her feet to stop the dog but he was just too strong. For a few seconds she was running, but her legs were moving too fast for her to catch up and she tumbled and then landed face down on the grass. This did nothing to deter Snowflake as he ran as fast as he could across the lawn, Aria wakeboarding behind him, bouncing across the ground.

'SNOWFLAKE, STOP!' Aria yelled, getting a mouthful of dirt for her trouble. But Snowflake was intent on having that squirrel for dinner and let out a howl of frustration, probably at the Aria-shaped anchor that was slowing him down – although evidently not by much. The lead was still tightly wrapped around her wrist and there was nothing she could do to free herself as Snowflake charged through one of the flower beds, which were still wet from the sprinkler that morning.

She bounced through a patch of bluebells that were just starting to bud and over another patch of grass, until Snowflake finally came to a stop as he tried to climb up a tree that the squirrel had scarpered up.

Aria climbed shakily to her feet, checking that all her bones were still intact. She seemed to be OK, although she unfortunately couldn't say the same thing about her dress – there was a thick mud streak complete with grass stains from the top to the very bottom. Her hair was matted and sticking to her face and, as she reached up to check her lips, she found a blade of grass stuck between her teeth.

She let out a little sigh.

She had chosen this dress this morning as it was the one she had been wearing when Noah had kissed her. Maybe it was petty but she kind of wanted him to see what he was missing. She hoped it might jog his memory in a positive way but that wasn't going to happen now. Still, if she could get back to the hotel quickly, she might be able to get changed before he arrived so she was at least clean.

She yanked Snowflake down from his quest to climb the tree and, given that the squirrel was now completely out of sight, the dog was a lot more willing to come with her than she had thought he would be. Maybe Lady Luck was back on her side.

Aria hurried back to the hotel and collared Jeremy, one of the porters, who was outside having a crafty cigarette, to take Snowflake back to Mrs O'Hare. Just then a car pulled up outside and her heart sank. Surely fate wasn't that unkind.

She turned round just as Noah Campbell climbed out of the car. God, he was so tall. She looked at his strong arms and remembered him holding her close as he kissed her under the shade of a willow tree in the garden, those hands stroking her face, making her feel adored. And then he'd left, just like all the other guests, and she didn't know what to do with that because Noah was the one man she had come to trust.

She couldn't drag her eyes away and noticed he was wearing a smart grey suit instead of the jeans he normally wore. She was vaguely aware of the taxi driver removing a pale blue suitcase from the boot and driving off.

Noah looked up at the hotel for a moment and Aria was frozen to the spot, hoping he would go straight in and not look in her direction at all. She was tucked into the side of the entrance; he might not even see her. But, like a moth to the flame, his eyes slid over in her direction.

CHAPTER THREE

For a fleeting second Aria thought she saw Noah's eyes light up at seeing her but that seemed to pass as soon as it had arrived. He didn't even seem to notice that she was covered in mud; he couldn't take his eyes from her face.

She had no idea what she wanted to say to him. She wanted to shout at him and hug him all at the same time. They'd been friends before this and she missed that, but she wasn't sure she wanted to be friends with him again. However, if she wanted his help with the hotel, she had to keep things professional between them.

'It's good to see you again,' Noah said. 'How have you been?'

'I'm OK,' Aria said.

Silence fell over them.

God, this was so stiff and formal between them.

'It won't be the same staying here without seeing your dad,' Noah said.

'I think that every day,' Aria said. 'The place seems so quiet without him. He made it what it is. I miss him so much.'

Noah took a step towards her, his arms moving as if he wanted to hug her, but he stopped himself.

'I'm so sorry for your loss. I know I said this at the funeral, but I am. He was a wonderful man.'

'Yes he was.' She paused. 'You knew he was ill; he told you that day that you left.'

Noah nodded. 'At lunch. I couldn't tell you. He wanted to enjoy a few days with Skye and Clover first, with all of you together.'

Aria nodded. She didn't blame Noah for that.

'Is that why you left?'

He didn't answer straight away, seemingly trying to find the right words. 'I didn't leave because he told me he was dying.'

'So why did you leave?'

She cursed herself because she didn't want to be antagonistic with him as soon as he arrived. She could have waited until he'd at least unpacked. But she suddenly did want answers, despite having told Kendra and herself that she didn't care. She wanted to know why he'd left because how could she ever really move on to them having a professional relationship when there was this history between them and this unexplained betrayal?

Suddenly Aria's walkie-talkie squawked into life.

'Noah Campbell is here,' Tilly's voice came over the airwaves loud and clear. Obviously she didn't know Aria was standing outside the entrance. 'Get your arse back here quick.'

Noah arched an eyebrow at the excitement in Tilly's voice and Aria felt her cheeks burn red.

'I've just been googling him to see what all the fuss was about,' Tilly went on. 'Bloody hell, this man is hot, his pictures don't do him justice.'

Noah's lips twitched with amusement.

'God, he looks like he was poured into that suit,' Tilly carried on. 'I'm not normally the kind of woman who appreciates a man in a suit. There's no personality in a suit. But hell, there is a ton of *personality* in those trousers. Have you seen the size of his thighs?'

Aria fumbled for her walkie-talkie before it could get any worse but Tilly was on a roll.

'I can see now why you were so excited about him coming back, the man looks like some kind of god.'

Aria pressed the button on the walkie-talkie to turn it off and silence fell over them.

'I wasn't excited,' Aria said. 'I just…'

Noah moved closer towards her and reached up to her hair to remove a stray leaf. 'I was looking forward to seeing…' he paused and seemed to correct himself '…to coming back here. Jewel Island has always been a special place for me.'

Her heart leapt at his touch, words stalling in her mouth. He'd said that the last time he was here too.

'You're here for a month this time?'

'Yes, initially. Probably longer.'

She was surprised by that. He normally only stayed for a few days here and there, never any long periods.

'How come you're staying so long?'

'I… have business I need to attend to,' Noah said, vaguely.

She wasn't sure what business would bring Noah Campbell to the island; beyond a few shops and restaurants, there was nothing that would attract a businessman like him. Unless he was meeting someone here.

His eyes cast down her dress and she saw the tiniest traces of a smile play on his lips.

'Is it fancy dress day today, Miss Philips, or is the zombie swamp monster look a new thing you're trying?'

She smiled at the gentle teasing but then her heart

dropped. *Miss Philips?* He had never called her that before. It had always been Aria. He had set a professional tone right from the off and she couldn't help feeling disappointed about that.

'I was... umm... walking a dog,' Aria explained lamely.

His eyes cast down her again. 'Shame about the dress, that was always one of my favourites on you.'

Her heart leapt. He did remember.

He stared at her for a moment and then took a step back. 'Miss Philips, we need to talk. Would you have dinner with me tonight?'

The use of her surname didn't fill her with good feelings. He was trying to draw a line between them and that kiss. Dinner was probably going to be where he officially dumped her, which seemed a bit weird when they had never been a thing in the first place.

She cleared her throat. 'I don't think that's necessary, *Mr Campbell*.'

His eyebrows shot up at her tone of voice.

'No, it really is.'

She stepped closer and lowered her voice even though there was no one around. 'I get it, you regret the kiss and you want to draw a line under it. You want to make sure I'm not under any illusions about what it meant. Trust me, I know what it meant to you. It was a mistake.'

He frowned. 'I can assure you; I absolutely do not regret that kiss. I'm... frustrated that we never got a chance to finish it but I could never regret kissing you.'

Her heart thundered in her chest. He didn't regret the kiss. 'But you left.'

He sighed. 'Something happened that made it very... difficult for me to continue with any kind of relationship with you. If you have dinner with me tonight, I'll explain everything. Come to my suite so we can talk in private. We can order room service. Shall we say eight?'

Why did he want to talk to her in private? Was he hoping to pick up where he'd left off the last time he'd stayed? Why was her mind suddenly going there? She wasn't going to sleep with him. He'd kissed her and left, why would she let him back into her life again like that? The frustrating thing was there had been many times she'd imagined what it would be like to sleep with Noah Campbell and that kiss had given her a glimpse of the passion he was capable of, and what it would feel like to spend the night wrapped in his arms. This was ridiculous. Maybe he really was just inviting her to his suite to talk. But either way she wanted to get to the bottom of all of this. She was owed an explanation and she was damned sure she was going to get one.

'OK.'

'Good.' He paused as if he wanted to say something else but then he took a step away from her. 'I should probably check in.'

He picked up his suitcase and he gestured for her to go ahead of him. She walked into reception and Tilly's jaw dropped open when she saw the state of her. Clover appeared out of her office and giggled when she saw her. Thankfully there was no one else around.

'What happened?' Tilly asked.

'Snowflake pulled me over when he was chasing a squirrel.'

'And Snowflake would be your dog?' Noah asked.

'No, he belongs to one of the guests,' Aria said.

He frowned a little. 'And is dog-walking one of the services you offer your guests?'

'No, but she asked if I would so...' she trailed off lamely. She liked to keep her guests happy but she knew some of them took advantage of that.

43

Noah turned his attention back to Tilly to check in. Thankfully her receptionist managed to regain her composure as she served her god-like guest. To his credit he never mentioned a word about hearing Tilly's affirmations of him over the walkie-talkie, he just chatted to her and Clover as normal.

When he was finished he turned back to Aria and the humour was now gone from his eyes.

'Eight o'clock?'

Aria nodded. 'I'll be there.'

She watched him go and only when he was safely in the lift did Aria feel like she could breathe again.

'Have you got a date with him?' Tilly gasped in shock.

'No, it's not a date, it's a… business meeting.'

It most definitely wasn't a date.

'About the hotel?' Tilly said.

'Yes,' Aria lied.

'Really?' Clover said, her attention piqued. 'Maybe me and Skye should come along too.'

Aria caught Tilly's eye and saw she was smirking at that prospect. Aria couldn't imagine turning up to her sort-of date with Noah Campbell, or whatever it was, with her two younger sisters in tow.

'It's not that kind of business meeting,' Aria said, awkwardly.

'Where is this *business meeting* taking place?' Tilly asked.

Aria cleared her throat. 'In his suite. We're having dinner.'

Tilly burst out laughing. 'It's a date. I saw the way he was looking at you. He likes you. You obviously like him – and why wouldn't you when he looks like that.'

Aria sighed with frustration. It was so much more than just his looks that she had fallen for.

'There's no point pretending it's a business meeting when

we all know it's a date,' Tilly went on. 'And if the date is taking place in the privacy of his own bedroom, it's not the kind of date you want your little sisters tagging along to.'

Clover smiled. 'Well, I'll definitely give that one a miss. I hope you have fun; you deserve it.'

Tilly nodded enthusiastically. 'And then come back tomorrow and tell us all about your night with Noah Campbell.'

Clover's face fell. 'That was Noah Campbell, the man that broke your heart?'

Tilly's face lit up with potential gossip and Aria wished that she hadn't told anyone about their kiss.

'He broke your heart? When was this, what happened?'

'He didn't break my heart. That would have meant I was in love with him and I most definitely would not fall in love with a man like Noah Campbell. My dad told him he was dying and he left me to deal with that on my own. What kind of man does that?'

'You weren't alone, you had us,' Clover said, quietly.

'I know, of course I did. I didn't mean that, but he was supposed to be my friend and it would have been nice to have a friend there to support me too. He told me once he doesn't have many friends and I thought at the time, how awful that his work travelling the world means that he can never make any real connections with people. But you know what I think it is? This is a man so scared of commitment that he runs at the first sniff of it. He tells lies to get what he wants and then moves on regardless of the people he hurts along the way. He fed me some lies about moving here and kissed me and it was all a ploy to get me into bed. Then he found out my dad was dying and he had some semblance of a conscience and decided it might not be a good idea to sleep with me and leave me after all. This is not a man who is good at longevity. I want children one day. I know I don't need a man to help me with that, but if I do have one, I want one who stays the distance, not flees at the first sign of trouble.'

She stopped talking, realising she was a lot more hurt over Noah's departure the year before than she'd thought. She also realised, as Clover and Tilly were looking at her with wide eyes and then shifting their nervous glances over to the lift, that Noah was standing behind her and most likely had heard every word she'd said.

She turned around and sure enough he was there. So much for being friendly and professional with him. He looked pissed off and she didn't blame him. He didn't move and she didn't know whether to apologise or not. She had been hurt by him leaving and he should know that.

He walked over to her. 'Aria, I may not have broken your heart, but it broke my heart to leave you. I appreciate my actions means that a relationship between us is completely off the table, and I regret that more than anything, but please don't think that walking away from you was easy because it was the hardest thing I've ever done.'

She stared at him in shock.

'I'll see you at eight and I'll explain everything then.' He turned to Tilly. 'I just came back to say, I left my laptop cable in Dubai so I've ordered a new one and it should be arriving today or tomorrow if you can look out for it.'

Tilly nodded numbly as Noah turned and walked away. He went inside the lift and the doors closed behind him.

Aria turned back to Clover and Tilly. She had no words at all. All this time she had felt betrayed and angry that he had left her but he hadn't wanted that at all. What the hell had happened all those months before?

'Holy hell, that's the most romantic thing I've ever heard,' Tilly said, fanning herself.

Clover nodded. 'He really likes you.'

'I think romance could definitely be back on the table tonight,' Tilly said.

Aria shook her head as she tried to dismiss the tumble of feelings racing through her heart, but there was a tiny sliver of excitement about their meeting that night that hadn't been there before.

Noah dumped his suitcase on the bed and then moved to the window that overlooked Sapphire Bay.

Aria Philips.

Christ, this woman had got right under his skin.

When the job got too stressful, hell, when life got too much, this place had become his haven in the storm. The quiet island life, the beautiful views, it helped him to take a breath. But he'd quickly realised that it wasn't Jewel Island that he kept returning to, it was her.

Kissing her had been like an explosion in his gut. Suddenly, and for the first time in his life, he'd felt like he was home. He had never felt so certain in his life that here was where he belonged. With her.

But it was only an hour later that everything had changed. He should have said no, he should have walked away. He'd been offered a deal that made no financial sense and it ruined any chance of him and Aria being together. But his friend had been desperate and he couldn't walk away from that.

He sighed and leaned a hand against the window.

Never mix business with pleasure was one rule he had lived by his entire life.

But now he was back he was second-guessing everything.

Maybe rules were made to be broken.

CHAPTER FOUR

Aria was nervously watching the minutes tick by on the clock in the reception. It was twenty to eight. She didn't want to turn up late as that would be rude, so she was wondering what time she could feasibly arrive at his suite without coming across as super keen. Maybe she'd leave it a few more minutes before going up. She was finally going to get some answers. She needed to get that straight in her head more than anything else before she could even think about moving on with him, but she'd replayed what he'd said to her in the lobby more than a hundred times. That was the Noah she had fallen in love with and it seemed his feelings for her were still as strong as ever. She'd be lying if she said she didn't have feelings for him. She had imagined, with rose-tinted glasses, how the evening would unfold many times, but whatever was going to happen, she couldn't help but be a tiny bit excited about it.

Skye came out of the kitchen wiping her hands and looking truly fed up. When their dad died, the hotel chef had quit and it had fallen to Skye to take over. She was a brilliant chef and the guests had all been commenting about how great the food was. It was obviously good for business, but Aria knew her sister was hating every minute of it. Skye was such a fiery, passionate woman and over the last year Aria had watched that sparkle fade away.

Aria looped an arm round her little sister's shoulders and Skye leaned her head on her. 'It won't be for much longer,' Aria said.

Skye looked up at her in confusion. 'What do you mean?'

'Tomorrow, the estate will be finalised and then we can talk about what we want to do. You could go back to Canada, if you wanted. We'll figure all this out somehow, so everyone is happy.'

Skye looked like she was going to say something but then there was a noise from the toilet that sounded like an animal in pain.

Tilly had been in there for a while now. Aria knew that Tilly always took a long time in the loo lately – just getting dressed was a massive chore, plus the cubicles were fairly small. She hoped that Tilly hadn't got stuck.

Aria hurried over to the toilet door and was just about to call out to Tilly when there was a loud grunt and a groan.

Her heart dropped into her stomach and she rushed in. 'Tilly, are you OK?'

'No,' Tilly gasped, 'I think I've gone into labour.'

'Oh my god, you're having a baby?' Aria said through the cubicle door, visions of delivering a baby here in the toilet filled her mind. What would she need? Hot towels were apparently a must. Or was it hot water and cold towels? God, she really should know that. Her dad had always been the designated first aid person, not that he'd ever used those skills for anything more than handing out plasters for cuts and blisters.

Tilly opened the door looking red and flustered. 'Yes, the last nine months might have been a kind of clue, plus there's this huge belly which might have given the game away.'

'I mean now, you can't have a baby now.'

'Believe me, this baby is definitely coming now. These contractions are bloody painful. No one ever tells you that when they talk about the wonders of having a baby. I think you better call the air ambulance.'

'Shit,' Aria said. 'Shit! What can I do, what can I get you?'

'The sodding air ambulance,' Tilly said, grunting again as she held her belly.

Aria ran back to the toilet entrance and shouted to Skye. 'I need you to call Theo, Tilly's gone into labour.'

'Oh god, is she OK?' Skye said.

'I'm not sure but tell Theo it's urgent. And get Jeremy to make sure the lawn out the front is clear of people, so Theo has somewhere to land the helicopter.'

'OK.'

She turned back to find Tilly holding onto the sink and groaning and panting. Aria put an arm around her, rubbing her back. 'Are you OK, what do you need?'

'I need Ben,' Tilly said.

Aria nodded and ran back to reception, bringing up the list of emergency contacts on the computer and quickly dialling Tilly's husband's number. There was no answer at the house and no answer on his mobile either.

Shit.

She ran back to the bathroom. 'I can't get hold of him, any idea where he might be?'

Tilly groaned. 'He's up at Moonstone Lake, there's no bloody phone reception up there.'

Shit.

'I'll take the buggy,' Aria said, running back out into the

reception and shouting across to Skye as she dashed out the door. 'I'm going to find Ben, stay with her.'

She hurried outside and jumped in one of the golf buggies, which they used to transport the guests to some of the holiday cottages owned by the hotel. Although, after the first few minutes of driving the thing, it became very obvious that choosing this mode of transport was a big mistake because the buggy was making very slow progress up the hills towards Moonstone Lake. Abandoning the buggy, she ran the last few hundred yards to the crest of the hill where the lake was nestled into the hillside. To her horror, she realised that Ben was on the far side. She raced as fast as she could around the lake, waving her arms in the air and yelling as loud as she could, but it didn't seem like he could see or hear her. Finally she got close and Ben looked up at her just as the helicopter flew overhead and landed in the grounds of the hotel. Ben must have guessed what it was right away without her saying a word because he abandoned his stuff and pelted back to the car, reversing it onto the road in a cloud of dust. He tore down the road towards her, stopping only long enough for Aria to throw herself into the passenger seat, and then he drove off. Aria's heart was beating so loudly and her breath so ragged that she couldn't even speak.

'Is she OK?' Ben said, as he accelerated down the road.

'I don't know, she says the contractions were painful, but I'm sure that's completely normal though.'

Ben floored the car, throwing Aria back in her seat and taking the bends of the road a lot faster than he should. But before they were even halfway back to the hotel, they saw the helicopter taking off and heading towards the mainland and Aria's heart sank that Ben had missed the chance to fly with his wife. She hoped someone had gone with Tilly and that she wasn't alone. Theo would be flying the helicopter so it wasn't as if he could hold her hand.

'Crap,' Ben said, taking a tiny side road. 'What time is it?'

Aria knew he was heading to the bridge that joined them to the mainland. At high tide the bridge became impassable and there was no way off the island apart from by boat or helicopter.

Aria checked her watch. Living on the island, she knew the tide timetables almost off by heart.

'It's quarter past eight.' Her heart dropped again when she remembered Noah sitting in his suite waiting for her. But there was no way she could ask Ben to drop her off at the hotel now. 'We have two hours until high tide, we might just be able to make it.'

He floored the accelerator again and they bumped across the island towards the bridge. The water was just licking the edges of the bridge as they arrived and Michael, the gateman, was about to move the blockades across the road, preventing people from driving on it until it was safely past high tide. Ben leaned on the horn and Michael leapt out the way as the car splashed onto the bridge, big waves rolling up the sides of the car as they hit the water at high speed. It wasn't really a big risk, especially as the sea was so calm – it would be another story if it was stormy. They rumbled over the bridge and reached the other side.

It wasn't too far to the hospital, thankfully. The way Ben was driving meant they got there extra quick. He parked the car badly in the car park and Aria joined him with running to the hospital. Ben checked in at reception and a nurse showed them where Tilly was.

'I'll wait here,' Aria said. If Tilly was pushing a baby out into the world, she certainly wouldn't appreciate her employer standing there watching it happen.

Ben nodded as he burst through the doors to be with his wife.

Aria sat down and looked at her watch. It was a quarter to nine. It was safe to say, when she'd been busy imagining all the different ways her night would go, never in her wildest dreams had she envisaged it would go like this.

'Hey!'

Aria looked up to see Skye had arrived with a cardboard cup of coffee in her hand.

'What are you doing here?'

'I flew with Tilly; I didn't want her to be alone. Being on a helicopter is a bit bloody exciting though.'

Aria grinned as Skye sat down next to her. 'Island life, it's never straightforward. We don't just call an ambulance; we have a helicopter to take us to the hospital. Was she OK?'

'I think a little scared. Theo looked her over and he seemed to think she was fine. She even said the contractions seemed to be slowing down on the ride over here.'

'Well, Ben is with her now, I'm sure she'll be OK.'

Skye took a sip of her coffee and winced. 'God, this stuff is disgusting. They really should invest in better coffee machines in places like this.'

'I don't know, I guess I'd prefer hospitals to spend their money on important things like machines and equipment for patient care, not visitor coffee,' Aria said.

Skye smiled. 'How did you get to be so bloody lovely?'

'I had great parents.'

Skye nodded. 'Yes you did.'

'And two wonderful sisters who I wanted to look after and make the world a better place for them to live in.'

Skye grinned. 'And we had this amazing older sister who was always a fantastic role model.'

Aria slipped her hand into Skye's. 'I missed you guys so much when you left.'

'We missed you too. It's good to be back.' Skye rested her head on her shoulder and they sat in companionable silence for a while.

Skye sat up. 'OK, enough of this mutual appreciation and love. If we're going to wait here for a baby that might take hours to arrive, let's play a game. Truth or Dare.'

Aria groaned. They'd played this many times growing up and it was always used to wheedle information out of each other that they didn't really want to share. 'Go on then, truth.'

'Did you really have a date with that git that broke your heart tonight?'

'It wasn't a date. He wanted to explain why he left and honestly I believe there was something more to it than we originally thought. He said it broke his heart to leave.'

'And you believe him?'

'Noah was always a wonderful, kind man and I knew him for several years before we kissed. What he did was completely out of character for him so maybe I should give him a chance to explain. Be open-minded.' Aria gave her a meaningful look. Skye was always so protective of her sisters; Aria had the feeling Skye wouldn't forgive Noah as easily as she would. 'And as it happens, I'm not even going to be there for our *date* anyway. I really need to call him; did you bring your phone?'

'No I didn't. I'm sure there are payphones around somewhere.'

'Yeah, I didn't bring any cash with me either.' Aria stood up to see if she could go and use one of the hospital phones when there was a loud guttural moan from the other side of the door. Aria promptly sat down again. 'I'll phone him later.' She turned back to Skye, determined to change the subject. 'Truth or dare?'

'Truth.'

'What's really going on with you and Jesse?'

Skye laughed. 'I change my mind, dare.'

'OK, I dare you to phone Jesse, as soon as we get back to the hotel, and tell him how you really feel.'

Skye laughed. 'You're so mean. OK. Truth. Jesse is... my missing piece, the other half of me that I never knew I needed. But some things are just not meant to be, are they? I'd rather have him in my life as a friend, or a friend with benefits, than not have him at all.'

'Jesse loves you.'

'As a friend,' Skye corrected. 'We're best friends who occasionally have amazing sex. He doesn't want more than that. And actually, in some ways, it's been good to be back here and have some space from him. It hurts sometimes to be with him but not be *with* him, if you know what I mean. Maybe this long-distance friendship is better – we get to see each other a few times a year and when I'm not with him I get to breathe and not look at him all day and pine for what I can't have.'

Aria gave her hand a squeeze. Love was never easy and smooth running.

'Your turn,' Skye said, changing the subject.

Aria decided to let it go. 'Truth.'

'Are you planning on selling the hotel?' Skye asked.

'God no, I don't want to do that at all. But I do understand if you and Clover want your share of the hotel so you can go back to your own lives. If that's what you want, we can talk to Francis tomorrow about how we can release some capital... Do you want that?'

'No. Well, I can't speak for Clover, but the Philips Hotel is our home and, even if we're not there, it's always nice to know we have this place we can return to. I don't want that to change.'

Aria let out a little sigh of relief. 'OK, your turn.'

'Dare.'

'I dare you to drink all of that coffee,' Aria said.

Skye laughed. 'I think I'd rather phone Jesse and tell him how I feel.'

It was quite obvious Aria wasn't coming. Noah stood up and blew out the candle on the table near the balcony. If he was completely honest with himself, it was probably a good job she wasn't. Tonight's meeting was about business and the hotel and he'd made it romantic in his head when there was definitely no place for that. He'd arrived here, determined he was going to keep everything professional between them, and then she'd mentioned the kiss and he'd done nothing but think about it in glorious detail ever since. He had to move past that; it was never going to happen again so he needed to stop dwelling on it. He absolutely had to keep things professional. It was very likely he'd be here for the next six months at least, so he couldn't let things get awkward between them when he had business to take care of.

He sighed, because the business with the hotel was the one thing he'd wanted to talk to her about tonight. Aria deserved some warning and now she wasn't even going to get that.

Why the hell had she not come?

But if he was still thinking about that kiss then she probably was too. Noah rubbed the back of his neck awkwardly. He knew he had hurt her when he had walked away after kissing her before and why would she put herself in a position to be hurt again? God, if she was going to avoid him altogether, that was going to make working here difficult.

Still, tomorrow she'd finally know why and he just hoped she wouldn't be angry with him. Maybe they could get past all of this and be friends again. He had a feeling that after tomorrow she would be needing a friend, and he intended to be there for her even if nothing else could happen between them.

CHAPTER FIVE

Aria felt awful about letting down Noah the night before. Of course it had been due to circumstances out of her control but still she felt bad. It had been gone midnight before she had been able to get back on the island after waiting for the tide to drop enough for her to cross the bridge.

She'd been desperate to call him but the hospital hadn't been keen for her to use their phone unless it was an emergency and cancelling a date hardly seemed to class as such. Ben had been too busy looking after Tilly to bother him about borrowing his phone so she'd done nothing and, in hindsight, perhaps she could have done more.

As it happened, Tilly's contractions had slowed and then stopped altogether, which apparently was fairly common. They were keeping her in overnight, but as she was a few weeks off her due date, they said they'd likely send her home again until her contractions started coming closer together.

Aria hadn't been able to stop thinking about Noah all morning. She had lingered around the breakfast hall deliberately in the hope that she might see him but he hadn't been there and she hadn't seen him around the hotel either. She had thought about going up to his hotel room but it was possible that he might be having a lie-in and she didn't want to disturb him.

But now Aria and her sisters were on their way to see Francis Cole about their dad's estate so she had bigger things to worry about. The future of the hotel kind of hinged on this meeting and she still had no idea what the twins planned to do. Skye had been pretty adamant that she didn't want Aria to sell the hotel, but it didn't mean that her sister would be willing to use any money left in the estate to help the hotel. And would they both leave once the estate was settled? Although if they'd planned to do that, they could have done it long before now.

And if there was money in the estate and the twins were happy to use it for the hotel, would there be enough to do all the things Aria wanted to do?

Maggie, Francis Cole's secretary, greeted them when they arrived and ushered them straight into Francis's office. But Aria stalled because in the office with Francis Cole was Noah Campbell.

'Oh sorry, we can wait outside until you're finished.'

'Actually, erm...' Francis moved round the desk towards them. 'Well actually, this meeting concerns Mr Campbell too.'

Aria frowned in confusion.

Noah held out his hand and introduced himself formally to Clover and Skye. He didn't shake Aria's hand, though she guessed introducing himself to her was a bit redundant when they had already kissed.

'Did Dad leave you something in his will?' Aria asked as she sat down next to Noah, Skye and Clover sitting down on her other side.

Aria supposed her dad might have left him a small gift. She

hoped it wasn't anything they had already cleared out and taken to the charity shop. There was a watch of his that was something of an antique, Aria wondered if it might be that.

Noah cleared his throat awkwardly. 'Something like that.'

Francis returned to his side of the desk and shuffled some papers around. Long minutes stretched on as the solicitor continued to move documents to different piles on his desk and look at a file on his computer.

Aria was painfully aware of Noah's leg next to hers and the warmth from his body. She leaned over to him and he turned his attention to her, his warm grey eyes locking with hers.

'I'm so sorry I didn't come last night. My receptionist went into labour and I ended up spending several hours in the hospital on the mainland waiting for a baby that never arrived...' she trailed off, realising she was rambling. She was nervous about what Francis was going to say and she just wanted to clear the air with Noah before they went any further. Regardless of what had or hadn't been about to happen between them the night before, and her complicated feelings towards him, it was rude to just not turn up and she wanted him to know she hadn't done it deliberately.

Noah didn't say anything and she didn't know if he was pissed off or not.

Francis cleared his throat and it suddenly occurred to Aria that the solicitor was nervous too. What on earth could he be worried about?

'Well, as you know, we are here to discuss the estate of Thomas Philips. This is in two parts. There is the money left in the estate and there is the hotel itself. There were a few debts to be paid, and various other probate fees, but the remainder of the estate comes to one million pounds.'

'Bloody hell, a million pounds?' Skye said.

'Where had he been hiding that?' Clover said.

'A million pounds,' Aria squeaked. That could save the hotel if the sisters were willing to pour all that money back into the business. She'd wanted to open a fitness centre and some kind of spa to attract a different kind of clientele to the hotel. With that kind of money they could renovate and decorate the whole hotel, including every bedroom. They might even be able to reopen the swimming pool which they'd had to close due to the high cost of running it. The possibilities were endless. OK, she might be getting carried away, she wouldn't be able to do *all* those things, and if her sisters didn't want to use their money to save the hotel, then that would change things. But even with just her third of the money she could do something wonderful in the hotel.

Francis pulled on his collar as if he really wasn't comfortable with what he was going to say next. 'As per the will, the money will be split equally between Clover and Skye.'

Silence fell over the room. Aria felt a lump in her throat. She waited for him to say 'and Aria' but those words never came. The rumours had been true, after all.

Francis hurried on. 'The hotel itself is a bit trickier as Mr Campbell bought seventy-five percent of the hotel during your father's lifetime. The other twenty-five percent has been left to Aria.'

Aria stared at him, blood roaring in her ears, her mouth dry. She didn't know which bit of this information she should process first. Right now she felt like she was going to throw up.

'This is bullshit,' Skye said, standing up. 'How can there be no money for Aria? Dad adored her. She's worked her arse off in this hotel all her life, how can Dad not have left anything for her?'

'But he did, he left the hotel… well, part of it. He knew that was her home so he gave that to her,' Francis said.

'We've lost the hotel,' Clover said, quietly.

Aria had no words. There was no money at all. No funds she could use to save the hotel and, to make matters worse, seventy-five percent of her home had been sold over a year ago and she'd had no clue.

She felt the lump in her throat become bigger, her eyes smarting with tears. Her great plans for the hotel suddenly lay in tatters. And in his last act before he died, her dad had made sure his real daughters had been provided for, not her.

She felt sick at that thought.

Clover and Skye were silent and Aria could only stare at the floor as tears welled in her eyes.

She stood up, suddenly needing to be anywhere but here. She didn't want to cry in front of Noah or Francis. She didn't even want her sisters to see her cry.

'Excuse me,' Aria mumbled and stumbled out of the office into the outer area. Maggie looked up in surprise as Aria hurried out into the street. She looked around, wondering where she could go, crossed the road and went up a little path towards Crystal Stream.

There was a large bush near the banks that hid an old bench on the very edge of the river. She moved round the leaves and sat down, shutting out the rest of the world behind her.

But she had only been there for a few seconds when Noah suddenly joined her, although he didn't sit down.

'I'm sorry Aria, I really am. I never wanted you to find out like this.'

'Why didn't you tell me? You let me walk in there and completely blindsided me with that. My dad died a year ago and you never thought to reach out to me at any time after he died.'

'I tried – after the funeral I told you to give me a call but you never did. I phoned you multiple times but you never took my calls. I figured you hadn't called because you were still dealing with your grief and all the paperwork and kerfuffle you had to deal with after his death. I didn't want to add to your stress by telling you this too.'

'Oh god Noah, I thought you wanted to talk about the kiss. I didn't call you because I thought you were going to tell me it was a big mistake and I didn't want to hear it. And I was still so angry that you left. I had no idea this was what you wanted to talk about.'

His eyes softened. 'Aria... that kiss... was everything but... I met with your dad after we kissed and that's when he told me he was dying and asked me to buy part of the hotel. How could I tell him I'd just been kissing his daughter and had invited her up to my suite later that night for hot shower sex? I couldn't take his hotel and his daughter as well. There seemed something terribly wrong with that.'

'If that's why you left, then you didn't know my dad at all. He adored you and he would have died a very happy man if he knew we were together.'

Noah stared at her. 'I didn't leave because of that. Your dad needed this deal done as quick as possible before he died or probate would have made it very complicated. I had so much to sort out to get that money available in such a short amount of time. I had to leave to meet with solicitors, get the contracts drawn up. And he'd forbidden me from telling you until everything was finalised. How could I get into a relationship with you and not be honest with you about this? I wasn't even allowed to tell you he was dying as he wanted time with you and your sisters first. There was no way I could stay and lie to you and tell you everything was fine. I didn't know what to do. God, I felt like such a shit for leaving, knowing what you were going to face, I'm so sorry. You have every right to be angry with me, about all of this, but please understand I did it for your dad.'

She swallowed. 'And now, we're business partners?'

He nodded. 'And friends, I hope we'll always be friends. But yes, business partners, nothing more.'

'We're not even that,' Aria said. 'You own seventy-five percent of my home. You have the final say about what to do with this hotel, you get to make all the decisions.' The tears welled back up in her eyes again. She had lost everything. 'This is my home – you have no right to it.'

'This is what I told your dad, that he needed to discuss this with you properly, that you shouldn't find out after he'd died.'

'I can't believe he didn't leave me any money,' Aria said, and then hated how selfish that made her sound.

'I can buy you out of your part of the hotel if you want the money instead. You'd have the same as your sisters,' Noah said.

That was where the money for Clover and Skye had come from, the sale of part of the hotel. Suddenly things were starting to make sense. Her dad had no money and he'd wanted to leave something to his daughters.

'No, you don't understand. I was going to use it to do the place up, I wanted the money to save the hotel,' Aria said, quietly.

'There's a letter, from your dad. Francis has it. I don't know what's in it but it might answer some of your questions. Maybe you should read it before you make any decisions.'

'There is no decision to make, I'm not selling my share of the hotel.'

'Good, although I wouldn't have expected anything less. I'm not here to take your home from you. I want to work with you to make it better.'

A new sick realisation hit her. Noah had owned seventy-five percent of the profits from the hotel for the last year. The hotel was barely making any profit at all. After all the wages had been paid, after all the stock had been bought, there was next to nothing left over. Whatever had been left over, Aria had poured into the hotel, paying for a gardener to come and take care of the grounds, paying for much-needed repairs. There had been many a month that she hadn't even paid herself a salary because the hotel needed the money more than she did. How was she going to find the cash to pay Noah what he was owed?

'There's no money,' Aria blurted out. 'Your profits for the last year, I can't pay you that.'

'You don't need to worry about that,' Noah said.

'Of course I do. You didn't buy into this hotel and expect to not get any money.'

'I bought into this hotel because Thomas was a friend and he wanted my help, and because I thought, maybe in some way, I was helping you too. This was not a decision based on money. You don't need to pay me anything.'

Aria sighed. This whole thing was a mess and she hated that she hadn't known any of this until today. 'I can't believe Francis didn't say anything.'

'He was sworn to secrecy too. Your dad didn't want you all to know until everything was finalised. A lot of this was to do with Clover and Skye. He'd asked them to come back and help at the hotel after he'd died.'

'Is that why they stayed?' Aria felt suddenly betrayed about that too. The twins hadn't stayed because they wanted to be with her, but because their dad had asked them to.

'I don't know why they stayed, but I think a small part of him was hoping they would fall back in love with the place. But he wanted them to make their own decisions about this, not feel pushed into anything. I know he was worried that your sisters would want their share of the hotel and you'd be forced to sell your home to give it to them, and he didn't want that. With the money I gave him for the hotel he was able to give them their share and you could still keep your home.'

Aria shook her head; she was still hurting over all of this. She felt so let down by her dad.

'Come back in and let's finish the meeting. Then we can go back to the hotel and talk everything through.'

Aria nodded and Noah stepped back, gesturing for her to go ahead of him. She stepped back out from behind the bush and he followed her. As they walked back across the road, Noah slipped his hand into hers and he was still holding it when they reached the office.

Her sisters immediately surrounded her.

'We'll split the money,' Skye said. 'We've talked about it, we'll split it three ways.'

Aria shook her head. 'No, the money is yours. You should go back to Canada, do something amazing with it, invest it in your ice cream shop. Clover, you should open up that dance studio you've always dreamed of. I have the hotel, my home, that's all I've ever wanted.'

'Ladies, please, let's resume our meeting,' Francis said, obviously feeling relief that the secret was now out in the open. 'I'm sure you have questions and I would be happy to discuss them with you.'

They all sat back down and Aria was vaguely aware that Noah was still holding her hand, something her sisters were sure to notice. She didn't know what it meant as he had quite obviously put the brakes on anything further happening between them, but she was glad of the support.

Francis sat back down behind his desk. 'I am sorry that I was unable to divulge this information before now. It was most unconventional as my clients are normally fully informed throughout probate, but I've known your dad since we were kids and he swore me to secrecy. It didn't feel right but I think your dad had his reasons for all of this.'

He picked up a blue envelope and Aria's heart leapt to see her dad's distinctive scrawl on the outside.

To my daughters.

'Your dad only wanted the best for all of you and I firmly believe he did all of this for the right reasons, even if you don't agree with them. He has explained everything in here. I can read it to you or… you could take it away with you and read it in your own time.'

Skye reached out and took the letter, sliding it into her bag.

Francis nodded. 'OK, well if you have any questions, now or in the future, I'm happy to chat things through with you. For now…' he cleared his throat awkwardly. 'Here are the cheques for the money.'

He slid two envelopes across the table to Clover and Skye.

After a few awkward goodbyes they were all back out on the street again.

They were silent as they made their way back towards the hotel, passing little shops and cafés. Half of them were open but some of them hadn't opened for the main season yet and probably wouldn't until the end of May. There simply wasn't enough of a tourist trade to warrant opening all year round. Aria felt some responsibility for that. The hotel was a failure; maybe it was time to admit defeat, take the money Noah was offering her and let him take over completely. He could probably do a much better job than she ever had and it might bring some life back into the island when it needed it the most.

They arrived back at the hotel and she quickly checked in with Katy, who was manning the reception, but nothing had happened since they'd left. Nothing ever happened.

She turned to her sisters. 'Shall we go up to my bedroom and we can read the letter together?'

Clover and Skye both nodded, silently. They were both clearly as shocked by the news as she was.

Noah caught her arm just as she was moving off. 'I know you need some time to think about all of this, but when you're ready and want to talk, even if that's at two in the morning, come and find me in my suite.'

She nodded.

They went up to her room, which had a small lounge area, a tiny kitchen and her bedroom. The sofas were soft and squishy and Clover flopped down on the corner section as Skye placed the offending letter down on the table.

They all stared at it for a moment.

'Go on Aria, you should read it first,' Skye said.

Clover nodded. 'Read it out loud to us.'

Aria sighed and picked it up. For something that seemed to hold all the answers, it was surprisingly light. She slid it open and pulled out the letter inside. It was one sheet of paper.

She sat down and started reading.

To my beautiful daughters,

I love you all so much and it breaks my heart that I will not be around to see you all grow and flourish. You are all such bright, amazing, young women and you could do anything and be anything you want.

Aria swallowed. She could hear her dad saying those words as if he was standing in the room with them. He was always so generous with his love and praise and she felt tears in her eyes at hearing those words again. She took a deep breath and carried on reading.

The hotel was always your mum's and my dream but that doesn't mean it should be yours. I want only the best things for you and I want you all to be happy more than anything else.

There was no money in the hotel, there hasn't been a profit for many years and in actual fact we were massively in debt. I didn't want to pass on this millstone and tie it around your neck so I took the decision to sell part of the hotel to pay off those debts and to release some capital.

Skye and Clover, I know you've always enjoyed coming home to spend time with the family and you will always have a place here but your dreams have always been somewhere other than Jewel Island. I want those dreams for you so badly, so take your share of the hotel and reach for the moon, chase those rainbows. Clover, you have always dreamed of opening your own studio, to teach dance, you can do this now. Skye, your home is in Canada, your heart is with Jesse, tell him you love him, fulfil your dreams.

Aria looked up at Skye to see she was blushing wildly. She never really spoke about her complicated relationship with her ex-husband – the night before had been the first time Aria had got some answers out of her – but it was quite clear to all of them, even their dad, that she was still crazy in love with him. Aria glanced back at the letter to see the next part was addressed to her.

Aria, the hotel has always been your home and every time we spoke about it you always had all these incredible ideas that I was never brave enough to implement myself. I hope you might be able to fulfil those dreams now. I sold part of the hotel to Noah because he knows this business, he has spent his life buying hotels, developing them and selling them on. I know with your passion and his experience you can make the hotel a success again. And maybe in a few years' time, if you wish to sell the hotel, you can get your share of the hotel then. Noah is a good man; someone I respect and like a lot. Don't be angry at him for any of this. He didn't want this but I begged him to do it. I think you will make a very good partnership.

I'm sorry if this is not what you wanted. I love you all and I was trying to do what I thought was best.

Dad x

Aria closed the letter and placed it down on the table. They were all quiet for a while.

'How do you feel?' Clover asked Aria.

'I'm not sure. Dad is right, this hotel was my dream. I never wanted the world like you two, I just wanted to make a success of this place, but I hoped to do it my way. I hoped if there was money left in the estate that we could use it to make the hotel better. I'm disappointed there is no money for me to carry out my plans. But I have Noah to help me so maybe that's better. He knows his stuff; he's been doing this kind of thing for years.' She sighed. 'I don't know, I have no idea what Noah will want to do or what his plans are. I suppose I will feel better once I've spoken to him about all of this. But I agree with Dad, this place was never your dream. You can take your share of the hotel and you can go back to your lives.'

The twins were silent for a while.

'I know we left but this was always our home,' Clover said. 'When Dad asked us to come back and help I kind of thought, yes of course. I dropped everything to be here and now it's been taken away from us.'

To Aria's surprise, Skye nodded her agreement.

'But this was not what you wanted to do with your life. Skye, you've hated being a chef again,' Aria said.

'I wouldn't say hated. I've loved being back here and working with you both again. I didn't know how much I missed it and you.'

God, this was such a mess.

They sat in silence for a while and Skye picked up the letter and read it quietly to herself again, Clover leaning over her shoulder to read it too.

'I should go and talk to Noah,' Aria said. 'It might make things easier when I know what we're dealing with.'

She left them alone, talking quietly to each other as she closed the door behind her. She went upstairs to Noah's suite and knocked on the door.

When he opened it, she saw his jacket and tie had been removed and his shirt sleeves were rolled up. He eyed her and she knew she must look like a state. To her surprise, he opened his arms to her. Without a moment's hesitation she stepped up to him and he wrapped his arms around her holding her close. God, this was exactly what she needed right now. She slid her arms around his back and they just stood there for the longest time. He moved his hand to the back of her neck, stroking her head gently. This was everything. She didn't know if she was ready to forgive him for leaving and move on, but they had been friends before all of this had happened and she wanted to be friends with him again.

Eventually he released her and stepped back, closing the door and guiding her over to his huge sofa. She sat down and he sat opposite her on the low coffee table, enclosing her hands in his. She looked down at where they were touching and frowned slightly. For someone who wanted to be strictly business partners, he was doing a bad job of keeping his distance.

'How are you doing?' Noah asked.

'I'm OK. I think. I still have the hotel so I can't really complain. It would have broken my heart if Dad had sold that to you outright.'

'I would never have taken that deal. I know how important this place is to you.'

'I think the worst part is that Skye and Clover have been hurt by this too. They didn't want to lose the hotel.'

His fingers stroked hers in the tiniest of movements. 'You always look out for everyone else before yourself.'

'They're my sisters, of course I'm going to look out for them.'

He paused as if he was going to say something but then changed his mind. 'Tell me about them.'

Aria smiled. 'Skye has always liked to cook, but it was puddings she loved the most. Even as a kid she was always making cakes and different desserts. She went to college and university and learned everything there was about food but it was desserts and sweet things that were her passion. She ended up in Canada and she opened up her own ice cream shop, one where people can help themselves to the different-flavoured soft whippy ice creams and all the different toppings you could imagine. She loved it. Every week she had a new dessert of the week. She instinctively knows which flavours go well together. She's been cooking for the guests for the last year and they all love her food, but I can see she's not happy. She wants to be doing silly stuff again.'

'And Clover?'

'Her passion was always dance as a child. She would walk around the hotel dancing; ballet, tap, Irish, jive, you name it, she was always moving. She fell into teaching yoga and Pilates as a way to pay for dance lessons but it was something she actually really enjoyed. She ended up working for a gym in London teaching fitness classes but she has always wanted to do it for herself. I think, in her heart, teaching dance would be the dream. Not to little kids who dream of being the next ballet star, but to normal people who want to get fit and have fun in a different way.'

He nodded, chewing on his lip as he thought.

'I guess they can follow their dreams now,' Aria said. 'And I want that for them, but now the hotel has been taken from them I'm scared they'll leave and never come back. What have they got here to come back for?'

'You,' Noah said without hesitation.

'But I'm not their real sister, you might have guessed.'

'Families come in all shapes and sizes: step-brothers, half-sisters, step-aunts, second cousins, single-parent families, children with two mums or two dads. There is no black and white, no right or wrong. The only thing that really matters in a family is whether you are loved and you have that in spades. Your sisters absolutely adore you and your dad loved you very much. What happened today doesn't change that.'

Aria rubbed her hand across her eyes, feeling tired. She knew what he said made sense but it didn't fill her with any confidence that it was true.

'You don't think you're enough?' he said, softly.

'My biological parents abandoned me on a ferry from Spain when I was only a few weeks old, I wasn't enough for them.'

'There are lots of reasons children end up getting put up for adoption, and not all of them are because their parents don't want them. Maybe they thought someone else could give you a better life than they could.'

73

Her parents had said the same thing, but that nagging doubt had never really gone away.

He was watching her carefully. God, this was a whole load of baggage that he shouldn't have to deal with.

'Sorry, we're going off at a tangent here. We need to talk about the hotel. What happens now?' Aria said.

'That's largely up to you, Aria, this is still your hotel, you're still the manager. There will be renovations – I think you know the hotel needs that – but the rest… You can still do it all by yourself and I can be a silent partner. You can run ideas past me if you wish and I can give you funding for those things that I agree with. Or I could have more of an active role. When I buy a hotel, I normally oversee the renovations, bring in a new manager or management team and some other new staff and then leave them to it for a year or so, checking back in on a regular basis. But once I have a good hotel manager, I'm happy for them to oversee the day-to-day running.'

'I'm not a good hotel manager, Noah. The place is a mess and we're not running at a profit. You'd be better off getting someone else in to manage this place,' Aria said, honestly. 'Someone who is far more qualified than me.'

'Passion, experience, knowledge of the area are all important qualities in a hotel manager, but I can help you. We could work together. I could base myself here, at least for the next year or two, but the hotel would still be your baby.'

Aria thought about it for a moment and for the first time that day she couldn't help but smile. To have the expert eye of someone with so much experience would be just what the hotel needed. It sounded exciting. And she wasn't going to lie, the thought of working alongside Noah for the next few years would be wonderful.

'I'd like that.'

He smiled.

She glanced down at where his hands were still wrapped around hers. She was so confused over her feelings for this man. She had fallen in love with him years before but buried those feelings deep after he'd left. She was still angry over him abandoning her and all the secrets that he'd kept from her but, now he was back and being so bloody lovely, all those suppressed emotions were bubbling back to the surface. She didn't know if she trusted him enough to let him back in, or if he even wanted that, but she couldn't help the ache in her heart when she thought about what they had missed out on. She absently stroked her thumb over the top of his hand.

He stared down at their hands and, with some obvious reluctance, let her go.

'And I think we need to keep our relationship strictly professional, not blur the lines,' Noah said. 'Business partners. Nothing more. It would get too complicated if there was anything else. If things ended between us then it would get very messy if we still had to work together.'

'Business partners don't hug or hold hands.'

'No, but friends do. We were friends before we became business partners. I think we could still be friends.'

What he said made sense but the ache in Aria's heart seemed to hurt even more at what he was offering. Once the dust had settled on this big news, didn't they deserve to have a second chance, take things slow but see if they had anything worth fighting for?

'You wouldn't want me as your boyfriend anyway, Aria. My ex-wife and I fought constantly. I made a terrible husband.'

She couldn't imagine that for one second. She wanted to discuss this some more but there was a sudden knock on the door.

Noah stood up and went to answer it. To Aria's surprise Skye and Clover were standing there. He immediately stepped back to let them in.

'Can I get everyone a drink?' Noah said, moving over to the minibar.

'Whisky please,' Skye said and Noah smiled.

He poured out four glasses and came and sat back down.

Clover sat next to Aria and took her hand.

'Are you both OK?' Aria asked.

'We've been talking,' Skye said. 'We want to buy back into the hotel. We'll give you all the money Dad gave us for a share in the hotel.'

Noah looked as surprised by this as Aria was.

'You don't have to do this,' Aria said, but her little heart was already filling with hope.

'The hotel belongs to our family, we want it back,' Clover said.

'If we do this, it would be a twenty-five percent split each, between the four of us,' Noah said.

'That's what we thought,' Skye said. 'Equal partners.'

Noah swirled the whisky around his glass for a moment and Aria wondered if he would even agree to it. To turn this hotel around would be a huge amount of work and if he only had twenty-five percent of the profits, there would be very little gain for him.

Noah looked up. 'I would have conditions before I would agree to this.'

Aria saw the fire in Skye's eyes. She obviously hadn't been expecting this. Skye had worked for herself for too long, she certainly wasn't used to taking orders. To her credit she didn't say anything.

'Clover, your money will be used to renovate the garden room downstairs into a dance studio. I'll need you to oversee that project and then take over all the fitness and dance classes for our guests, come up with a daily schedule. It's also something we can offer to the islanders too.'

Clover's face lit up.

'Skye, there is an old wooden lodge at the end of the gardens that was once a café. I'd want your money to be used to renovate that into an ice cream café and I'd need you to run that side of things for me. I want somewhere special for the guests to go for dessert, somewhere with great views and access to the beach too.'

There was silence from Skye.

Aria stared at Noah, her heart filling with love for this wonderful man. He'd just made both her sisters' dreams come true. Tears filled her eyes for probably the tenth time that day.

Skye lifted her whisky glass. 'Deal.'

Clover held up hers too. Noah and Aria joined them.

'To being equal partners,' Noah said.

'Equal partners,' they all said, chinking their glasses together.

CHAPTER SIX

They talked for hours, coming up with ideas and plans, and Noah had loved to see the passion for the hotel from the sisters, especially in Aria. Today had not turned out how she'd planned at all but she seemed to be heading down this new path with great gusto and determination. He was probably going to have to rein her in on some of her ideas but for now he was just happy to see her smiling again.

Skye stood up. 'I have to go and get everything ready for dinner.'

Noah stood up too. 'Tonight won't be the last time you'll be cooking in that kitchen, but I promise you, I'll have a replacement for you soon.'

Skye nodded and left the room.

'I better go too,' Clover said. 'I presume you'll want to go through the accounts at some point.'

'Yes I would,' Noah said.

'Then I better make sure everything is in order for you.'

'I wouldn't worry too much about that. I already know the hotel isn't running at profit so I wouldn't bother trying to dress it up to make it look better. Hit me with the facts and I can look at ways we might be able to save money.'

Clover nodded. 'I'll get you all the paperwork tomorrow.'

She shut the door behind her, leaving him and Aria alone.

Noah sat back down and she stared at him. The atmosphere crackled in the air between them. She glanced over at his bed just briefly and his heart thundered in response.

She stood up. 'I should go too, there's always lots to do.'

'Yes, I have a ton of phone calls to make. I've already booked some builders and decorators to come, so they should be starting the day after tomorrow, I think. I'll check in with them.'

Her face fell a little. 'Yes, erm… of course.'

Noah could see Aria was going to be one of those hotel managers who needed to be kept in the loop about everything.

'Why don't you have dinner with me tonight and I can discuss my plans for the renovations with you?' Noah said.

She smiled again. 'I'd like that.'

She moved to the door.

'And you'll definitely show up this time,' he teased.

She grinned. 'Of course. I don't have any more pregnant receptionists to look after.'

He glanced over to the table near the balcony where the candle was still sitting in the middle from the night before and then his eyes found his bed. It had never looked so inviting as it did with Aria standing mere feet away from him. He turned back to her. 'Maybe we should have dinner in the main restaurant tonight.'

That was one of his better ideas. Lots of people, no chance of him being inappropriate with his new manager.

She actually smirked like she knew this was torture for

him and was finding it amusing. 'I think that's probably a good idea.'

She reached for the handle and then turned back and reached up and stroked his face. Christ, the feel of her fingers on his cheek was heaven. He wanted to pull away, he wanted to tell her that this was not appropriate for business partners, but he couldn't do it. It took every ounce of willpower he had not to haul her close and kiss her again.

'Thank you.'

He cleared his throat but still he didn't pull away. 'For what?'

'For... being there for me today, for giving me back hope again and mostly for what you did for my sisters. You've made their dreams come true and you didn't have to do that.'

'This is their home and I know that your dad would have wanted them involved too, if that's what they wanted.'

'I know, but you could have just taken their money and given them twenty-five percent each. What you offered them was so much more than any of us could have hoped for.'

'I want this place to be a success almost as much as you do, and for that to work I need everyone involved to be as passionate as you are. I wanted to give them something to get excited about so they're not just sticking around out of loyalty.'

'Well, you've certainly given them that. And you've made their decision to stay an easier one, so thank you for that too. I would have missed them so much if they'd left.'

'So I've made their dreams come true, but what about yours? What are your dreams?'

What was he doing? He'd drawn a professional line between them and now he was asking her how he could make her dreams come true. But although it wasn't a good idea for anything to happen between them, it didn't change the feelings he'd had for her for the last four or five years. He wanted her to be happy, even if he couldn't be with her.

'For the hotel to be a success,' Aria said, without missing a beat.

He smiled. 'Do you have any dreams that are just for you?'

She hesitated and shook her head. He gave her a meaningful look.

'I don't think it counts as a dream, more something I want to do at some point in my life. And I'm not sure I need your help for it anyway, it's something I can do on my own,' she said.

'Try me.'

'It's not something I could do for a few years. I have this place and I want to make it a success, I want to make my dad proud, I want to build a successful business for my sisters, I want to bring life back to the island again. You've given me that hope. I felt so lost this morning when I found out but I'm excited about all the possibilities now.'

Noah watched her for a moment and decided he'd come back to her dreams another day.

'So you're happy?' he asked.

Her eyes cast down to his lips and then she let her hand fall from his face. 'Mostly. I'm excited about working with you on this and getting some of your expertise on a project that means so much to me. I'm loving the fact that Skye and Clover are going to stay but... I hate that *we* never even had a proper chance. I still feel so conflicted over you leaving and the secrets but I felt like we had something special and we missed out on that.'

'I know,' he said, softly. 'That's the worst part of this. I wanted to say no to your dad so badly because I wanted to see where it would go with you, but he begged me to do it and I couldn't turn him down. But I just don't see how we could have a relationship now. The next few months are going to be busy and stressful and we will argue a lot. That's hardly the best start for us, is it?'

'I suppose not.' She stared down at the floor and she looked so crestfallen he just wanted to reach out and hold her. But he'd already blurred the line of professionalism today. 'Although, don't you think working alongside each other would be a good test for a relationship? If we could get through that, we'd know we could face anything together.'

God, he wanted to give it a go more than anything. He wanted to kiss her again, he wanted to spend time getting to know her properly and, when they'd talked about growing old and grey together, there was a huge part of him that wanted exactly that. He felt like he belonged here with her. But there was a part of him that knew he wasn't good at relationships. He had argued constantly with his ex-wife and, although he had no experience of what a loving relationship was like, having never grown up in one, he was pretty sure it wasn't supposed to be filled with arguments. He was the sort of person that people fell out of love with very easily and where would it leave them if or when it ended? He owed it to Thomas to see this project through and working alongside Aria every day after they had broken up would make things very difficult.

'You know what.' Aria lifted her chin defiantly. 'You're right, it wouldn't work between us. If I'm with a man, I'd want to be with someone who knew I was worth the risk, not someone who is too scared to take a chance. You walked away from me before and that hurt, I'm not going to give you the chance to hurt me again. We'll be business partners, nothing more. Let's forget dinner tonight. You can meet me in my office tomorrow and we'll discuss your plans for the renovations then.'

With that, she turned and walked away. He was about to call her back but this was for the best. Strictly professional. He walked back into his suite and closed the door, leaning his head against it. So why did letting her go feel like the biggest mistake he'd ever made?

CHAPTER SEVEN

Later that afternoon Aria went back down to the village with Snowflake in tow. God, Noah Campbell was infuriating. Infuriatingly likeable, that was the main problem with all of this. He was sweet and lovely and kind and, if she was completely honest with herself, she'd fallen a tiny bit in love with him many years before. And the annoying thing was that she was pretty sure he felt the same. Well, maybe he didn't love her but he certainly felt something for her that went way beyond a simple kiss. And she understood that working alongside each other and having a relationship could be complicated, but she also knew that many couples had met their partner or spouse at work. So it wasn't always the negative experience that Noah thought it would be.

She stopped to take a picture of a large flower bed filled with tulips of every colour; she'd upload it onto the hotel's Instagram account later.

Aria thought back to what Noah had said earlier about being a terrible husband when he was married before. She wondered if *that* had more to do with his reservations about their relationship than just the potential awkwardness of getting involved with someone he worked with. She knew he held a lot of the responsibility of their failed marriage on his shoulders, though she didn't know all the details.

She'd never had a serious relationship before. Of course there'd been men that she'd dated for a few weeks or months, but nothing that you could ever class as life-changing. When her relationships had come to an end she might have been a bit sad if it was the man who had ended it, or a bit relieved if it was her who had finished it, but she'd never felt guilt that the relationship hadn't worked. She'd never felt like a failure. But she knew that Noah had felt those things because he'd told her so not long after he'd got a divorce. She wondered if that still lay heavily on his mind.

If that was the case, her heart went out to him. That was a heavy burden to carry.

She shook her head. No, she didn't want to feel sympathy for him. The man was an ass.

Except he wasn't, not at all. He had hurt her when he walked away after they'd kissed but there'd been circumstances out of his control and secrets he'd been sworn to keep. He had done all of this for her dad, despite not wanting to take the project on, and she couldn't help but love him a little bit more for that.

She let out a little sigh of frustration.

She knew he was worried about working alongside her if something did happen between them and it went wrong, but she was more concerned with how torturous it was going to be to work alongside him and not have anything happen between them at all. How did you fall out of love with someone when they were there, every day, being so bloody lovely all of the time?

Aria spotted Izzy Quinn sitting on a wall near the fountain, looking a bit forlorn.

She walked straight over to her.

'Hey Izzy, you OK?'

Izzy looked up at her, seemingly carrying the weight of the world on her young shoulders.

'Yeah, I'm OK.'

Aria sat down next to her. 'Except you're not.'

Izzy sighed, stroking Snowflake's ears who had flopped down next to her. 'I'm just worried about Mum.'

'Is Delilah OK?'

'Oh, health wise I think she's fine – unless she's keeping that from me as well. The doctors all seem happy with how she's doing. I just worry about the stress of her not having a job. She shouldn't have to worry about that, she needs to focus on getting better.'

'She has a job,' Aria said. 'Whenever she's ready she can come and work at the hotel. If that's next week or next month, there will always be a job for her.'

'Thank you. I suppose she's worried what we will do in the meantime. Even if she comes and works for you, it'll be a month before she will get paid.'

'We can pay her in cash, on a daily basis if necessary. And if you guys are short of food, you can come to the hotel for breakfast and dinner, no charge. All of our employees eat for free and, as she is pretty much an employee already, she can take advantage of that now – both of you can.'

Izzy stared at her. 'Really?'

'Yes, and let me tell you, Skye's food is amazing, her desserts and puddings are simply heaven. You should definitely come along for those alone.'

Izzy smiled and Aria was relieved to see it.

'Thank you. I'll tell her,' Izzy said.

'You're both welcome any time.'

'Thanks. Oh look, there's Abigail.' Izzy waved at her friend. 'I better go. Thank you.'

'Anytime,' Aria said.

Izzy ran off and Aria watched her go. She was sure Noah would have something to say about Aria giving away free food but right now she didn't care.

Aria stood up, tugging Snowflake gently to his feet, and they made her way over to the greengrocers. She picked up a melon, sniffing the glorious sweet scent.

'If you buy two of them, I'll give you the third free,' Madge said, as she came to the door.

'Well, that sounds like a bargain and I'll have some of these raspberries too,' Aria said, tying up Snowflake and following Madge back inside. Seamus, one of the islanders, was in there, deliberating over a punnet of strawberries. Aria liked Seamus; he reminded her of Santa with his bright clothes, round belly, white beard and jolly outlook on life. He had an opinion on everything too, and because he'd been born and raised on the island people would often listen to whatever he had to say.

Madge's husband, Toby, came from the back carrying a tray of large dirty potatoes.

'We heard the news, love,' Toby said, dumping the tray on one of the shelves and giving her a sympathetic look.

'News?' Aria said, blankly.

'About the hotel, that your dad sold it off to some Scottish billionaire.'

'He's not Scottish,' Aria said. She paused in denying that Noah was a billionaire; she had no idea about his finances.

'Oh, I thought with a name like Campbell...' Madge trailed off.

'Well he certainly hasn't got an accent and does it really matter where he's from?'

'We heard your dad gave all his money to Clover and Skye and left you with nothing,' Toby ploughed on.

Seamus turned around, his eyes wide, not even pretending he wasn't listening.

Wow. News certainly travelled fast and not even accurately. Clearly, now that Francis was free to spill her dad's secrets, he had let it slip to a few people and it had been embellished and exaggerated in the last few hours. Well, in fact, he only needed to have mentioned it to Maggie, his assistant, and the whole island would know by the end of the day.

'That's not entirely true,' Aria said as Madge deliberately took her time bagging up the fruit so she could hear the gossip from the horse's mouth. Seamus wandered closer.

Part of her wanted to tell them to mind their own business but she didn't want anyone to think badly of her dad or to start reading into rumours as to why he had left her nothing.

'Dad left me part of the hotel because he knew it was important to me. He didn't want my sisters to feel obligated to stay if they didn't want to, and he didn't want me to have to sell the hotel to give them their share. So this seemed like the wisest course of action to him,' Aria said, taking the bag of fruit from Madge. 'But actually Clover and Skye have decided to stay here and have bought their share of the hotel back.'

Obviously that wasn't official yet but it would be soon.

'Well, that's good,' Seamus said. 'Skye's food is amazing. The hotel will benefit from having both of them there.'

Madge and Toby exchanged doubtful glances, apparently not as won over as Seamus was.

'And who is this Mr Campbell that is swooping in here and changing everything?' Madge said.

'He hasn't changed anything yet,' Aria said.

'Oh, you mark my words, he'll be changing everything,' Madge said.

'Noah Campbell is very experienced in the hotel business; he knows what makes a hotel work. Dad didn't just sell part of the hotel to some random man, he chose Noah specifically because of his skills and experience.'

'We looked him up, he buys hotels, does them up and sells them on,' Toby said. 'And do you know who he sells most of his hotels to? Starburst Heights Hotels. That big faceless chain of near-identical hotels. We don't want that sort of thing here.'

Aria's heart sank; she hadn't realised that. 'I'm sure that's not his intention. Philips Hotel has charm and character, he wouldn't want to take that away.'

'I'm sure the owners of those other hotels hoped that too.'

'Well, Starburst Heights Hotels are one of the most successful hotel chains in the world,' Seamus said, encouragingly. 'Maybe it wouldn't be the worst thing to have one of those chain hotels here – it would bring a good trade to the island.'

But Madge and Toby obviously didn't think it would be a good thing at all. Aria didn't blame them.

'That hotel has been here for nearly a hundred years, it's part of this island. We don't want to see it changed,' Madge said.

Aria couldn't imagine anything worse for the tiny Jewel Island than for the hotel to be bought by Starburst Heights Hotels. They did not need a big brash resort that was one of many clones. She would rather continue running the business alone, without Noah, than for it to be sold to Starburst Heights. But she didn't want to be disloyal to Noah and start insulting his plans before he'd even been there a day. She would talk to him about her concerns, of course, but right now she needed to present a unified front to the islanders, try to put their minds at ease.

'Look, the hotel needs updating, things need to change, it's not working right now,' Aria said. 'I have thirteen rooms occupied and that includes Noah's. The hotel has seventy rooms. It's the Easter holidays and the weather is glorious. Right now, I'm willing to do anything to help the hotel increase its guests and that will help the island too.'

Madge shook her head sorrowfully. 'They won't like it.'

'They' being the self-appointed town council for the island, which Madge was a part of. The council members believed they were the ones in charge of all the decisions on Jewel Island. They probably wouldn't like *anything* that Noah and Aria were going to do with the hotel.

'Then maybe you can have a word with them, because something needs to change. The island is dying and we have to do something to save it – even if we have to sell our souls along the way,' Aria said.

'And what about the festival of light? We always have fireworks every year to celebrate the festival of light. I suppose the big party won't be happening now *he's* in charge,' Toby said.

Aria sighed. 'It's nothing to do with Noah, we just don't have a lot of money right now.'

'I'm sure there'll be plenty of money for gold chandeliers and marble floors though,' Madge said, begrudgingly.

'Most of the money for the renovations will be coming from his pocket so he can spend it on whatever he thinks is best for the hotel, and that includes marble floors if he wants. I'm not going to ask him to put his hand in his pocket and pay out for a big party. Do you have any idea how much a firework display actually costs?'

Seamus turned to Madge. 'If you want a big party with

fireworks, then maybe the town council can pay for it for a change instead of looking to the hotel to pay for everything.'

Aria couldn't help smiling. She couldn't have said it better herself.

But Seamus wasn't finished. 'Her dad spent his whole life giving to this island, maybe it's time the island gave something back.'

Madge and Toby stared at Seamus and Aria used the distraction to grab her fruit and leave before they could find anything else to pick fault at. She was untying Snowflake just as Seamus walked out.

They headed down the road a little, away from prying ears. 'Thanks for that,' Aria said.

'Oh, no problem.' Seamus shrugged. 'They make me so frustrated sometimes with their take, take, take attitude. If they want this island to survive they have to help too.'

Seamus saw one of his friends and hurried over to them with a quick wave goodbye in Aria's direction. Aria continued down the road to her godmother's bakery.

God, she'd had so much hope after her meeting with Noah earlier and now it felt like her bubble had well and truly burst. Surely the islanders didn't want the hotel to stay as it was, limping along with next to no guests? Although the thought of it becoming another Starburst Heights Hotel made her feel sick. That was the very last thing she wanted. This was her home.

And now she would upset the town council by refusing to have the traditional festival of light party too. But there were so many more important things to spend their money on; a party just for the sake of it seemed a bit excessive.

And although she knew most of the islanders would understand, she wanted the town council to get behind the changes in the hotel. She didn't want Noah to come up against confrontation before he had even started. If they knew what the plans were for the hotel that might be easier rather than rumours and hearsay fuelling a fire. Maybe they could have a small party for the festival of light, drinks and a few nibbles, just to get the locals on their side. Then, once they were suitable happy from the free drinks, she could show them the plans for the renovations, sell them the exciting changes.

Although the town council would never be happy.

She rolled her eyes at how quickly rumours had spread since that morning and how fast people had made their minds up about what was happening.

She had to laugh that they thought Noah was a billionaire. She'd never really thought of him as having loads of money before. He was just Noah. But if he was buying and selling hotels, he must have some money to his name. Not many people could produce the kind of money he'd needed to buy seventy-five percent of the hotel at a drop of a hat. And earlier, when she had moaned about not having any money left to her in the will, Noah had offered her half a million without batting an eye. If he had sold many of the hotels he'd bought to Starburst Heights, he must have made some decent money over the years. Oh god, what if he *was* a billionaire?

Suddenly there were more potential reasons why he hadn't wanted to pursue a relationship with her. She was a woman who had next to nothing. If he was a billionaire he could have any woman he wanted; rich, successful, glamorous women who he would be proud to have on his arm. Maybe for him the kiss had been just a kiss, nothing more, and here she was expecting him to jump into a proper relationship. No wonder he was back-pedalling away from it.

Aria tied Snowflake up outside The Vanilla Bean and stepped inside. Her godmother was busy serving so she scooted through to the kitchen and put the kettle on. She was sure Kendra would want to hear all about her meeting, if she hadn't already heard on the grapevine. She poured out two mugs of tea and placed them on the table.

There were some peanut cookies cooling on a tray and Aria helped herself to one as Kendra came back into the kitchen.

Her godmother eyed Aria stuffing her face with the cookie. 'Is it really as bad as I've heard?'

Aria shook her head and sat down at the table. 'I'm not sure what you've heard as it seems to have been embellished quite a lot since I found out this morning. But let me tell you the truth and you can decide whether it's bad or not.'

Kendra sat down opposite her, clutching the mug of tea as Aria explained everything.

'Well that's not as bad as I'd heard,' Kendra said when Aria had finished. 'But I don't like the idea of this Noah Campbell owning part of your hotel.'

'I'm actually excited about working with him to make the hotel better.'

'Will you be as excited when he starts making lots of changes you don't agree with?'

Aria knew there would be lots of things happening around the hotel that she wouldn't necessarily agree with, and she would fight against the changes she felt strongly for, but she knew he had a wealth of experience in making hotels successful and she had to remember that.

'Noah is a good man, he's very clever and he knows his stuff. I'm certainly going to try to be open to his ideas.'

Kendra's gaze softened. 'You really like him?'

Aria shook her head. 'We're business partners. I respect him.'

Kendra studied her for a moment. 'I always knew you had a little soft spot for him but this is something more for you, isn't it? Especially after what happened between you before.'

Aria let out a little sigh. 'I do like him, but nothing is going to happen between us.'

'Well, that's very sensible, but do you really think you can work together and not let anything happen?'

'That's down to him. I think he'd like to keep things professional.'

'I looked him up,' Kendra said.

'God, I wish people wouldn't do that. I hope that my life and the kind of person I am would never be judged by some articles someone had found on Google. There is a lot more to him than that.'

'That may be the case, but from what I can see, a place like Jewel Island and Philips Hotel would never be the sort of place that Noah Campbell would buy. He buys these massive hotels in big cities. This is quite a detour for him and something must have made him decide to buy it,' Kendra said, giving Aria a meaningful look.

'Because Dad begged him to.'

'Or maybe there was another reason.'

'He loves Jewel Island,' Aria said.

'And maybe he loves something else too.'

Aria rolled her eyes.

Kendra laughed. 'Maybe you need to keep an open mind about that as well.'

Aria walked back to reception to find Katy still there, manning the desk. She looked well and truly bored and was quite obviously trying to read a book surreptitiously. There wasn't a customer in sight.

'What are you reading?' Aria said, leaning on the reception desk.

Katy quickly tried to hide the book underneath some papers but Aria gave her a look; it was a bit late for that.

Katy sighed. 'The new one from Velvet Steele.'

Aria tried to suppress a smirk. Velvet Steele was famous for having a sex scene almost on every page. Her characters had incredible stamina and would have sex every single chance they got. She was hugely popular across the world.

'Don't judge me,' Katy laughed. 'I love to escape with stuff like this. My own sex life is completely lacking, so I can live it vicariously through the pages of this book.'

'No judgement here. I've read them too and I know what you mean. Besides, reading is supposed to be an escape and whether that's in the pages of a twisty spy thriller, or something like this, what does it matter?'

'I agree. Mrs O'Hare gave it to me, she said I needed... fulfilment.'

Aria laughed. 'She's a saucy one.'

'She is. Does she really just sit in her room and watch porn all day?'

'Well, judging by the noises that come out of there, yes. Her husband is a vicar, maybe he's a bit more... buttoned-up than Mrs O'Hare would like and she comes here a few times a year to get her fix. I have no idea why she watches so much of it while she's here. Maybe you can ask her,' Aria said, playfully.

Katy laughed.

Aria could hear voices coming from the little office just off reception that Clover had commandeered as her own.

'Who's Clover with?'

'Skye.'

'Oh.'

Aria wondered whether they were discussing the hotel or

just having one of their twinnie chats. She hesitated over going into the office to join them. It was a strange thing to feel left out of her own family; she knew her sisters loved her but there was nothing quite like the bond of a twin and she simply wasn't a part of that.

The business of the will and the hotel was still playing heavily on her mind and would probably be something her sisters would still be thinking about, so it was quite likely they were talking about that rather than anything else. Deciding that she wanted to know if they had any concerns, she knocked on the door of the office and then cursed herself. She shouldn't have to do that for her own sisters. If Clover had been in there alone, she would have just walked straight in.

Clover came to the door in confusion and was then seemingly even more confused to see Aria.

'Why did you knock?'

'I didn't want to interrupt a private conversation.'

'It's not private, you silly lump, we don't have secrets from you.' Clover stepped back to let Aria in and then closed the door behind her, but Skye looked awkward.

'Are you both OK?' Aria asked.

'Yes, just talking about our plans for the new dance studio and dessert café,' Skye said, leaning against the desk. 'I'm thinking of names already, maybe Sundae Funday or Ice Cream Fundae, or The Emerald Ice House. I'm sure I'll come up with something.'

'I love those. So you're both happy about staying?' Aria said and sighed with relief when they both nodded.

'What Noah did was… wonderful,' Clover said.

'He's a kind man,' Aria said. 'And he wants you to be passionate about this place.'

Skye fiddled with the sleeve of her shirt. 'Is there something going on between you two?'

Aria's eyebrows shot up at the way the conversation had suddenly turned. She glanced at Clover, who was obviously worried about the answer too. This was what they'd been talking about.

Aria sat down.

'No, there isn't,' she said, honestly.

Her sisters exchanged glances.

'But you were going to have that date with him last night,' Clover said. 'And I heard what he said to you yesterday, it's obviously he has feelings for you.'

Aria sighed. 'It wasn't a date. He wanted to tell me about his deal with Dad ahead of our meeting with Francis so that I was prepared. And he might have feelings for me, but nothing is going to happen. I'm still hurt over how he left and he wants to keep things professional between us. And as it happened, the *date* never took place anyway thanks to Tilly's emergency trip to the hospital.'

'He was holding your hand today in the meeting,' Clover said.

'As a friend. We're friends. I've known him for a very long time.'

'We just think that it's not a good idea for you two to get involved with each other,' Skye said. 'He's here in a business capacity and it would… muddy the waters if you two were to have some kind of relationship. We don't want any business decisions to take place in the bedroom. We're equal partners now, or we will be. We want to be a part of it all too.'

Aria thought carefully how to word what she was going to say. 'You will be heavily involved, of course you will, but there will be times that me and Noah will meet and discuss things without you. I don't want to sound like a twat here and pull rank, but I'm still the hotel manager and I don't think I can defer to you for every little decision.'

She watched Skye glance over at her sister. Aria hoped to god they understood that.

'OK,' Skye said, slowly. 'But it would still be weird if you were to get together. It would shift the dynamics between us. Also, we then have the awkwardness of you working with him if it all goes wrong.'

Why did everyone assume it would go wrong? Why could Noah and Skye not focus on the positive instead of the negative? They could get together and live happily ever after. But as it happened, none of that mattered. Noah had put the brakes on before it had even started.

'He hurt you so badly last time,' Clover said. 'We don't want you to get hurt again.'

'Not least because I'll have to beat the crap out of him if he does and that could make our equal partnership a bit awkward too,' Skye said.

Aria smiled at the protectiveness of her sisters.

'I can assure you nothing is happening between me and Noah Campbell,' she said. 'You don't have to worry about things being awkward between us. I will be professional in all my dealings with him in regards to the hotel. I want this hotel to be a success as much as you do and I won't let anything ruin that.'

Her sisters seemed satisfied with that.

Except Aria hadn't been professional with him earlier. She had been hurt that he hadn't even wanted to try having a relationship for fear of it going wrong and had practically flounced off. She couldn't let things get weird between them, that was exactly what her sisters were worried about.

Aria gave a little sigh. Maybe the fact that nothing was going to happen really was for the best.

CHAPTER EIGHT

Noah finished his bowl of soup and sat back for a moment. He'd barely placed his spoon down when the bowl was whisked away by a girl who couldn't be any older than sixteen. He'd like to think it was efficiency but it was probably more to do with the fact that he was one of only a handful of guests in the restaurant that evening and the two waiting staff had next to nothing to do.

From his corner booth he could see the whole of the restaurant and the spectacular view of the sun as it set into the sea, leaving tangerine and candyfloss-pink clouds dancing across the sky. The restaurant should have been packed and the fact it wasn't had absolutely nothing to do with the food – the soup was one of the nicest he'd ever had and he'd eaten in a lot of fine restaurants around the world.

Movement across the restaurant caught his eye and his heart leapt as he saw Aria coming towards him. God, she was incredible. Her dark hair was loose, a sleek ebony curtain tumbling over her shoulder. She was wearing a pretty summer dress that seemed to float and shimmer as she moved. But there was something else that sparkled about her as she moved through the tables, smiling at her guests and stopping to check on some of them. She just glowed.

Finally she was at his table and her smile seemed that much bigger for him. It filled him with so much warmth.

'Can I join you?'

'Of course.'

He hadn't expected that at all – they'd not exactly left on good terms earlier – but he quickly shifted over to make room for her.

She slid into the booth next to him and for a second he could feel her warmth, the gentle touch as her leg brushed against his, her sweet coconut scent washing over him before she realised she was sitting a bit too close and scooted a bit further away.

'What did you order?'

'Steak,' Noah said.

'That sounds good.' Aria waved over the efficient waitress. 'SJ, can you ask Skye to do me a steak as well please, she knows how I like it.'

'OK,' SJ said and scuttled off in the direction of the kitchen.

Aria smiled at him, tucking a lock of her hair behind her ear. She was nervous and he didn't like that.

'You seem to talk to some of the guests like you know them,' Noah said, gesturing to the people she'd said hello to on her way through the restaurant.

'I do. Most of these are regulars and come every year, sometimes two or three times a year,' Aria said.

Just then an elderly woman in a long purple velvet cloak swept into the room. It was a woman he recognised but he couldn't think of where from. Then it hit him. Sylvia Steele.

Aria saw him looking at her. 'That's Mrs O'Hare, she's... slightly eccentric.'

He got the feeling she was being diplomatic.

'I know her actually, we've met before. She has stayed in hotels all round the world and we've bumped into each other on several occasions.'

'Oh really?' Aria's eyes lit up. 'I don't know a lot about her, other than... well, she spends a lot of time in her room.'

'Oh, well she's probably working.'

Aria laughed. 'I don't think so, not judging by the noises that come out of her room.'

Noah wasn't sure what she meant but at that moment Sylvia drifted over to their table.

'Noah, how lovely to see you here,' Sylvia said as Noah stood up and kissed her on the cheek.

'It's good to see you too, how's work?'

'Oh, you know, the usual,' Sylvia laughed. She glanced at Aria and her eyes lit up. 'Are you two together?'

Noah smiled at the way she'd got straight to the point. 'No, I'm here in a business capacity.'

'All work and no play, Noah dear. It wouldn't hurt you to have a little fun while you're here.'

He smirked. 'I'll keep that in mind.'

'And if you need any tips...'

'I'm sure I've got that department covered.'

'I bet you have,' Sylvia laughed and then moved off to her own table.

Noah sat back down again.

'You do know her,' Aria said, in delight.

'Yes, we've had dinner a few times, although I didn't know her under the name you said. But maybe she has moved on to another husband now.'

Aria's eyes widened. 'What does that mean? How many husbands has she had?'

'She was on her fifth the last time we met, but that was a

few years ago. Although she's always kept her maiden name before now.'

'Five husbands?' Aria laughed. 'And what work does she do? She looks like she's well past retirement age.'

'She is, I think she's approaching eighty. Although, if you don't know what work she does, it's probably not my place to say.'

'Now that has me intrigued,' Aria said, her eyes sparkling.

'Why don't you ask her one day, I'm sure she'd tell you.'

'I think I will.'

Aria fell silent for a moment and it felt a little awkward between them when it had never been that way before.

She gazed out of the windows that stretched up the entire side of the restaurant. 'Another glorious sunset tonight, we do get some beauties here.'

He stared at her. She was attempting polite small talk. He could manage that. They'd had years of friendly, simple conversations before… before their conversations had become more serious, before his feelings had deepened, before he had kissed her.

'It's one of the many things about this place that brings me happiness,' he said, not taking his eyes off her.

She turned to look at him and then quickly looked away, a smile playing on her lips. 'Mr Campbell, do I need to remind you we're going to keep things strictly professional.'

He suppressed a smile at her playful tone.

'I was commenting on the view,' Noah said. He absolutely had not been talking about the view and they both knew that.

She cleared her throat. 'Why don't you tell me your plans for the renovations?'

He could do that at least, even if it was the last thing he wanted to talk about with her. 'Well, the outside of the hotel is actually in good shape.'

She nodded. 'Dad didn't believe in change but he never let things fall into disrepair. We get some bad winters here and he always made sure the outside of the hotel was fortified and maintained.'

'It's just the inside that needs decorating and updating. New flooring in the lobby, I was thinking a marble finish.'

She winced.

'What?'

'Nothing, it's just that… I'm not sure some people would think marble floor is in keeping with the character of the hotel.'

'Who are "some people"?' Noah asked.

'Well, the island town council for a start.'

'The island town council? I didn't realise I had to run everything past them too.'

'You don't, of course you don't,' Aria quickly back-pedalled.

He watched her for a moment. 'I get the impression that you spend your life trying to make everyone else happy.'

She frowned. 'I wouldn't say that.'

He stared at her, wondering why she couldn't see what he could. He had fallen for this amazing woman many years before but now he was here more permanently he felt like he was peeling back the layers he hadn't seen before.

She sighed. 'All my life, I've kind of felt like I've never really fit in. I'm not sure why. Maybe because I was adopted and this family, this place, was never meant to be mine. But I've always felt like I needed to keep everyone happy in order to be accepted.'

'And how has that worked out for you?'

Aria smiled, ruefully. 'Well I guess I've earned a reputation for always saying yes.'

'Did it help you to fit in?'

'I've always been accepted by the locals. But some of the older generation don't like the young folk growing up and getting ideas above their station. The older folk are in charge and they like us young uns to know it. I think that feeling of not belonging comes from me, not them. Of not knowing where I came from or anything about my birth parents and why they dumped me. And I'm not sure that can ever be fixed.'

He had a sudden overwhelming urge to reach out and hug her. They'd had a similar start to their lives. His parents hadn't wanted him either and those kinds of scars never really went away, no matter what.

'I didn't have the best childhood either,' Noah said. 'And I know it has impacted on me and my relationships so I'm probably not the best person to give advice. But I think you need to carve your own path in life. There is no point being someone you're not to simply fit in. You should embrace your differences. And pursue the things *you* want, go after what makes you happy, follow *your* dreams for a change.'

She smiled. 'I like the sound of that.'

'I just think that the only opinions that count when it comes to the changes in the hotel are yours, your sisters' and mine. And if someone tries to push their opinion on you, well maybe you tell them where to stick it.'

She stared at him with wide eyes and then burst out laughing. 'I'd love to tell a few of them where to stick it.'

'Be bold, Aria, show them who's boss.'

She laughed again and he loved the sound of it.

'OK, back to the floor. Marble would be expensive,' she said.

'It's classy,' Noah countered.

She pulled a face. 'I'd prefer a cosier finish, some new carpet perhaps, maybe a nice plain royal blue.'

'We want to upgrade the hotel – a marble-effect floor

would make it look plush, in another league from where it is now.'

'You mean it would make it look like a Starburst Heights Hotel?'

Noah frowned. 'You make that sound like a bad thing. They are one of the most successful hotel chains in the world.'

'Is that really where you see this place, another uniform chain hotel?'

He thought about this for a moment. He hadn't really considered what would happen when the hotel was finished and a big success again. Would he sell his part of the hotel and move on? The year before, his plan had been to retire to Jewel Island, get a little cottage overlooking Sapphire Bay, get himself a dog, maybe spend the rest of his life with a wonderful woman – he glanced at Aria for a moment. Then, agreeing to that deal with Aria's dad had ruined all of that. Could he still settle here when all of this was done? Would Aria still want him to? But that wasn't the question here.

'Would I sell the hotel to Starburst Heights? No, that wasn't my plan.' He watched her sigh with relief. 'But that still doesn't mean it wouldn't benefit from a touch of class. If you want you can have some blue carpet in the bar or as a large welcome mat in the entrance. Or we could look at blue carpet in the bedrooms. But the lobby is the first impression and it wouldn't hurt for new guests to think the hotel is elegant as they walk up to their bedrooms.'

The steaks arrived at that point and Aria tucked straight in, chewing as she thought.

'I'm going to let you have that,' she said.

That surprised him; he'd thought he would have to fight her for it. She glanced at him and must have seen the look on his face.

'I think there is going to be a lot I don't agree with about the changes you're going to make to the hotel,' Aria said. 'But the way I see it, the hotel is not working as it is and you have a wealth of experience when it comes to stuff like this, so for the most part I think I will have to bow down to your expertise. Doesn't mean I'm going to hand you the hotel on a plate, I will fight for the important things, but...' she shrugged. 'Pick your battles, I guess.'

He stared at her for a moment. She was different to other hotel managers or staff he'd worked with in the past. They would either fight him for every little thing or just hand the hotel over and walk away. Aria cared, and that was an important quality, but she also recognised the hotel needed to change, despite any sentimental attachment she might have to the place because of her parents. She caught him staring and he quickly diverted his attention to his steak which melted in his mouth.

'This is so good.'

Aria nodded as she carried on eating. 'Skye knows her stuff.'

'I'm kind of regretting saying she could be in charge of ice creams and desserts if she cooks like this,' Noah said.

He dipped a bit of steak into the dauphinoise potatoes and then paused with his fork halfway to his mouth as he realised Aria was staring at him and definitely not in a good way.

'What?'

'Don't do that,' she said, all warmth gone from her voice. 'Don't promise one thing and then take it back. Skye is beyond excited about her ice cream café. Don't take that away from her.'

'I won't, I'm not,' Noah said. 'I would never go back on my word. The offer still stands. I'm merely saying she is clearly an exceptional chef and that's one of the things that would ensure the hotel gets good reviews. But I know many great chefs, I can find someone just as good to replace her.'

Aria evidently thawed a little and resumed her eating. 'I'm sorry. I just want this to work, for all of us.'

'I want that too.'

She nodded. 'So tell me what your plans are for the bedrooms.'

'New carpet throughout, new curtains or blinds, lick of paint. I think some of the bathrooms will need completely new suites, new tiling, showers, toilets, sinks. Basically a complete overhaul in every room. The rooms could do with some new furniture and some new artwork too.'

'There's a shop in the village that sells paintings, really lovely modern stuff, quirky too –some of them are quite funny and the guests might appreciate that. Also, if they like the paintings, that could give some business to the art shop if people want to buy their own copies.'

'I'll have a look at them and see if they are suitable.'

Aria carried on eating for a moment. 'How long will it take?'

'For everything? Maybe three months. I'd like to hold a big reopening maybe at the end of July and hopefully attract a big crowd for the summer holidays.'

She bit her lip thoughtfully.

'What are you thinking?'

'Nothing. Well, it's just that we have the spring festival of light in two weeks, I'm wondering if we could do something special for that.'

'I've never been here for that, tell me about it.'

'It's something we've had here on the island as far back as I can remember and for many years before that. There's a parade with lanterns that goes from one end of the island to the other. It starts on the east side and travels to the west, to recreate the path the sun takes. It ends here at the hotel and there's normally fireworks to celebrate, although we didn't do that last year... for obvious reasons. The parade is pretty spectacular though, the lanterns are lots of different shapes and sizes and the costumes are wonderful. All the children from the local school get involved. It used to be a big draw for the tourists. The hotel always used to be full and we'd open up the gardens to let people camp there.'

Noah smiled slightly; he loved seeing her passion and enthusiasm. But then his smile faded. 'I'd rather not push the hotel when it's not looking its best or there's builders and decorators everywhere. Sure-fire way to get bad reviews is to have noise and mess for people to complain about. The fewer guests the better over the next few months. I won't cancel anyone who has already booked, although we need to make it clear to them that there will be some disruption. But I'd rather we didn't take any more guests on until all the work has finished.'

'We can't turn guests away.' Aria looked horrified at this prospect.

'We can if it's for the best in the long run. Have you seen the most recent reviews for the hotel? The guests are not exactly singing our praises. We don't need to add fuel to the fire.'

He had an idea for how he could distance the hotel from those reviews but he knew he'd need to broach that subject very carefully.

But Aria was not to be deterred. 'It's only one weekend. What if we were to invite people to stay, do a special offer for the weekend of the festival of light? Maybe we could hold a small party. We don't need to worry about fireworks. We could put up boards in the lobby showing people all the changes and plans so they can see what's coming and hopefully pique their interest enough to persuade them to book for the grand reopening. I reckon the islanders would love to see our plans too. I'm sure we could get a few of the bedrooms finished by then. Well, if not the bathrooms, the rest of the bedroom could be decorated. I know the lobby won't be done by then but we could decorate it for the festival of light, put fairy lights everywhere. Drape material over the ceiling and walls to make it look like the inside of a marquee, but also to hide a multitude of sins. We hold off on doing any of the big renovations to the main areas of the hotel until after then. But we let everyone know it's under new management and things are changing.'

He couldn't help smiling; her enthusiasm was infectious. But like many things she had suggested in the last few hours, he was going to have to rein her in.

'Why is this festival so important to you?'

Aria was quiet for a moment. 'The island is dying, the restaurants and shops are closing, and I feel a huge sense of responsibility for that. I wonder if doing more for the festival of light might help bring more custom to the island.'

'Admittedly, the hotel isn't looking its best right now. But the islanders have to take some responsibility for the lack of tourists too. What are they doing to help the island? What are they doing to help the hotel? Are the locals eating in your restaurant on a regular basis?'

Aria shook her head.

'Did they ever pay to use the pool before it was closed?'

'No.'

'Have any of them ever used the hotel to hold a party for a birthday or some kind of celebration?'

'No, well Elsie did, but the islanders don't have much money.'

'But they're not helping themselves when they stay closed for most of the year.'

She nodded to concede this.

'It works both ways. And as wonderful as all of your plans for the festival sound, it might be a bit ambitious to organise something like that, especially in the space of two weeks. A party would take a lot of planning and organisation and we have no idea if anyone would even come.'

'They'll come. Dad had a lot of wonderful, loyal friends, you being one of them. If we invite them, they'll come.'

'OK,' Noah said slowly. 'If you can take care of that, that's a start. But what we really need is some bloggers and travel journalists, that kind of thing, to get the word out to the right people. But we need to keep it small.'

'A drinks reception then. And I'm sure you know some people in that field that you could invite along in return for some free accommodation and a free cocktail.'

He did know a few trusted journalists who would give him column space in a 'coming soon' kind of way.

'Oooh, we could have Skye run some kind of dessert station, to show people what kinds of things she'll be selling in her new ice cream café, get her to come up with some weird and wacky creations to celebrate the festival of light.'

'Not a bad idea,' he said, then shook his head at the fact that he was getting swept along with Aria's madcap schemes. But this could be a good way to drum up enough interest for the grand reopening in July, let people know that something good was coming. 'OK, so how about we focus all of our renovations in the next two weeks on the bedrooms? We won't do the bathrooms as that would take too long – or maybe we do one bathroom so we can show photos of what's to come. We need to order curtains and carpets.'

Aria nodded. 'I know someone on the island who might be able to help with carpets.'

'Really? You have a carpet shop on the island?'

'I know, I think everyone was surprised when Nick opened up a carpet shop here. He's hardly going to be overrun with customers, but he'd sold carpets his whole life and when he retired here he thought he'd carry on doing what he does best. He only opens part time but it'd be good to support the islanders.'

He frowned. 'Whoever we use, it needs to be made, delivered and fitted within two weeks and we'd need enough carpets to do all the bedrooms in the hotel.'

'Well, I'll talk to him, see what they can manage. It would be good to keep some of the work local.'

'Only if he can cope with the demand and produce the kind of quality the hotel needs.'

'I'm sure he can,' Aria said, loyally.

'We'll need to talk to Skye about the desserts. And we'll need someone who can dress up the lobby, make it look dramatic and effective.'

'I definitely know someone who can help with that. Mira Coleman, Jewel Island's florist. You should see Mira's shop, it's so pretty inside. Her job used to be decorating hotels for weddings and parties. We always get her to dress the hotel for Christmas and other big events and I know she does some of the shops and restaurants in the village too.'

'OK.' He let out a little sigh, not knowing why he had agreed to all of this. He glanced at Aria. Except he did know why.

'Have I talked you into something you really don't want to do?' Aria said, giving him a sympathetic smile.

'I think this won't be the last time this will happen over the next few years,' Noah said.

They had finished their steaks by this point and the ever-efficient SJ whisked their plates away.

'Well, I think we should have a dessert,' Aria said, picking up the menu.

'I don't think I could manage another mouthful,' Noah said. 'That steak was divine.'

'You need to try the desserts, then you'll know why you are letting Skye be responsible for that. Ooh, how about the candyfloss crème brûlée?'

'Sounds like sugar overload.'

'You'll see. Surely candyfloss appeals to your inner child. You can relive your misspent youth.'

'I've never actually had candyfloss before,' Noah said and then regretted it immediately.

'You've never had candyfloss?' Aria was as aghast as if he'd told her that his hobby was taxidermy.

'No.'

'You never went to the fair and had toffee apples, or hot doughnuts or candyfloss as a child? Surely that's a rite of passage?'

He took a swig of his water. 'I didn't have the most conventional of childhoods.'

She stared at him, clearly not sure what to say to that. 'I'm sorry.'

'Don't be. The experiences of my life shaped me into the man I am today. The path I took has led me to here and I don't regret that.'

She smiled slightly and then she slipped her hand into his underneath the table and gave it a brief squeeze.

SJ suddenly arrived at the table to take their dessert order and, although she couldn't see them holding hands under the table, Aria quickly dropped his hand anyway. 'Could we have two crème brûlées please?'

SJ moved off to the kitchen and the moment seemed to have passed.

'Every child should have candyfloss, even thirty-three-year-old ones,' Aria said.

Noah decided to move on before she asked him any questions about his childhood that he really didn't want to answer. 'Is there anything else you'd like to ask about the renovations?'

She thought for a moment and then her face fell a little.

'How much is all this going to cost?'

'You don't need to worry about that,' Noah said.

'Of course I'm going to worry about that. You can't be expected to pay out for all the renovations. We're supposed to be equal partners.'

'Some of the money will come from Skye and Clover buying back into the hotel, that money will come in very handy.'

'But… I'm not contributing anything.'

'But that doesn't matter.'

'So you don't care that you'll be spending thousands of pounds on doing this hotel up with no way of getting that money back? Because if this is normally how you do business, you'd be in a lot of debt right now.'

She was right, of course, this was not the norm for him. He would usually buy a hotel outright, do it up, sell it on and make a good profit along the way. But he could never sell this hotel, it belonged to Aria and her sisters. He might, at some point, sell them his twenty-five percent but he'd never make his money back doing that. This project was going to be a lot more complicated than any other deal he'd done in the past, not least because many of his decisions would be led by his heart.

'When this hotel is a success, fully booked, it could be earning upwards of seven thousand pounds a night – that's forty-nine thousand pounds a week. Of course there will be outgoings, salaries, overheads to take from that, but it still leaves a nice profit for me. And maybe I won't get all my money back in one go like I have with previous hotels, but twenty-five percent of the profits for the next twenty or thirty years is fine by me.'

She stared at him for a moment.

'You make it sound like you're here to stay,' Aria said.

'Maybe I am. Remember that day we kissed, I told you I'd like to settle here one day? That hasn't changed. I suppose it all depends on how things go over the next few months whether it will become permanent. If it doesn't work out, I can still receive my profit from a distance.'

'I remember that conversation, of course I do, because it was followed by one of the most incredible kisses in my life. You said you were going to move to the island. We talked about growing old and grey together.'

He swallowed.

'I'd still like that,' he said, softly. 'It's not a good idea to start something when we are working so closely together, but maybe when all this is done with, if you haven't decided you hate me by then, we could try picking up where we left off.'

Asking her to wait didn't exactly seem fair and asking her to trust him again felt like a step too far, but he was surprised when her whole face lit up in a smile. 'I'd like that too,' she said.

He took her hand under the table and entwined his fingers with hers. Her smile grew. It felt like a promise of what was to come.

SJ came up then with their desserts but this time Aria didn't let go of his hand. He knew it was dangerous ground but at least they were on the same page.

CHAPTER NINE

Aria walked out of her office the next morning to find Tilly leaning over the desk talking to Xena, one of the young receptionists.

'Tilly, what are you doing here? Ben said you'd be at home resting until the baby comes.'

Tilly sighed, dramatically. 'I know but I'm so bored. Daytime TV is rubbish and Ben isn't even there as he doesn't want to start his paternity leave until the baby is actually here. This little one has obviously gone back to sleep and will probably be in there for another year at least, if not forever. I could work here for a few hours. He'd never know.'

Aria laughed. 'Absolutely not. I'm not being responsible for you going into labour again. You wouldn't want me as a midwife, I'd panic at the first sign of blood. Besides, Ben would kill me.'

'I bet you're short-staffed since I left?' Tilly said, clearly not giving up.

'We're doing OK,' Xena said. 'We're all doing a few extra

hours here and there. But Mr Campbell said he will bring in some new staff soon, so it won't be for long.'

'I feel awful,' Tilly said. 'And so embarrassed. I flew to the hospital in an air helicopter to be told to just go home.'

'Sounds like good advice: go and put your feet up,' Aria said. 'Make the most of the quiet before your whole world changes. Sleep, because by all accounts you won't get any once the baby gets here.'

'Thanks for that inspiring talk,' Tilly said, glumly.

'And you shouldn't feel bad. I've had nine months to find a replacement for you, so if it's anyone's fault it's mine. Besides, I think Delilah is going to come and work for us in a week or so. And in the meantime, we're all pulling our weight. Clover is doing a few hours tomorrow and I'll be covering reception too. We'll work it out. And Xena is right, Noah is going to bring some people in to help, in all areas actually, so you don't need to worry at all.'

Just then Noah walked into the reception area and stopped when he saw Tilly. 'Tilly, good to see you, how are you feeling?'

'Fine, fed up, embarrassed that I caused such a fuss, bored, huge, did I mention fed up?'

Noah grinned. 'I'm sure you won't have long to wait. And you have nothing to be embarrassed about. It's better to be safe than sorry with childbirth and it'll be something to tell him when he's older.'

'The helicopter trip was pretty cool; I just wish I'd had longer to enjoy it.'

'Well, I was going to talk to Theo about maybe offering helicopter trips to our guests,' Noah said, which surprised Aria; it was the first she'd heard of it. 'Maybe you can be one of the first people to trial it for us, if it gets off the ground. Once the baby's here of course.'

'Wow, I'd love that.'

He turned back to Aria. 'My assistant Angel will be arriving tomorrow so I'll need a bedroom.'

'Of course.'

'Angel will be here for as long as I am, so it will be fairly permanent, I'm afraid.'

'Not a problem.' It wasn't as if they were overrun with guests.

'That's great, thank you.' He touched her arm and then quickly snatched his hand back when he realised what he was doing. He moved away and Aria turned round so she wouldn't have to watch him leave. She noticed Mrs O'Hare watching her with interest. Aria blushed and directed her attention back to Tilly.

'Well, I better get on, I have a ton of emails to reply to and I need to sort out the staff rota for the next week or so,' Aria said. 'It was lovely seeing you, Tilly, and if you really want to stay, I'm sure Mrs O'Hare could do with some company.'

Aria walked inside her office but to her surprise Tilly followed her in and closed the door.

'You OK?' Aria said.

'Angel, eh?' Tilly said.

'What's that tone of voice for?'

'Well, I've had a bit of time to myself over the last day or so and, well, I've been looking into my new boss in a bit more detail.'

Aria groaned. 'And I'm sure Google has given an accurate representation of his life. Also, he's not your boss. He owns twenty-five percent of the hotel, he's an equal partner with me and my sisters.'

'Well, he's still technically my boss, all four of you are. And don't get arsey and defensive. I was doing this for you. Knowing that you were supposed to be going on a date with him before I messed everything up and seeing the way you two were looking at each other, I decided to see what his reputation was with women.' Tilly grabbed her phone from her pocket and swiped a few things. 'I typed in "Noah Campbell girlfriend" and look what comes up.'

Tilly turned the phone around for Aria to look at. It showed images of Noah with several different women at various glamorous parties.

'This doesn't prove anything. These could be people who have worked in the hotels he has developed. They could be friends or random women who he ended up having a photo with.'

'They all look very pretty, don't they?' Tilly said.

Aria swallowed. 'Yes they do, but still…'

'This woman turns up in a lot of different photos with him.' Tilly pointed at a beautiful blonde, who was wearing a figure-hugging dress in every picture. 'I wonder if *she* is his wonderful assistant Angel.'

'OK, so that could be Angel. It doesn't mean anything. Noah has been pretty adamant that nothing can happen between us because it would make it very awkward to work together so I hardly think he's sleeping with his assistant. And I'm sure he has had lots of girlfriends over the years but…'

Tilly took the phone back. 'I'm going to do a search for Noah Campbell's assistant.' She swiped at the screen a few times and then turned it back to face Aria. There was one photo of the same woman sandwiched between Noah and another young man. But, as Aria stared at it, she couldn't take her eyes from the sight of Noah's hand, which was quite obviously on the woman's bum.

'OK, I mean, that's fairly damning but… we have no idea who this woman is and whether this photo was just taken from an unfortunate angle.'

Tilly gave her an exasperated look.

Aria shook her head. She remembered having dinner with Noah the night before and him talking of staying here on the island with her and growing old and grey together. Whatever had happened before, whoever he had been with, he was here now and she was not going to judge him on his past. He could have had a hundred girlfriends before he came here but that did not detract from the wonderful man he was now.

'I just don't want to see you get hurt,' Tilly said. 'I see the way you look at him and I don't think you're going to get what you want out of this. He stays in these places for a few months, maybe a year, apparently has a bit of fun while he's there, and then moves on.'

Aria remembered what Noah had said the night before about whether him staying here would be a permanent thing. He'd said that if it didn't work out he could still receive his profits from a distance. That didn't really show a commitment to stay. God, why was she second-guessing everything?

'I'm not getting anything out of this,' Aria said. 'Nothing is going to happen between us.'

And maybe that was for the best – that way he couldn't break her heart again.

'OK, OK, I'm sorry, I shouldn't have said anything,' Tilly said. 'I'll leave you to your job.'

'Look, thanks Tilly, I do appreciate your concern.'

Tilly gave her a small smile and left.

But as Aria set to work answering her emails, she couldn't get the image of the very beautiful Angel out of her mind.

It was a glorious day, with a spectacular view of Sapphire Bay outside the office window, and the sun was blazing outside, but Noah could feel himself getting more and more agitated.

He had spent the last three hours going over the accounts of the hotel with Clover and it was quite clear that running the hotel to a budget or making cost-effective decisions was not Aria's strong point.

'Are you seriously telling me that in the last year since your dad died, Aria has only paid herself a monthly salary five times?'

'Yes, it seems that way. I don't understand it. I always do the payroll and she's always on it, but then I have to send it to her to check and she's obviously been taking herself off it on a regular basis. I never realised.'

'And when she has paid herself it's always been the minimum. This month here she was paid less than your seventeen-year-old receptionist,' he pointed to the screen.

'She must have been changing the figures,' Clover said, defensively.

Noah shook his head. 'But she has enough money to pay a full-time gardener.'

'She says it's important that the gardens look nice for the guests and I suppose I'm inclined to agree with her.'

'I agree that appearances are important, but not at the detriment of her wages,' Noah said. 'From now on all salaries will be approved by me, not her.'

Clover shook her head. 'You'll have to clear that with her. She's still the manager around here and she's my sister – I'm not going behind her back and reporting to you instead. Besides, do I need to remind you that we are all equal shareholders? You're not in any position to start bossing me around or trying to take control.'

Noah suppressed a growl of frustration, although there was a tiny part of him that admired Clover's loyalty. And she was right, he had a twenty-five percent share in the hotel and he needed to remember that. Normally he would have full control because the hotel was a hundred percent his. It was going to be hard to get used to not having the final say.

He decided to move on.

'And what about all these outgoings? She buys fresh bread every day from the bakers in the village, she buys muffins too. Why is Skye not making this stuff for the hotel?'

'Because Aria firmly believes in buying everything locally. If the hotel stopped sourcing its produce from the village, then almost every shop would close. We are their single biggest customer and they need the business.'

'We're not running a charity.'

'Well, you'll have to bring that up with Aria too,' Clover said, folding her arms.

He was going to have some serious words with Aria Philips. He turned his attention back to the screen.

'And according to the petty cash records, she's been paying to have this delivered over the last few months. The village is literally a five-minute walk away, ten minutes at max. Why does she need to have a few rolls and cakes delivered?'

'Ah well, that is charity. There's a boy in the village who has adopted a donkey after he saved it from being slaughtered and he needs the money to look after it. Well, he needs the money to pay me to look after it. I've kind of adopted a few horses, and a cow too, and that's pretty much where all my wages are going. Now the donkey is in the same field... Sorry, that's a long story that I'm sure you don't want to hear.'

Noah stared at Clover in disbelief. 'The hotel is not even breaking even right now, let alone making a profit, and Aria's spending money every day on saving a bloody donkey?'

He stopped himself from saying any more because it wasn't fair to take his frustrations out on Clover. And really he'd expect nothing less from Aria. One of the many things he had fallen for was her kind and generous heart, he couldn't expect her to change who she was just because there were times it didn't suit him. He needed to talk to her, though – they needed to prioritise their outgoings or the hotel could very easily fall into debt again.

'I think the reason the hotel is not making a profit is more down to the lack of guests than Aria spending a few pounds a week on a donkey and ordering fresh bread and muffins, which the guests love by the way,' Clover said, loyally. 'I think you should be finding a way for us to get more guests and make more money rather than focussing on us spending less.'

'You're right, of course, our biggest challenge right now is getting guests through the doors, but there has to be a bit of movement on both sides if we're to be successful.'

Clover nodded to concede this.

'I think I better talk to your boss,' Noah said.

She smiled. 'I think you better had.'

He stood up and stretched. 'Thanks for this.' He moved to the door, then paused and turned back. 'By the way, what are Aria's dreams?'

It was such a casual question, and not one that showed the importance of something so big. Clover was clearly surprised by it herself.

'What an odd question.'

He moved back inside.

'Yesterday she thanked me for making your dreams come true and I wondered what *her* dreams were,' he explained. 'I asked her but she said it's not something she could do yet. Something she wants to do with her life.'

Clover pursed her lips. 'I feel bad that as her sister I don't know that. She's always been so focussed on this hotel, and I assumed she was happy here. It makes me sad to think she might have dreams and aspirations beyond these walls but has never had the chance to pursue them.'

'I think she's very happy here, she said to me once that she could never imagine leaving Jewel Island, so I presume it's something she could do as well as run the hotel.'

Clover shrugged. 'No idea. But I do wonder why you want to fulfil her dreams when you're supposed to be keeping things professional between you?'

She gave him a pointed look.

'Yes, well. Thanks for your help,' he gestured to the paperwork.

She nodded and he walked out the room. Christ, if he'd thought Clover was the quiet, sweet one of the twins, he'd got that wrong.

What couldn't he help with that would be unprofessional? He was determined to find out what Aria's dream was so he could give her that if nothing else.

He wandered into the restaurant, which was empty at this time of day. He helped himself to a coffee from the machine and smiled to himself. If he had his way, people would pay for coffee in the lounge area if they wanted one but, actually, having a machine where people could help themselves whenever they wanted one was a really nice touch. He supposed muffins were a nice touch too.

He went back out into the reception. Mira, the florist Aria had mentioned the day before, had already started work on the lobby. He wasn't sure what brief she'd been given but it seemed to include a lot of fairy lights. He turned and knocked on Aria's office door. There were two offices here with connecting doors. He knew one used to be Aria's dad's office and wondered if it would be disrespectful if he started using that one.

'She's not in there,' Xena, the seventeen-year-old receptionist, said. Xena had blue hair, a nose piercing and was wearing a black t-shirt that had tiny metal studs around the collar. It hardly seemed like the professional look he wanted for the hotel.

'Any idea where she might be?'

'I think she's out in the gardens talking to our gardener, Stephen.'

Of course she was. Why send an email to your staff when you could wander through the gardens and talk to them face to face.

He took another couple of swigs of coffee and then stepped outside. The warmth of the day hit him straightaway, while out on the horizon the turquoise sea sparkled under a blazing sun.

He wandered through the gardens a little and he had to admit they were beautiful. It was certainly something the guests would appreciate. He spotted Aria talking to a man in his fifties as they admired the tulips that were blooming in every colour.

Noah held back, watching her laughing with Stephen; she was just so bloody endearing.

Aria noticed him and waved him over.

'Noah, this is Stephen, our very talented gardener. Stephen, this is Noah, my partner... erm, business partner, I mean,' Aria blushed.

Noah stuck his hand out and Stephen shook it. 'The gardens look spectacular.'

'Gardening is my passion,' Stephen said, slowly.

'I can tell, there's a lot of love amongst these plants.'

Aria smiled at him.

'If you've finished here, could I talk to you for a bit?' Noah said to her.

Aria nodded, falling in at his side, and as they made their

way down the path she slipped her arm into his as if it was the most natural thing in the world. He could hardly have professional business discussions with her when her body was pressed up against his.

They approached the willow tree where they'd kissed and she gave him a little smile.

'Is what you want to talk to me about the kind of thing you might discuss under the branches of a willow tree?'

He grinned. 'We should save this place for really important discussions.'

She smiled and they carried on walking. She looked over her shoulder, presumably to make sure that Stephen couldn't hear them.

'Stephen used to be the village dentist. He did that his whole life and then about eighteen months ago he had a really bad stroke, it nearly killed him. Luckily he survived but it left him with shaky hands which meant he couldn't really carry on being a dentist anymore. He still struggles with his speech, as you might have noticed. He has to really concentrate to get the words out so it's not ideal for any job where he has to deal with customers. He has no experience or skills in any other occupation so there weren't really a lot of jobs he could do. Fortunately, his love of gardening doesn't require him to speak or have a steady hand or deal with customers, he can just be out here by himself, and we've obviously benefitted from having him here. Mum was always the keen gardener and when she died Dad did nothing with the garden other than hire a few teenagers now and again to do a bit of weeding and mowing. It was the perfect solution to have him here.'

Noah found himself smiling. It was almost as if Clover had primed Aria for why he wanted to talk to her. But hearing Stephen's story made every last bit of frustration he had with her fade away. The world needed people like Aria, who looked out for other people when they needed it the most. He couldn't be angry with her for being one of the kindest people he'd ever met.

'I was just coming to talk to you about why you haven't been paying yourself a wage most months,' Noah said, gently. 'But Stephen is the reason for that, isn't he?'

She paused before answering. 'Not just Stephen, the hotel needs the money more than I do. I have everything I need. I live in the hotel, I don't have to pay bills, I eat in the restaurant or use the food from the kitchen to make myself a sandwich. What do I need money for?'

He couldn't even argue with that. It was a refreshing change from most of the people he worked with who wanted to make as much money as they possibly could.

'I need to talk to you about some changes we need to make to the hotel,' Noah said.

'Sure.'

He'd go in with the easy stuff first. Well, *easier*.

'I'd like the staff to wear a uniform.'

'Are you kidding?'

'No, it's more professional. Then the guests know who is working here and who isn't.'

Aria sighed. 'We all wear name badges and I think it makes the guests feel more comfortable and relaxed around us if we're not all dressed like clones.'

'Your receptionist is sitting in there with metal studs around her top.'

'The guests love Xena, she is friendly, kind, always goes the extra mile for the guests. Don't you think that kind of thing is more important than what she's wearing?'

'I have never been in a hotel before that didn't have a uniform,' Noah said.

'Well, you have now.'

'It doesn't have to be anything elaborate, just a nice jacket and shirt for the reception staff, and maybe you. Black clothes for the waiting staff. Maybe a nice lilac for the cleaning staff.'

'Are you determined to strip away all the character from this hotel? The guests come here because we are different, friendly, relaxed.'

'The guests don't come here at all.'

Aria was silent for a moment and he winced over that unintentional slap round the face.

'What other changes did you want to make?' she said.

'I think we need to change the hotel name.'

Aria didn't say anything but her arm slipped out from his. She thrust her hands in her pockets and stared at the ground as they walked.

Crap.

'If people look up Philips Hotel on Jewel Island, we have an average of three stars in our reviews,' Noah went on. 'That isn't good. That alone could put people off from coming here. If we have a new name we can distance ourselves from that. I also think we need the kind of name that sells the beauty of this place, the incredible views, the prettiness of the island.'

'What did you have in mind?' Aria said, quietly.

'How about the Sapphire Bay Hotel?'

She thought about it for a while. 'It's nice.'

'But?'

'No, it sounds very pretty.'

Her voice was strained; she obviously wasn't happy with it.

'You don't like it?'

'It's just that the hotel, all of this, was my mum and dad's dream, their hotel, and now it's mine and my sisters', carrying on their legacy. The Sapphire Bay Hotel says nothing about that.'

He stopped and caught her arm so she was facing him.

'I totally get that, but you hold onto the memories of your parents in your heart, not with a name. We want people to judge us on how we are running the hotel now, the new changes we're going to make, not on some old reviews of an old hotel. Those reviews will have a huge impact on whether guests stay or not, regardless of how much we improve the hotel now. And don't you think something pretty like the Sapphire Bay Hotel is far more enticing than the Philips Hotel?'

'Yeah, I suppose. We need to talk to Clover and Skye about this but I know you're right. Doesn't mean I'm happy about it though.'

They had reached the hotel by this point and Noah noticed Sylvia sitting in the reception watching them. Aria was making her way up towards where her dad's old apartment was and where he presumed she now slept. He followed her up the stairs.

'Anything else?' Aria said.

'I need to talk to you about the outgoings for the hotel. We need to tighten the purse strings a little, at least until we can start getting more guests through the doors.'

'OK, I'm open to suggestions. We've made a lot of cuts here and there, closed the swimming pool because it was too costly to run. We installed solar panels to help with the running costs, which the islanders hated. We even did a deal with the local fisherman that he would supply fresh fish to us in return for a free meal every night. I know we need to make some changes, so I'm happy to listen to ideas. What did you have in mind?'

It suddenly seemed petty to bring up the muffins, bread and the 'save the donkey' fund, but he knew he had to.

'I notice that you're buying muffins every day. What's that for?'

'I always put them in the bedroom when a new guest checks in and we put them out for breakfast every morning. The guests love them.'

'You put them in the bedrooms of every guest?'

'Yes, did you not notice yours?' Aria asked.

'Yes, I did, but I thought it was something special you'd put there for me,' Noah said, awkwardly.

She smiled. 'No, but I'm glad you felt special because of it, that's how we aim to make all our guests feel. I have stayed in a few hotels and B&Bs around the UK in my life and they were all perfectly nice, but the one I remember was this tiny B&B in Littlehampton that put a fresh muffin in my room every day of my stay. It's those little touches that make the guests feel welcome and make them come back.'

'OK,' he said, slowly, not entirely sure he agreed with that. 'But why isn't Skye making them? And the bread that you're buying daily?'

'Because Skye has enough to do with making breakfast and dinner. And because the bakery in the village makes the best bread, muffins, scones and other baked goods I've ever tasted.'

'I think, going forward, we need to look at where we source our food and produce from. If we were to buy our food from wholesalers or some of the bigger chains, it would be a lot cheaper for us and—'

'Absolutely not,' Aria said.

'Even if we were to go to somewhere like the big supermarket chains for our food deliveries, we could get great deals – you know, buy two loaves get the third free kind of thing. Over the year we would save—'

'Let me just stop you there,' Aria said, unlocking the door to her room and stepping inside. He followed her in. 'This is not one of those times where you tell me all the reasons why I should go along with your brilliant idea and I eventually cave and bow down to your experience. I'm absolutely not going to change my mind on this. I'll let you have stupid uniforms; I'll dress everyone in flamingo pink if that's what you want. I'll change the name to the Noah sodding Campbell Hotel if you think it will help attract tourists, but we are not buying our food from off the island. Everything – the bread, the cakes, the fruit and veg, the meat, the sauces, everything that Skye needs to cook breakfast and dinner – we buy from the local shops. And if there is something that I absolutely need that I can't get in the village, I know that most of the shopkeepers will be able to source it for me. The quality of food we get locally far surpasses the stuff you see in the supermarkets where it has probably sat on a shelf or in a warehouse for far too long. The food here is fresh and a lot of it, like the stuff from the bakery, is made fresh every day. A lot of the fruit and veg is grown on the island too. But much more than that, the shops need us, and I refuse to spend the hotel's money somewhere else. Without us they would close, and how attractive do you think a closed village with no shops or restaurants would be to all the new tourists we're going to bring here?'

He stared at her, her hands on her hips, her eyes flashing furiously. God, he loved her passion. But it was safe to say that the conversation hadn't gone according to plan.

He cleared his throat. 'A simple no would have sufficed.'

'But it doesn't with you, does it? You just keep chipping away until I agree with you. Well, it's not going to happen this time. I would rather we turned all the heating off and provided all the guests with fur cloaks to wear in the winter than do this. And if these are the kind of suggestions you're going to come up with, then I think we need to look very seriously about continuing this partnership because it's simply

SUNRISE OVER SAPPHIRE BAY

not going to work.'

'Hang on a minute,' Noah started but Aria was seemingly not finished.

'No, we are clearly coming at this from very different angles. You want to turn this hotel into something it's not, with marble floors and pretentious uniforms, and I was prepared to go along with all of that in the hope it would bring more guests to the hotel. But I was doing all this to save the island, not the hotel. And I don't think you fully understand that. This place is my home, these people – for all their quirks, nosiness and irritations – are my family, and you don't seem to realise the importance of that.'

Unknowingly, she had hit a low blow with that final comment. He had no idea what it was like to be part of a family. Of course she wouldn't want to let down the people of the island. The success of this hotel would impact on more than just him and the Philips sisters, and he'd never really considered anything beyond that. His ex-wife always said that he thought about everything through a business perspective where there was no room for emotion – although she hadn't seemed to care about his shrewd business mind when she'd been spending all his hard-earned money. But maybe, if he was going to settle here one day, he needed to start thinking with his heart not his head.

'I'm sorry.'

Aria let out a little huff of frustration and turned away. She went to a cupboard and pulled out a pair of flip-flops. 'I swear if you make a comment that these are not professional, I may never speak to you again. My feet are killing me.'

'I wouldn't dream of it.'

She hopped around for a moment while she changed her shoes. He looked around at her living space. It was small, but cosy with brightly coloured accessories. It suited her very well.

'Nice place.'

'Thank you.'

'I came up here once or twice when your dad lived here. It's changed a bit now.'

'It probably hadn't been decorated since Mum died. I had to make it mine when I moved in here.'

'Where were you living before?'

'One of the cottages in the grounds. When Dad died, I knew I needed to be closer in case there were any issues.'

'Are there any other staff rooms up here? I should probably move into one of them if there is, rather than occupying a suite that could be used for a paying guest.'

'No, you might as well stay where you are for now, there's no one who can afford the suite prices anyway. We've never had more than a handful of people using them. There's a couple checking into one of the other suites the day after tomorrow who are here for their honeymoon, but there are four suites so you're not going to be in the way. I have a spare room in here, but… I don't think it's a good idea for us to be living in such close quarters. Besides, the fire alarm doesn't go off up this end of the hotel, so if there was a fire, you'd burn to death,' she joked.

He scowled. 'There's no fire alarm up here?'

'Well, I have a smoke detector, but no, you can't hear the hotel fire alarm up here if it goes off. It's no big deal. Whoever is on reception when the alarm goes off is instructed to call me before anything else.'

'Well, that's one of the first things we need to fix when the builders and decorators get here.'

She smiled at his overprotectiveness. 'You worry too much.'

'Of course I worry about you, Aria, you're... important to me,' Noah said.

She reached up to stroke his face. She didn't say anything but she didn't have to.

'And I'm sorry about before. I didn't think through the repercussions and I—'

She let her hand drop. 'It's fine. Now you know. If you really are going to live here, these people will become your family too, best not to piss them off too much.'

That was true. He couldn't imagine actually having a family and what that would be like, but it would certainly make a nice change.

'You have a lot of fire inside here,' Noah said, pointing to her heart, as he decided to change the subject.

'I do when it's important.'

'But the things you want, your dreams, are equally as important. You worry so much about the villagers and everyone else and I think sometimes you forget about yourself. Why is Aria so unimportant to you?'

She stared at him in surprise.

'Your dream – you won't pursue it because you have to look after this place, you have to look after your sisters and the staff and the villagers.'

'I can't let everyone down. There's just not enough time to dedicate to it. We barely have enough staff as it is. With Tilly off for the next six months, we don't have enough reception staff to cover all the shifts and there always seems to be so much work to do.'

'But I can help you with that. Let me share the load so you can have a few days off a week to pursue the things that make you happy.'

She smiled. 'I appreciate the gesture, I really do, but this thing I want to do is bigger than just devoting myself to it a few days a week. And what about the things that make you happy?' Aria deftly turned the tables on him. Her dreams were obviously not something she wanted to get into right now. 'Becoming a hotel manager at some tiny remote hotel can hardly be your dream.'

'Being with you makes me happy, Aria. That has been my dream for far too many years.'

She stared at him, her eyes wide, and he knew he'd crossed over the line that he was so carefully trying to keep in place. He cleared his throat and stepped back away from her.

'So, we have a honeymoon couple checking in soon?' Noah said, deciding to change the subject.

'Yes, Cal and Lottie.'

'Maybe we should get them some champagne and flowers to celebrate.'

She grinned. 'Now that's the spirit.'

CHAPTER TEN

Aria was in her office when Noah walked in. He seemed a bit stressed, as if he was in a rush. He'd certainly lost some of that carefree attitude he'd had before he'd been coerced into buying this place.

'Just to say the builders and decorators will be here tomorrow, so if we can let all the guests know that there might be some noise and disruption.'

'Will do. Are you OK?'

'Yes, I'm fine,' he smiled. 'There's a lot to do. I'll be relieved when Angel gets here actually, he can share the load.'

She frowned in confusion. 'Angel's a man?'

He grinned. 'Were you expecting a woman?'

'I thought you might have a very glamorous assistant.'

'No, I don't need one of those, I just need one who's competent and efficient. Angel has that in spades.'

Aria nearly let out a big sigh of relief. Although that still didn't answer the question of who was the mystery woman she'd seen in lots of photos with Noah.

'I better go, I have a Skype call in a few minutes,' Noah said.

He rushed off in the direction of his bedroom and Aria was left wondering why he wasn't taking the call in her dad's office next door. Unless he wanted privacy for some reason.

She stood up and walked into reception and noticed Mrs O'Hare was still sitting there, laptop poised on the table, notebook and pen in her hand, Snowflake snoozing at her feet. She had been there quite a bit over the last few days observing the comings and goings. Normally Mrs O'Hare spent most of her stay closeted in her room with her porn so it was a surprise to see her out here for such a long time.

Aria wandered over to talk to her. 'Mrs O'Hare, are you OK?'

'Oh yes, dear, and please call me Sylvia. Mrs O'Hare makes me sound so old.'

'Is everything OK in your room?'

'Yes, of course, I was just heading back there now actually. Could you grab Snowflake's lead for me?' Sylvia picked up her laptop and other belongings and stood up. 'Sometimes real life is much more interesting than what's on the screen. Very inspiring.'

Aria picked up the dog lead and Snowflake heaved himself to his feet. 'What's inspiring?'

'You and Noah Campbell. I've been watching you two over the last few days and…' she fanned herself. 'The chemistry is smoking.'

Aria suppressed a grin. 'Mr Campbell and I have a professional relationship only.'

'Don't give me that. At my age, I've seen it all and you two have the makings of a great romance story. I'd have to change a few things, make him sterner, more grumpy. Maybe set it in the Victorian times. I think you'd be a widow left to run your husband's hotel after his death. Mr Campbell would be a businessman who wants to buy the hotel off you. Maybe your exhusband was a bit of a brute and Mr Campbell shows you a tenderness that you never had before. Sparks fly, inside and outside the bedroom.'

'Well that sounds like a lovely story,' Aria said. 'And not based on real life at all.'

'Some of it has been embellished, of course, but there's no denying you two have the hots for each other. I think our real-life Mr Campbell is in love with you.'

Aria smiled at her rose-tinted view on life. 'So you write stories?'

They had arrived back at Sylvia's bedroom by this point and she opened the door and then gestured for Aria to come inside. Once the door was closed and Snowflake was snuggled up on his bed, Sylvia turned back to her.

'Yes, romance stories, erotic romance mostly. I'm Velvet Steele, dear.'

Aria stared at her and then felt the smile spread across her face. 'Are you really?'

'Yes, it's not really a big secret. Many people know, but I don't go blabbing it to everyone. I have to retain an air of mystery, you know.'

Aria laughed. 'Of course.'

Sylvia sat down in a big armchair and gestured for Aria to sit opposite her.

'Sylvia, as we're being open, can I ask, are you really sitting in here watching porn every day?'

Sylvia laughed, a big booming laugh. 'Well yes, but for inspiration, you see. My own love life...' She hesitated. 'It would be disloyal to my wonderful husband to speak ill of him but let's just say things in the bedroom are... nice. And I need a bit of saucy inspiration for my stories. Clive, my husband, he doesn't know what I do.' Aria raised her eyebrows in surprise. 'Oh, he knows I'm a writer, but not that I write this kind of stuff. So I come here a few weeks of the year and write out as many sex scenes as I possibly can during that time with some films on in the background to help the juices flow.' She laughed at her own innuendo. 'The creative juices, that is. And then when I get back home I can write the rest of the story around the sex.'

'Why does your husband not know about the kind of stories you write?' Aria said. It seemed odd to be married and not tell your husband everything. But then she wasn't married so who was she to judge?

'What you have to understand about Clive is that he is a lovely kind man, but he likes things very plain, very safe, very normal. He's a vicar, or at least he was, and he has just led a very quiet life. I don't think he needs the shock of discovering his eighty-two-year-old wife has a secret kinky side.' Sylvia smiled and shook her head fondly. 'Forty years ago, if you'd told me I would have ended my days being married to a man like Clive I would have laughed you out the door, but I have had five husbands in my life, before Clive, who were complete rogues. Yes, they were good in the bedroom, but they broke my heart. Some cheated on me, some stole from me, one of them even tried to kill me. And let me tell you, after that, I'd take safe and normal any day.'

'Wait, are you serious?' Aria said, leaning forward in her seat.

'Oh yes, threw me overboard while we were on his yacht. I was twenty-five at the time and had won gold in several regional swimming championships. Something he didn't realise. I just kept swimming until another boat picked me up, which was about half an hour later. It was in the summer too, so the water wasn't that cold. No damage done, dear, you don't need to look so shocked. And he served ten years at Her Majesty's pleasure, so all's well that ends well.'

'Why did he try to kill you?' Aria said, still absolutely horrified. She had led a very sheltered life and thankfully no one had ever tried to kill her.

'We'd had a fight, about money, which was our usual thing we fought about, and he just picked me up and threw me over. He was always quite an aggressive man – he never hit me, but he generally just spent his whole life being angry at everything.' Sylvia laughed at Aria's expression. 'You see, nice safe Clive is looking more and more attractive now, isn't he?'

'I suppose so,' Aria said.

'You don't need to worry about stuff like that with your man,' Sylvia said.

'My man?'

'Noah. Now there's a man who could take care of his woman in the bedroom. But someone who would treat you like a complete queen too. Such a gentleman.'

'But we're not—'

'I know, why is that? You're both crazy about each other, any fool can see that.'

Aria sighed. She hadn't really been expecting to have this conversation with one of her guests, she'd thought she and Noah had been more discreet than that. But Sylvia O'Hare was certainly a savvy old woman and she must have spotted something. There was no real point denying it.

'It's complicated,' Aria said.

'The best ones always are. So tell me, why are you not swinging from the chandeliers with that wonderful man instead of hanging out with this old bird?'

Aria smiled and told Sylvia all about the deal her father had asked Noah to take, about him leaving after he'd talked of moving to the island to be with her. She didn't mention the kiss, that seemed too private.

'So you see, he's here in a business capacity. We're going to be working alongside each other for the next few months at least, probably for the next few years, trying to get this place sorted, and he thinks it would be awkward if we were to start something.'

'Oh that's rubbish, some of the strongest couples I know met at work.'

'Well exactly. I'm more than happy to give this a go, but he's holding back.'

'I think you should walk straight into his room stark naked and see how much restraint the man has then,' Sylvia said.

Aria burst out laughing.

Sylvia sat back in her chair and poured herself a tumbler of whisky. She offered the bottle to Aria but she shook her head. Sylvia took a sip. 'I would suggest he's holding back for more than just complicated work reasons.'

'That's what I thought. I know he was married before and that didn't work out.'

'Yes, to Georgia, she was a horrid woman.'

'Do you think that's the reason he doesn't want to pursue another relationship?'

'It could be. It's got to have made him wary of making the same mistakes again. He never loved his wife – he cared for her maybe, but he was never *in* love with her.'

Aria frowned. 'Then why did he marry her?'

Sylvia smiled and shook her head. 'That's complicated.'

Aria sat back in her seat with a sigh of frustration. 'What do I do, Sylvia? We've sort of made this tentative pact that once the hotel is finished we'll give things a go then, but that seems very far away. I'm falling for him and it's driving me mad not being able to do anything about it.'

Sylvia swirled the whisky around in her glass as she thought.

'What would your heroines do in my situation?' Aria asked.

'They'd walk into his room stark naked, just like I suggested,' Sylvia said.

Aria laughed.

'Some of my heroines might try to make him jealous by flirting or pretending to be with another man.'

'Yeah, but I'm not really a playing-games kind of woman.'

'No you're not, but you are the kind of woman who listens and cares. Those are good qualities. And maybe you need to dig a little deeper to understand why he's really holding back and then you can help him move forward.'

Aria sighed. 'Maybe stripping naked would be easier.'

'Maybe it would be, but I get the feeling that Noah would definitely be worth the effort.'

Aria nodded her agreement. She thought so too.

Aria popped the pizza on the table and Skye flopped down on the sofa next to Clover.

'Ah, it's so nice to have someone else cook for me for a change,' Skye said, easing a knot in her shoulders.

Clover scooped up a slice, put it on a plate and passed it to Skye, then did the same for Aria before getting a slice for herself.

'We need to do this more often,' Aria said, taking a bite. 'We're always flying around from one job to the next and some days I feel I barely see you. If you're going to stay, we need to set aside time, at least once a week, I think, just us.'

'A family meeting,' Clover smiled. 'Just like we used to have.'

Aria smiled. They used to sit around the table every night for dinner and talk about their day, what they had learned in school, funny things that had happened. It wasn't just a time for the children to talk, their parents would tell them about things that had happened in the hotel, unusual guests, stuff that was happening on the island or in the wider world. She missed that.

'Yes, exactly,' Aria said. 'So, in keeping with tradition, tell me something positive about your day.'

Skye swallowed a bite of pizza. 'I spoke to Jesse. That's always a positive thing.'

Aria smiled. 'And how is he?'

'He says he misses me. I told him all about the ice cream café. He didn't say a lot about that at first but then he soon started trying to help me come up with different names for it.'

'Do you think that he was sad because you opening up the ice cream café here made it obvious you weren't coming back?' Aria said, softly.

'I don't know,' Skye sighed. 'I'm not sure what he wants, to be honest.'

'You,' Clover giggled.

'I don't know if he does, not like that. We got married so I could stay in Canada, but we agreed it would only be a year until I could get all my working visas sorted. When the year came to an end, it was him who sorted out getting the divorce. There was never any question about us staying married. So I don't think he does want that kind of relationship at all.'

'So you'll just stay as best friends who kiss and have sex?' Clover said.

Skye shrugged. 'I guess. I'm here now and he's not going to come here. Well, he might visit, but not to live. There's Bea to think of too.'

'How is she?' Aria said.

'Good,' Skye smiled. 'I talked to her as well. I miss her almost as much as I miss her dad. Anyway, let's move on because this is becoming less and less positive the more I think about it. Clover, what was your positive thing?'

'My positive thing was I spent a few hours today thinking about my new dance studio and the kinds of things I'll need and planning it all out. I'm so excited about it, I can't tell you. This is everything I've ever wanted. I'm still going to work on getting the hotel established as a wedding venue but this is something I can really look forward to and get my teeth into. The garden room is so perfect for it, I can't wait to see it once it's all finished.'

Aria smiled with love for her sister. 'I'm so glad we were finally able to give you what you want.'

'What about what you want?' Clover said. 'Do you know Noah asked me what your dreams were today and I'm ashamed to say I didn't know.'

Aria shook her head. 'I've never had big aspirations like you two. I know that makes me dull, but I always knew I wanted to stay here and run the hotel. I want to travel a lot more,' she looked out the window at the sun disappearing into the waves leaving damson and flamingo-pink clouds in its wake. 'There's a whole world out there to explore, but that kind of thing comes down to time and money and we don't have any of that right now. I want to have children, and as you know I want to adopt. But this island, the hotel, my wonderful family, I don't need more than that.'

'I love that you want to adopt a child,' Clover said. 'So many people wouldn't want to do that.'

'I have a wonderful life here and I couldn't have asked for better parents and sisters, but I do often think what my life would have been like if I'd stayed with my biological family. Mum and Dad always used to tell me that my real parents gave me up in the hope that I would have a better life than the one they could give me. I think there are a lot of children up for adoption who might have been born in the wrong location or to parents who couldn't really provide for them. I'd love to give a child a safe and secure home, and a life with opportunities just like I had. And to bring them to lovely Jewel Island.'

'That's lovely,' Skye said. 'But why does Noah want to know what your dreams are?'

Aria tried to wave it off. 'I just think he wants us all to be passionate about something in the hotel. I think he was hoping he could provide that for me in the same way he'd done that for you two – you know, start a pottery club for guests if that was something I was passionate about. It's no big deal.'

Clover watched her for a moment, clearly deep in thought, and then thankfully changed the subject. 'What's your positive thing, Aria?'

Aria thought for a moment about the day she'd had, her stupid row with Noah that morning and Tilly's depressing warning about Noah's reputation with women. It hadn't been the best day. And then she thought about Mrs O'Hare.

'Today, I sat with one of our guests and talked to her, properly. Just like Dad used to. It always used to frustrate me a little that he would spend hours talking to the guests when there was so much paperwork and admin that needed to be done. But I forgot that one of the reasons Mum and Dad wanted to open a hotel was because they loved meeting different people. Do you remember we used to have dinner with some of the guests and Mum and Dad would always ask them questions about their lives? It was always so fascinating. And with bills to pay and empty rooms, I've forgotten about that along the way. I learned something today about Mrs O'Hare that just made me smile so much. She is a very interesting woman and has led a wonderfully colourful life and I think sometimes taking the time to actually talk and listen to our guests can be beneficial to both parties.'

Skye nodded. 'I like that. I always used to talk to my customers in my shop in Canada. When people have something fun and tasty to keep them happy, it's a lot easier to talk to them. We'd get loads of tourists in the shop and I always liked to chat to them about where they'd been, what they were going to do next. You get to travel the world or live different lives vicariously through other people.'

'Exactly,' Aria said. 'And we can keep Mum and Dad's legacy alive by doing that.'

They were silent for a while as they finished tucking into their pizza.

'I saw you arguing with Noah today,' Clover said. 'Is everything OK?'

'Yes, it's fine. He just wants to make some changes that I wasn't that keen on,' Aria said.

'Like what?' Skye said, wiping her mouth.

'Uniforms for the staff, our suppliers, nothing really important,' Aria said. She didn't want to bother them with the whole row; she got the impression they were already wary of Noah after what he'd done to her the year before and she didn't want to give them any ammunition to dislike him even more. 'He does want to change the name of the hotel though.'

'What?' Clover said, in disbelief.

'I know, but he does have some valid points.'

She explained about the bad reviews and how Noah wanted to put some distance between the hotel and them.

'That's fair enough. What does he want to call it?' Skye asked.

'The Sapphire Bay Hotel.'

Skye clearly mulled it over in her head. 'It's pretty. I like it.'

'It does sound very lovely,' Clover said.

Aria's heart sank a little.

'You don't like it?' Clover said.

'I do,' Aria said. If her sisters weren't bothered about losing their name from the hotel then maybe she shouldn't be either. 'It'll take some getting used to, that's all.'

'And we're going ahead with the party for the festival of light?' Skye asked.

'Yes, just drinks and nibbles. But we thought you might want to do some kind of dessert station to show our guests the kind of things that will be on offer in your new café.'

'I can do that,' Skye rubbed her hands together, gleefully. 'I'd be very happy to do that actually.'

'Are we doing fireworks?' Clover said.

Aria shook her head. 'Not this year, it's too expensive.'

'Oh, that's a shame. I always remember the festival of light parties from when we were kids, they were so much fun.'

'Yeah, I know, but we don't need to spend thousands of pounds on something that will have very little or no gain for us. I'd like to keep outgoings as low as possible for the next few months at least, until we can increase the number of guests that come through our doors. We hardly have anyone coming that weekend at the moment, no more than two or three rooms I think have been booked. I told Noah that I'd get loads of Dad's friends and all the old loyal guests to come, but I emailed them all today and so far I've had no replies. I mean, we still have just over a week until the festival but it might be too late now to get a big surge of bookings.'

Aria wasn't sure what she would do if she couldn't get more bookings. She had persuaded Noah to go along with the party and she needed it to be a big success. She didn't want to give him any reason to leave. The hotel needed him just as much as she did.

CHAPTER ELEVEN

Aria stared at Clover in shock, and then at Sparkle the donkey, who was standing next to her, staring at Aria with large brown eyes, her coat shining in the early morning sunshine.

'What do you mean, you're bringing her into work?' Aria said.

'All the horses are picking on her and I don't want to leave her alone with them. Look at this bite mark on her back. One of them, probably Zeus, took a chunk out of her yesterday, and I have nowhere else to put her.'

'Well, we can't leave her in the gardens. Poor Stephen would do his nut if he found a donkey chomping away at his prize roses.'

'I thought I could…' Clover trailed off as she gestured to the hotel.

Aria felt her eyes widen. 'You want to take her inside? Are you insane? Noah would actually kill me. He has an important visitor coming today, someone he's hoping to secure sponsorship with. I can't let a donkey in there and ruin everything. Besides, what about the mess?'

'Sparkle is house-trained,' Clover said and then hurried on when she saw Aria's expression of disbelief. 'I know that sounds ridiculous but she is. She was kept in that old lady's house before Neil had her. I've had her inside my cottage several times overnight and I swear she's never gone to the toilet inside my house before.'

'You let Sparkle inside your house?'

'She doesn't like to be alone. When I bring her in, she sleeps in the kitchen and she's perfectly happy, and then I let her back outside in the field in the morning.'

Aria smiled with love for her sister. 'You are one of the kindest, loveliest women I have ever known and I love you, but you're not bringing a donkey inside the hotel.'

'I thought we could put her in the swimming pool room. There's no water in there and the floor is tiled, so it's easy to clean *if* she makes a mess. I have some food for her,' Clover gestured to the large bag she was carrying. 'We can shut the doors; no one ever goes in the pool room so they won't know she's there. She's very quiet and well behaved and it's only for a few hours. Neil is going to collect her after lunch and take her for a walk around the island until I get off work. I promise, there won't be any trouble. Noah need never know.'

Aria could almost feel herself wavering and she couldn't believe she was so easily swayed.

'Is this going to be a daily thing?' she asked. 'Because it's not very professional.'

'No, I promise. I'm going to pay someone to separate the field into two parts so Sparkle will have her own field.'

'Clover, that will cost a fortune.'

'I know, but what can I do? I can't kick Sparkle out; poor thing has already been through so much. Neil did the right thing adopting her and bringing her to Jewel Island, but he can't keep her where he lives, so she has to stay with me.'

'OK, OK. I know I'm going to regret saying this, but you can put her in the pool room. But only for today. You'll need to find somewhere else for her tomorrow.'

Clover leapt forward and hugged her. 'Thank you, I promise she'll be good.'

'Take her round the back, at least you won't have to put her in a lift to take her down.'

Clover hurried off with Sparkle happily following and Aria shook her head. What had she just agreed to? She smiled as she walked inside because she knew if her dad was still alive, he would have agreed to the same thing and probably taken some carrots down to the donkey at lunch time.

She looked around and noticed Mira, the florist, was busily getting the reception area ready for the festival of light, draping swathes of chiffon material in different colours across the ceiling, interspersed with fairy lights. She'd only been there such a short time and although there was still lots to do, it was already starting to look magnificent.

Aria was just about to go over and talk to her when she heard footsteps behind her, coming from the entrance.

She turned to see a very smart young man in a suit, carrying what appeared to be a laptop bag.

'Hello, I'm looking for Mr Campbell,' the man said.

This had to be Angel. If she'd had to guess what Noah's assistant looked like, it would be this: tailored, expensive-looking suit and shoes, perfect hair, shirt buttoned up to the neck, smart blue silk tie. This was a man who oozed professionalism and that would be one of the factors that Noah would look for in an assistant.

'You must be Angel, I'm Aria,' she said and hugged him, though she didn't know why. Maybe it was relief that Angel wasn't a beautiful blonde in a figure-hugging dress after all, or maybe because Angel was a sort of friend of Noah's. She felt awkward as soon as she'd done it, especially as Angel didn't hug her back.

She stepped back and the man cleared his throat. 'I'm not Angel, I'm Dr Howell. I have an appointment with Mr Campbell,' he said, haughtily. Obviously not a fan of being hugged.

Crap, this was the man Noah was meeting about sponsorship for the hotel. Aria had thought that he was due in the afternoon.

'Oh, I'm so sorry, I thought you were coming later. Let me just see if I can find Noah for you,' Aria said. She noticed that another man had come into the entrance and was watching her. He looked vaguely familiar. He was dressed in jeans and a blue t-shirt with a guinea pig in a sombrero on it; he was clearly a tourist.

Dr Howell sighed heavily and Aria hurried off. Noah had started using her dad's office now and again so she tried there first. Luckily that's where he was, responding to some emails. She quickly shut the door behind her.

'Dr Howell is here.'

Noah's face paled. 'Crap, he's not supposed to be here until two.'

'Well, he's here now and he's pissed off.'

'Why is he pissed off?' Noah said, desperately tidying up the office.

'Because I hugged him.'

Noah paused mid-tidy. 'Why did you hug him?'

'Because I thought he was Angel.'

'Why are you hugging my assistant?'

'Never mind that, just get out there and greet Dr Howell in a much more professional manner than I did.'

He hurried out the office, straightening his tie.

Aria watched Noah rush over to greet Dr Howell and she

stepped back as he ushered him into the office and closed the door. Something told her Dr Howell would not be parting with his hard-earned money today, but then he'd not exactly arrived in a good mood anyway.

She turned her attention to the man in the guinea pig t-shirt who had wandered over to the reception desk.

'Hello, how can I help you?' Aria smiled.

'Well, I believe that man took something of mine,' the man said. He had the kind of eyes that held permanent amusement.

'He stole something of yours?' Aria said, horrified. Could she really charge into the meeting and call the man a thief?

'In a manner of speaking. That man took my hug.'

It took her a few seconds to catch on. 'Oh my god, *you're* Angel?'

And suddenly she knew where she recognised him from. He was the other man in the photo with Noah and the blonde lady. No wonder Google had thrown up that photo when Tilly had Googled Noah's assistant.

'Yes, Aria?' he asked.

She nodded.

'Pleased to meet you,' Angel said and held his arms out for a hug.

Aria laughed. 'Oh stop it, I'm in enough trouble as it is for hugging Dr Howell. I can't go around hugging more strange men.'

'I'm not strange.'

'You're wearing a guinea pig t-shirt.'

Angel looked down. 'Ah this is cool, not strange.'

She smiled. She liked him immediately.

'You're not what I was expecting for Noah's assistant.'

'You were expecting someone stuffy like our Dr Howell in there?'

Just then the office door opened and Noah and Dr Howell came out. Aria suppressed a giggle that they'd nearly heard what Angel had said.

'Well this is the lobby. At the moment we are getting ready for the festival of light, an important event in the island's calendar, hence why we have all these decorations,' Noah said, glancing over in their direction and then doing a double take at what Angel was wearing. He shook his head, which made Aria laugh even more. Noah turned his attention back to Dr Howell. 'Why don't I take you upstairs to show you some of the bedrooms and talk you through the work we're going to do.'

Aria waited for them to disappear inside the lift before she burst out laughing.

'I take it back; you're exactly the kind of person Noah needs as an assistant. Someone who can counterbalance his serious side.'

Angel's smile dropped a little. 'He means well. I think Noah cares too damned much, that's the problem. He wants everything to be perfect and especially with this place because he knows how much it means to you, Aria.'

'I know. I love having Noah's skills and experience in renovating this place but sometimes I wish it wasn't Noah who had bought it and it was someone else instead.'

'Yeah, it has to make things complicated,' Angel said, he dipped his head to look her in the eyes.

Aria smiled. He knew.

She lowered her voice. There was no one around but Clover would be back to man the reception at any second. 'Noah told you about us.'

Angel grinned. 'Well, last I heard there was no "us", but I knew he wanted to change that, he just wasn't sure how, what with all of this.' He gestured to the hotel.

'Well, we're not there yet. This place is taking precedence but... I'm hoping he'll have a change of heart. And soon.'

His smile grew. 'Well that's... hopeful.'

Just then Clover appeared from the kitchen, carrying a piece of paper. Evidently Sparkle had been safely deposited in the pool room.

'Who is writing these menus?' Clover said, pen in her hand as she crossed out various things. 'Potatoes does not need a bloody apostrophe. And neither does tomatoes.'

'I think it's Jeremy,' Aria said. 'Skye tells him what we're having and he writes it down.'

'And I have to type it up after spending half an hour correcting everything.' Clover looked up and blushed when she saw Angel. 'Sorry, I didn't realise anyone was here. I'm ranting about apostrophes in front of our guests.'

'Clover, this is Angel, Noah's assistant. Angel, this is Clover, my sister.'

'Wow! I mean hello,' Angel said and Aria couldn't help smiling when Clover blushed even further. 'And grammar, punctuation and spelling are important, it definitely needs ranting over.'

Clover smiled. Punctuation was a personal bugbear of her sister's. Aria knew if she found a kindred spirit they'd be friends for life.

'In fact, I have several t-shirts you might like" Angel bent down to unzip his suitcase and pulled out a red one that said, 'Grammar Police. To serve and correct.'

Clover laughed as Angel rummaged around in his suitcase that seemed to be filled with t-shirts with different slogans printed on them.

'Or how about this one?' He held up a t-shirt that said, 'Synonym, a word used in place of the one you can't spell.'

'And this is my favourite, although you might not be a fan.' He held up a t-shirt that simply said, 'Theiyr're.'

Clover burst out laughing. 'I love it.'

Aria smiled at the way her sister's eyes were shining. Angel had a wonderful sense of humour and it seemed Clover appreciated it too.

Angel stuffed his t-shirts back inside the suitcase and zipped it up.

Clover saw Aria watching her and cleared her throat. 'Let me get you checked in; I believe we have you in the suite next to Noah.'

Angel glanced at Aria, with a smirk. 'I think a room not directly next door to Noah might be a good idea.'

Aria found herself blushing furiously.

'Oh really?' Clover asked in confusion.

Angel flashed Aria another smirk.

'Noah has dreadful insomnia,' Angel said. 'He ends up watching TV at very early hours in the morning. I've learned the hard way not to have the room next to him anymore as he keeps me awake with his… night-time activities.'

Oh god. Angel didn't want to hear the banging of the head-board, should she and Noah actually get together.

'OK, well, Angel, you can have one of our club rooms on the other side of the hotel. After the suites, they are our nicest rooms. There's one that overlooks Ruby Falls – it has a lovely view.'

'That's where Clover lives, at Ruby Falls,' Aria said, although she wasn't sure why she felt the need to share that.

'Well that sounds perfect,' Angel said. 'I love a good view.'

Clover blushed and handed over the room key. 'It's room forty-four, you can find it on the second floor. The lift is over there.'

'Thank you,' Angel said. 'And once I dump my stuff, I think I'll have a look around the hotel myself, familiarise myself with my new home – at least it will be for the next few months. Clover, it was nice meeting you. You too, Aria.'

Angel walked off to the lift and Aria smiled as she watched him go.

'I like him,' Aria said.

'I do too,' Clover said.

Aria couldn't help but smile even more about that.

Aria had spent a while emailing everyone who had ever stayed at the hotel in the hope they might want to come and snap up a bargain weekend for the festival of light. None of the regulars had replied so far, so she was casting the net wider. She heard laughing outside her office and, needing a break, she wandered outside to see what was going on. There was Angel chatting away to Clover, or rather flirting with her, and Clover was laughing loudly. Aria doubted anything would happen between them – Clover guarded her heart too fiercely for that – but it was nice to see her happy and relaxed with a lovely man, regardless of how far it did or didn't go.

Noah arrived back in reception with Dr Howell. Angel cleared his throat and stopped leaning over the reception desk and Clover moved to the other side of the desk and started doing something on the computer as if Noah was the boss and he'd just caught them messing around – although in many ways he was.

'I must say, this hotel is lovely,' Angel said loudly and deliberately, probably for Dr Howell's benefit. 'Although what's with the donkey in the swimming pool?'

Noah paused as he walked past the desk. 'Donkey?'

Behind Noah and Dr Howell, Clover started signalling frantically to Angel, waving her hands and doing a slitting motion across her throat. Angel's smile fell off his face as he realised he'd revealed something he shouldn't.

'Yeah, there's a, umm… mosaic-type picture of a donkey near the pool, I wondered what the significance of it was,' Angel said, quickly.

'Ah right,' Noah said. 'Well we're heading down that way ourselves in a minute, we'll have to have a look for it.'

'You're going to the swimming pool?' Clover said in alarm.

'Yes of course, why?' Noah said.

'Well, it's empty right now,' Aria said. 'It probably doesn't look its best.'

'That's OK, we just want to give Dr Howell a feel for the place,' Noah said.

Dr Howell looked like he'd already got a feel for the place and he wasn't impressed.

They started heading off towards the lift that would take them downstairs.

Crap. Aria glanced at Clover, who was looking panicked. She had to do something.

'Why don't you take Dr Howell through the gardens and round the back,' Aria called after them. 'That way he can see all the spring flowers and the amazing views.'

'Good idea,' Noah said and gestured for Dr Howell to follow him out of the entrance.

As soon as they had gone Aria turned to Clover. 'Go and get Sparkle out of the pool room, quick.'

'Where shall I put her?' Clover said.

'I don't care, just anywhere she won't be found,' Aria said. 'I'll man the reception. Angel, you can go and help her.'

'I take it Noah doesn't know about the donkey?' Angel said.

'No he doesn't, but since you decided to tell him, you've just signed yourself up to the relocation team. Now go.'

Angel and Clover took off at a run, heading into the lift that went downstairs.

God, what a mess.

Aria moved behind the desk just as Sylvia came up to her.

'So, have you put your plan of attack into motion yet?'

'My plan?'

'You know, strip naked and walk into Noah's bedroom?'

Aria burst out laughing but quickly stopped as Skye came out the kitchen.

'What are you laughing at?'

'How Aria can get—'

'More people to come to the festival of light,' Aria quickly corrected.

Sylvia looked between Aria and Skye, the penny dropping.

Just then the lift from downstairs opened on the lobby and Aria had never been so happy to see Clover before, even if she was accompanied by a donkey.

'Clover, what are you doing?' Aria said, as Angel escorted the donkey out the lift and Clover encouraged it forward with handfuls of hay.

'Well we couldn't go out the back door in case we bumped into Noah and Dr Howell, so the lift was the only answer.'

'What are you going to do with her?' Aria asked, looking around frantically.

'What about the dining room?' Angel suggested. 'They've already been in there.'

'Hell no,' Skye said. 'People eat in there, that's unhygienic.'

'There's no one in there now,' Clover pleaded.

'Absolutely not,' Skye said.

Clover turned to Aria but she shook her head. 'No, I agree with Skye on this one.'

'We need to be quick,' Angel said. 'They'll be back up here in a minute.'

'My office,' Clover said, desperately.

'Fine,' Aria said. 'But someone will need to stay with her to keep her quiet.'

'I'll do it,' Angel said, trying to lead Sparkle forward. But the poor donkey had seemingly had enough and was refusing to move.

'I'll get a carrot,' Skye said, running off towards the kitchen.

Sylvia was watching the proceedings with undisguised glee.

'Come on, Sparkle,' Clover begged, pulling on the rope a little bit.

The lift suddenly clanged into action as it went downstairs.

Skye came running back out of the kitchen brandishing a big carrot and waved it under Sparkle's nose. The donkey went to take a bite and Skye moved it out of her reach, forcing Sparkle to take a few steps forward.

'That's it, she's moving,' Aria shouted, triumphantly.

'The lift is coming back up,' Angel said.

They were now just a few metres from the office door. Aria ran forward to open the door and then started saying encouraging words to Sparkle as Angel tugged gently on the headcollar and Clover started pushing the donkey from behind. Sylvia came over and started stroking the donkey's nose as Skye waved the carrot around manically but no amount of cajoling, begging, pleading, pushing and pulling could get Sparkle to go through the door.

And that's how Noah found them a few seconds later, trying to manhandle poor Sparkle into a tiny little office.

Noah stared at the scene before him in shock, Dr Howell stared at them in disgust.

No one moved, no one said anything.

Oh God, this was not going to end well. Noah would be furious. But to Aria's utmost surprise, Noah suddenly burst out laughing. He bent over at the waist laughing so loudly and so hard that Aria couldn't help joining in. Noah was still laughing when Dr Howell stormed out in a huff.

CHAPTER TWELVE

'I can't believe my own assistant was in on this disaster,' Noah said, throwing evil glares across the table at Angel. Fortunately, it was like water off a duck's back as Angel just shrugged and carried on eating.

'You know I can't resist a damsel in distress,' Angel said.

'Hey!' Clover said, indignantly.

'I was talking about Sparkle,' Angel said.

Noah smiled to himself. He liked Angel. He was smart and organised, but he was also a good friend and was one of the few people Noah trusted. He was also a sucker for animals.

Neil had come to collect the donkey earlier and Angel seemed almost sad to let her go. Aria had talked to Stephen to ask if there was a small area of the gardens they could put aside for Sparkle. It seemed the hotel had just gained its own donkey.

'I'm sorry we lost you the sponsorship,' Aria said, next to him.

They were having a late lunch together with Clover and Skye. The hotel didn't currently offer lunch to its guests as

160

Skye was the only chef and she was already working long hours making breakfasts and dinner. It was something Noah was keen to change when he could get a few chefs to work in the kitchen. But it meant that for now they had the dining room to themselves.

Under the table, out of sight of everyone else, he squeezed Aria's hand. He was pushing the line he'd drawn between them, but he was having a hard time staying away from Aria Philips.

'It's fine. Dr Howell was never going to sponsor our hotel anyway; he made his mind up about the place as soon as he walked in. I could see he was less than impressed as he was walking round.'

'Well, he clearly couldn't see the potential of the place,' Aria said. 'It will look wonderful when all the renovations are complete.'

'It's probably not a good idea to bring people here who you want to impress until the place is finished,' Skye said.

'Maybe not. But we are inviting bloggers and travel journalists for the weekend of the festival of light to show them our plans and that the hotel is changing. I kind of thought Dr Howell would see the potential, just like Aria said. I want people to be excited about the new hotel now, drum up a bit of interest for the official reopening in the summer.'

'Well I think you need to pick who comes here more carefully,' Skye said. 'We don't want people to start saying negative things about us before the hotel has had a chance to shine.'

'Dr Howell was on me,' Angel said. 'I'm always on the lookout for people who might want to sponsor or endorse our projects. Dr Howell approached me, and although I did think that this hotel might be smaller and not as urban as he would like, he wanted to come and have a look and I didn't see the harm. Admittedly he hasn't left with the greatest impression but I can't see that one man is going to cause us any problems. But I promise I'll be more picky from now on.'

Noah smiled. Angel was honest and owned his mistakes; he liked that about him.

'Anyway, let's move on. I think we should have a progress report. Firstly, I have someone who is going to help out on reception arriving this afternoon. She's on loan to us for a month or two until we can get a few more members of staff. Her name is Zoe and she has been a receptionist, head receptionist and assistant manager for several hotels around the world for the last eight years.'

He noticed Angel mutter something under his breath. There was a mutual feeling of contempt between Angel and Zoe. Zoe could be rude sometimes to other members of staff but she was good at her job and the customers always loved her.

'I have someone from the island who is going to take up the job of receptionist,' Aria said. 'Delilah, but she won't be able to start for another week or so.'

'OK, does she have any experience?' Noah asked.

'No, but we can train her. She'll be a hard worker, and loyal. She's worked for the same department store on the mainland for the last ten years. I know she'll fit in here perfectly.'

Noah smiled to himself. Delilah sounded like another charity case but, after finding a donkey in the hotel that morning, he wouldn't expect anything less.

'OK, well, Zoe can stay until Delilah finds her feet. We'll probably need more than just Delilah anyway as Katy and Xena are only working part time, but we'll see how we go. I also have a chef arriving tomorrow, Basia, I've borrowed her from one of my other hotels too. She has an amazing talent with food. She'll be here for three months until I can employ a few more people to take over from her. They are both very experienced but, Clover, if you could work with Zoe and, Skye, if you could work with Basia for a few days, just so they know where everything is and how everything works. I'm sure they will both settle in very quickly.'

Skye and Clover nodded.

'And what do you think about the new hotel name?'

'I think it could work,' Clover said, carefully.

'I like it,' Skye said and then pulled a face when she saw Aria's reaction. 'I'm sorry but I do. Dad would have wanted us to do whatever it took to make this hotel a success again. He wanted you to make all the changes that he was never brave enough to do himself, he said that in his letter, and I don't think he would have wanted us to cling to the past, especially not at the detriment of the hotel. The Sapphire Bay Hotel is a beautiful name and I think it will sell very well.'

'I know,' Aria said, sadly. 'You're right. Doesn't mean I'm happy about it though.'

Noah gave her hand another squeeze and she flashed him a brief, grateful smile.

'OK, good. We'll get the sign ordered and all the new stationery and hopefully we can have that installed for the festival of light.'

There was so much that needed to be done before the festival and he had no idea if they could achieve it all by then. He wasn't going to fool himself that the hotel would be finished by then, far from it, but at least, he hoped, it would be semi presentable.

'The builders and decorators will be here shortly. I'm aiming to have at least twenty bedrooms finished for the festival,' Noah went on. 'Not all the bathrooms, as ripping out whole suites and putting in new ones and then retiling would take quite a lot of time, but we will certainly be able to

163

get one or two of them finished so at least we can show people what the room will look like when it's completely done.'

They all nodded, apart from Angel who carried on eating. He glanced up at Noah and quickly swallowed. 'Sorry, should I be taking notes, because you know, priorities.' Angel gestured to his food and Noah rolled his eyes and shook his head. Clover giggled.

'Have you had a chance to look at the rough plans I've drawn up?' Noah asked the sisters. They all nodded again. 'Any problems or ideas you want to discuss?'

'You haven't mentioned the pool. Are you going to reopen it?' Clover asked.

'I'm not sure. It's a big expense. I thought maybe it would be something we could do next year once we have started to increase the number of guests.'

'Having a heated swimming pool would help to encourage more guests,' Aria countered.

'I know.' He pierced a tomato on his plate and ate it as he thought. 'What if we were to add some more solar panels, either on the roof or in the gardens, and use them specifically to heat the swimming pool, at least in the summer months? Then we could open the pool for at least four or six months of the year and build up to a full-time pool a few years down the line.'

'That sounds like a good compromise,' Skye said.

'We'd have to remove the donkey though,' Noah said and they all laughed. 'And there's something I never thought I'd say.'

Angel flipped open his laptop and started surfing through the internet with one hand while eating with the other, as if he wasn't engaging in the meeting at all. With any other person, Noah would consider this rude, but he knew that Angel would be looking up solar panels or swimming pools or some other vital information.

'How are we doing with the plans for the festival?' Noah asked.

'I have lots of desserts planned for the dessert bar, and I'll also do a few nibbles too,' Skye said. 'I don't really know enough about wines to order anything special in. We sell a few bottles and glasses of house wine with dinner so I can order more of that, but if you want something special you'll have to let me know.'

'I think we'll need to employ a bar manager eventually to handle that side of things,' Noah said. 'But I'm going to bring someone in for the festival, maybe someone who can do cocktails. Angel?'

'On it,' Angel said, typing away furiously on his keyboard and miraculously still finding time to eat.

'Mira should be finished with decorating the lobby in the next few days,' Aria said.

'OK, good. I have six people potentially coming to stay for the weekend who will be able to plug us in various magazines or blogs. Aria, how are we doing on the rest of the guests?'

She paused for a moment while she ate a slice of cucumber. 'Umm... not sure on the total numbers but it's all in hand.'

He frowned slightly as Aria and Clover seemed to exchange glances but then the look was gone and he wasn't sure if it had even been there in the first place.

'Well, some of the rooms won't even be habitable so we don't want the hotel to be filled. And how are you doing with your plans for your own projects?' Noah asked Skye and Clover.

'There's not really a lot involved in mine,' Clover said. 'The room needs redecorating and a new floor. It will need a new sound system and some mats, but really it will just be a space to dance and do yoga and other classes. It's already very bright because of the large windows that face out onto the garden. So if you're happy for me to use your builders and decorators, it's something that we could finish fairly quickly once they have the time to do it. I don't suppose it will be done this side of the festival but that's OK. The good thing is, I won't be spending anywhere near my share of the money so the rest can be ploughed into the hotel.'

Which was something he'd been counting on.

'That's good. Yes, by all means talk to my team. You're right, it's not a priority this side of the festival, but we will get it done as soon as the festival is over. Skye, how are you doing?'

'Well, I've had a ton of ideas, like having booths with brightly coloured leather benches and brightly painted wooden tables. Kind of a retro vibe to the place, but with some modern twists. I thought we could serve milkshakes too and I've had lots of ideas about the different desserts.'

'Any idea of pricing for the renovations and furniture?'

'I'm afraid I've not had too much time to look into it. I'm cooking breakfast and dinner and it just takes up a lot of my time.'

Noah nodded. 'Well once Basia is here and settled in, you can get started on your project properly. I think we'll need to strip out all of the old furniture and floor and we can start painting it. If you can have a think about colours, so at least we can make a start.'

'I might be able to help with that,' said a voice from the doorway.

Noah looked up to see a man who resembled a bear. He was huge and his mass of dark curly hair and beard completed the rugged animal look. His accent was definitely not British; if Noah had to guess, he'd have said Canadian. The man was

166

carrying a motorbike helmet in his hand, which he deposited on a nearby table.

Skye's head whipped round and she let out a little squeak.

'Who's that?' Noah whispered to Aria.

'That's Jesse, Skye's ex-husband.'

'Ex-husband? Do I need to beat him up?'

Aria laughed. 'We won't be needing any heroic actions just yet.'

Skye suddenly leapt up and ran across the dining room, throwing herself into Jesse's arms. He wrapped his arms around her and she reached up and kissed him on the lips.

'Well, that's definitely a lot more friendly than I'd be with my ex,' Noah said, staring at them in surprise.

'Their relationship is complicated,' Aria said.

'What are you doing here?' Skye said, seemingly over the moon at seeing her ex again.

'You said you needed some help, so here I am,' Jesse said.

Skye took his hand and brought him over to the table. 'This is my wonderful friend, Jesse. This is Noah who I was telling you about and Angel, his assistant.'

Noah stood up and shook Jesse's hand and Angel followed suit.

'And you know my sisters,' Skye said.

Aria and Clover both stood up to hug him.

'It's good to see you again,' Aria said.

'Have you come to take Skye back home?' Clover said as she hugged him too.

Jesse laughed. 'There's no trying to get Skye to do anything she doesn't want to do. No, I came to see what I could do with turning that shack into a dessert palace of dreams. I'm a carpenter, builder, decorator,' he explained to Noah. 'And I'm at a loose end for the next few weeks so I could help out here if you need me to.'

'Of course we need you,' Skye said, and then more quietly, 'I need you.'

Noah watched the look they shared; it was clear there was a lot more than friendship between them.

'We would definitely appreciate any help you can give us,' Noah said. 'I'm sure Skye will have lots of things you can do down in the shack. We can't really spare anyone from my team until the festival of light is finished, but it would be wonderful to at least make a start on the ice cream café.'

'I'd be happy to,' Jesse said, sitting down as if he was a part of the team already.

Noah looked around the table. They all had their parts to play and somehow they had to make it work.

CHAPTER THIRTEEN

Aria was walking through the village the next day when Madge accosted her outside her shop.

'We had a meeting last night about the festival of light and I told them what you said.' Madge tugged on her green waistcoat importantly and pulled herself up to her full height, which must only have been about four feet. 'And against my better judgement, we have decided to fund the fireworks if the hotel agrees to hold the party. You will have to organise it with the firework company yourselves as it will be set up on hotel property, but we will give you a cheque to cover what it costs.'

Aria instinctively went to say thank you and how grateful she was but she stopped herself. *Be bold.* 'Against your better judgement?'

'Well, it doesn't seem right to me. The hotel has always funded the party and the fireworks. The town council work very hard to fundraise money for the island and it doesn't seem right that we should give that money to the hotel. The money is to benefit all the islanders.'

'And what benefit do you think the hotel gets from holding a party where we provide free fireworks and free food and drink? We would be doing this for the islanders, not for us.'

'Well, I... umm,' Madge bristled. 'I would think that holding a prestigious event like that would attract guests to the hotel.'

'It doesn't. Nothing is attracting the guests to the hotel right now. The only thing that will get people to come and stay is if we completely redecorate every single room and communal area like the lobby and dining areas. That's where we should be focussing our money, not on parties. However, as you are willing to pay for the fireworks, I will talk to Mr Campbell and see if we can accommodate a small party on the night of the festival of light.'

There was no need to tell Madge that she had already discussed this with Noah.

Aria waited a moment, giving Madge a meaningful stare.

'Thank you,' Madge mumbled.

'You're welcome.'

Aria walked off and couldn't help the smile from spreading on her face at the way she had turned the tables on Madge. Noah was right, the islanders had to take some responsibility.

She let herself into The Vanilla Bean and waved at Kendra who was serving two customers. Aria went through to the kitchen, flicked on the kettle and looked back into the shop at the couple who appeared to be buying lunch. There were quite a lot of day trippers who came to the pretty island, explored the beaches, visited the shops and cafés and then left when it got dark. The island was still a big enough draw to make people want to come, but they didn't want to stay. She knew the hotel was partly to blame for that but there was also not a lot for the guests to do once the sun went down. The cafés and shops were closed and only one or two of the restaurants were open in the evenings, and mostly only at weekends. There was a pub that was generally filled with fishermen or a handful of locals, but there was never any entertainment. They needed to do more and this had to be a whole island affair, it wasn't just down to the hotel.

As the nights were getting warmer, maybe they could offer a beach barbeque to watch the sunset. They could erect a big screen out in the gardens, provide deckchairs and play different movies, sell popcorn, offer blankets. She needed to talk to the islanders about what they could offer too. If the pub could do a pub quiz once a week that would be something. Maybe she could persuade the restaurants to take it in turns to open at least one night a week, so there was always one restaurant open on any given day. And, once Skye's ice cream place was open, that would be a good draw too; a lot of people liked going out just for dessert.

The island had a lot of history as well. There were the ruins of an old fort at one end of the island, plus several shipwrecks in the nearby waters that were rumoured to be old pirate ships. Maybe the islanders could do some history or ghost walks around the island.

Kendra walked into the kitchen after finishing serving her customers and smiled at her. 'I can see that brain sparking away with hundreds of ideas. What are you thinking?'

'Just some ideas for what we could offer visitors to the island after dark. Everywhere pretty much shuts down here and we need to give people reasons to stay a bit longer.'

Kendra poured out two mugs of tea. 'I think doing up the hotel will help; your dad should never have let it get so dated and tatty.'

Aria felt immediately defensive, even though she knew her godmother was right.

'But it's not just down to the hotel, is it? We're not the sole

171

reason tourists have stopped coming here. Half the shops and restaurants won't even bother opening until summer and will close again as soon as the summer holidays are over. If there's nothing for the tourists to see and do when they stay here, then they'll go off the island to have some fun. It works both ways. There's only so much I can do.'

Kendra nodded in agreement. 'Maybe you need to say all this at the village meeting this afternoon.'

Aria straightened in her seat. 'Do you know what, I think I will.'

'Oh wait, if you're going to set the cat amongst the pigeons, then I need to be there for it. But I have a dentist appointment this afternoon, so I can't come.'

'That's OK, might be best if you don't see me make an idiot of myself.'

'I think you're right though and it needs to be said. The future of the island can't rest just on your shoulders.'

Aria nodded as she thought about what she was going to say.

'How's it going up there anyway? I've seen loads of vans and trucks arriving all day,' Kendra said.

When Noah had said that the builders and decorators were due that day, Aria had been expecting a handful of people. What she hadn't been expecting was an entire team of people skilled in all areas of renovation. She had so far counted over fifty of them who had arrived en-masse, with more due later. Noah had held a big meeting in the garden room and detailed his plan for the next two weeks at least, which mainly involved the bedrooms. She had to hand it to the man, he clearly knew what he was doing.

'It's going well. I'm looking forward to seeing what the hotel will look like when it's all finished.'

Kendra studied her; her eyes narrowed for a moment. 'But you're not happy.'

Aria sighed and let the smile fall. 'I'm not unhappy but there are some changes I'm not thrilled with.'

'Like?'

'He wants us all to wear uniforms.'

Kendra pursed her lips. 'I don't think that's necessarily a bad idea.'

'Yeah, I suppose it's not the worst thing in the world, but we also had a stupid row over him wanting to use suppliers from off the island.'

'I do understand where he's coming from. It would be a lot cheaper in the long run. I appreciate your loyalty, and I know many of the other islanders do too, but from his point of view of course he will be looking at ways to save money.'

'I understand it too but I told him that I absolutely would not be doing that.'

Her godmother nodded. 'What else?'

'He wants to change the name of the hotel. He's thinking about the Sapphire Bay Hotel instead.'

Kendra's eyes softened. 'And you don't want to do that.'

Aria shifted in her chair. 'I just feel with the renovations and changes and now the hotel name, he's removing everything that shows all the hard work and love that my parents poured into the hotel. I know it needs to be updated but some of these changes seem too far even for me. It's been the Philips Hotel for over thirty years. I'm just not sure I'm ready to let go yet.'

'But you're not letting go of your parents, you will always have them. It's just a name and you and Clover and Skye still have that name too. The Sapphire Bay Hotel is really very pretty.'

'I know,' Aria said, sadly. 'I just wish Dad was here to ask him if it's OK.'

'Your dad would have been proud of what you're doing, and he trusted Noah to turn this hotel around. So maybe you need to trust him too.'

'I do. It's just a lot harder than I thought.'

Kendra took a sip from her tea as she stared off into the distance for a while. 'There is a solution to this.'

'There is?'

Her godmother stood up and retrieved a cheque book from the nearby dresser. 'I've just sold my flat in London, I made a nice profit from it too, but I have no idea what I'm going to do with the money. I thought about investing it somewhere, but I could invest it in you.'

Aria stared at her for a moment. 'What are you suggesting?'

'That I give you a cheque for half a million pounds and you buy Noah out of his share. I would be your partner then instead of him. I'm not going to get involved in any changes, that would be all down to you and your sisters. But I would get twenty-five percent of all profits once the hotel starts making some money.'

'I can't take your money from you,' Aria protested. 'You should do something fun with it, or at least something sensible for you.'

Kendra started filling in the cheque. 'This is sensible. I'm investing in my future and I believe in you. I know you will make this work, but you can do it your way without interference from someone who doesn't know the hotel or the island.'

Aria thought about it for a moment. 'I'm actually really excited to be working with him on this. He has a lot of experience that I simply don't have. I could use your money and pay to have all the renovations done myself but where would I go from there? How would I advertise or market it? I wouldn't have a clue where to start.'

'But you could learn those things.'

Aria shook her head. 'Like you said, Dad chose Noah for a reason and it wasn't just for the money. I trust him and of course there will be things that he does that I don't like. But we both want this hotel to succeed and he has a lot of experience in doing that.'

Kendra handed the cheque to Aria. 'I think you're right; Noah is probably going to be the best thing for this hotel. But in case you change your mind, the offer still stands.'

Aria stared at the cheque made out to Noah. Right now she wasn't remotely tempted to take her godmother up on her offer. Despite everything, she was enjoying working with Noah and she was prepared to see this through to the end. But if there were many more rows like she'd had with Noah the day before, there might come a time when she needed it. Kendra gave her an encouraging nod and she slipped the cheque into her pocket.

Aria walked down towards the village hall, following the road that led along the coast, the sun glittering and dancing across the almost mirror-calm sea. Little white sailboats peppered the horizon and a couple of fishing boats were trundling out to sea in the hope of making a catch.

She looked ahead to the village hall, standing proudly amongst the shops and restaurants. It was an old building that by all accounts had stood there for hundreds of years. It hadn't changed in all of that time, apart from a bit of redecoration here and there. It reflected the attitudes of some of the villagers too; they didn't do change either.

There was a village meeting about the festival of light today and everyone was expected to attend. Which meant that there would be thirty or forty stalwarts and everyone else would make their excuses or just not bother turning up at all. Aria always went to these meetings, to fly the flag for the hotel and make sure she was kept in the loop with any developments on the island. She liked to sit near the back and listen rather than take part. She'd answer questions if she was asked, and she'd occasionally suggest some ideas, but she had never addressed the islanders with her own point of concern or query. Until today. She had no idea why she was nervous.

Noah was right, she was a people pleaser. She didn't like to rock the boat. She had spent her whole life wanting to be accepted, wanting to fit in, and so she had tried to keep everyone happy. But not today.

She walked into the village hall to the hubbub of small groups of villagers chatting before the meeting started. Seamus came over and greeted her, shaking her hand as if he hadn't seen her in months, not just a few days.

'Welcome Aria, thank you for coming.' Seamus gave her a genuine smile and then looked over her shoulder. 'Is your Mr Campbell not with you?'

'I'm afraid he isn't.' Noah had offered to come with her to the meeting, introduce himself to the locals, but Aria didn't want to expose him to the criticism and the sniping just yet. Well, actually most of the islanders were lovely, but the ones who weren't would certainly make their opinions known.

'That's a shame, we would have liked to meet him.'

'He's very busy right now, but he promises to come along to the next one,' Aria said, realising she had just committed Noah to the next meeting whether he wanted to come or not.

'Well, we look forward to it,' Seamus said and then gestured for her to sit down.

'I'd like to say something today at the meeting,' Aria said, so there was no chance of her backing out. 'Maybe at the end before the meeting closes.'

'Of course,' Seamus said.

She sat down at the front and slowly other people took their seats too. As predicted, over half the hall was empty but she knew a lot of the villagers would read the minutes when they appeared in their email inboxes and she was sure word would spread too.

Aria Philips getting too big for her boots, that almost made her smile.

The meeting started and there was much talk about the lanterns and how the lantern team were busy repairing and making new lanterns ready for the procession and had been for several months. There was also talk about the visiting groups that would be bringing their lanterns to the island to represent the nearby local towns. There was much excitement amongst the villagers about the festival, even more so now there was going to be the usual party with fireworks at the hotel. Aria wondered if it would be noticeable that the villagers were likely to be the only ones there. So far she'd not had any luck attracting new guests to stay that weekend, even with a discounted price, though that was not something she had shared with Noah yet. Would it matter? With no extra guests, there would be enough finished rooms for all the journalists to stay in. The bloggers and journalists would see the festival of light and the fireworks. They'd see the hotel and the plans for all the changes, that was the important thing. Except, financially, the villagers would be coming to a free party, eating free food and drink and there would be no money coming into the hotel to cover the expenses. Their first big event and it wouldn't earn them a single penny.

She made a snap decision and raised her hand to speak.

'Yes, Aria?' Seamus said.

'Could those in contact with the visitors coming to the festival of light share with them that the hotel grounds will be open to campers as it was many years ago? Five pounds per tent per night and eight pounds per person if they want breakfast at the hotel the following morning, as long as they book ahead.'

Stephen was not going to be happy about his precious gardens being trampled on but the hotel owned a large field near Emerald Cove that wasn't really in use. She could put any campers in there. There were no facilities to speak of, but, as it was only one night, it hadn't seemed to put people off before.

'Thank you, we'll pass that on,' Seamus said, nodding to his wife, Kathy, who was furiously taking notes.

And, feeling bold, Aria carried on. 'And we're actually running a special at the hotel that weekend, seventy-nine pounds including breakfast. The details are all on the website but if you could at least mention it to them, some of the visitors might want a bit more comfort than sleeping in a field.'

There were a few whispers from the villagers and she distinctly heard someone mutter that the visitors wouldn't find comfort at the hotel.

'We are working very hard right now to improve the hotel and, while some of the renovations and building work will take several months, a good number of the bedrooms will be completely redecorated by the time the festival of light happens. It would be nice to show as many people as possible that the hotel has changed. We are rebranding as the Sapphire Bay Hotel and I know the guests will love it,' Aria said.

Suddenly the hushed whispers in the room got very loud.

'You're rebranding?' Madge said, incredulously, standing up so everyone could see her. 'Why was the town council not informed?'

Her friend, Betty, nodded sagely next to her.

'I'm informing you now,' Aria said, hesitantly. She hadn't been expecting this.

'We should have been consulted about something as important as this,' Madge went on.

'It has been the Philips Hotel since before you were born,' Betty said. 'Your dad would be so disappointed in you if he knew you were changing the name.'

That was a low blow.

'I like the name,' Julia from the chemist piped up. 'The Sapphire Bay Hotel is a very pretty name; it reflects the island perfectly.'

'I think it's lovely,' Kathy said.

'Me too,' Frank from the butcher's said.

'I think a new name is a wonderful idea,' Seamus said. 'And the Sapphire Bay Hotel is perfect.'

Aria had the satisfaction of watching Madge deflate in disappointment that no one apart from Betty agreed with her.

'I think we should put it to a vote,' Madge said, though without the confidence she'd felt a few moments before.

'I don't think that is necessary,' Seamus said. 'Aria is the manager of the hotel, and she is free to call it whatever she damn well pleases. She wouldn't come down here and tell us how to run our businesses so we shouldn't think we have the right to interfere in hers.'

There were several nods of agreement. Nonetheless, this was going to make it all a bit awkward when Aria wanted to say her part at the end of the meeting. She hadn't even got to that bit yet and she had already pissed off a few of them.

Madge slowly sat down.

Aria cleared her throat. 'My dad left me a letter saying he wanted me to make the changes in the hotel that he was never brave enough to make himself. Despite what some of you think, I know he would be very excited about the new developments in the hotel.'

'I think he would be very proud,' Seamus said, softly.

The meeting went on for a bit longer – there was talk about the bridge onto the island needing some repair work – and then things seemed to come to an end.

'Aria, I believe you wanted to say something?' Seamus said. 'Or have you already said it?'

'No, I, umm… still have something to say,' Aria said, standing up and turning to face the islanders.

There was quiet as every pair of eyes in the room stared at her, some encouragingly, some not.

She cleared her throat. 'I've seen many day trippers come to the island over the last few days but none of them stay. I know that the hotel is partly or even largely responsible for that, but we have to give them something else to stay here for. I feel that many of the islanders have already given up. Some of the shops and cafés only open during the summer months and then close again after the end of the summer holidays. There are many restaurants that are not open in the evenings during the week and only open on weekends. We have to give visitors pubs and restaurants that are open in the week too, not just weekends. I realise it costs money, with bills and staff wages, and to stay open all week for one or two customers would be ridiculous. But I thought we could come up with a rota so that we have at least one restaurant open on any given day throughout the week. The shops need to start opening earlier in the season too, give the tourists something to visit.'

She paused and looked around the room. It was hard to judge what kind of reaction the villagers were having to her plea. She decided to press on.

'But we need to do much more than that. We need to offer something else to attract the tourists to come to the island. It's a beautiful place but I don't know if that is enough. We could do historical tours around the old fort, or ghost stories about the pirate ships which are supposedly sunk around the island. We could offer workshops like pizza-making or ice-sculpting or flower-arranging, show off the amazing skills of the islanders. We could offer boat tours around the island to see the different wildlife. There is so much potential for the island and, while we are going to do our very best to improve the hotel and bring the tourists back here, there is only so much we can do on our own. I feel that the islanders have to take on some of that responsibility too.'

There was silence for a while and then everyone started chatting between themselves. Aria couldn't tell if they were positive or negative conversations. She glanced over at Madge. She didn't exactly seem happy but Betty actually looked quite animated as she talked to Madge. Betty used to be a history teacher, so giving historic talks might be right up her street.

'Quiet please,' Seamus said and everyone fell quiet. 'I agree with Aria on this. It's a bit of a tricky situation as many of us cannot afford to stay open throughout the year to cater for the odd winter tourist, but it is having an impact on the amount of people that come here. People have stopped coming to the hotel and many of us thought that was down to the dated décor and old carpets, but maybe the island is partly responsible too. There is nothing for them here. There used to be pottery painting and rockpool talks, amongst many other things, and now there is nothing. Many of the islanders have left, they've given up on us, but Aria hasn't and if she can fight to save us then we can too. She can't do all of this alone and she shouldn't have to. This is our home and we all care about it. It's time to show that.'

There were nods of agreement from many of the villagers, which Aria was relieved about.

'Let's have a think about ways we could attract tourists to the island and then we could feedback at the next meeting and maybe start implementing some of them. If those of you who own a café, pub or restaurant would be willing to open one extra evening a week, and if you have any preferred days, can you let me know and I will come up with a rota,' Seamus went on.

Aria sat back down as a few comments and questions started getting thrown about.

At least she'd tried. The rest was up to them.

CHAPTER FOURTEEN

When Aria arrived back at the hotel, there was a team of men inspecting the floor of the lobby area. That was a surprise, as Noah had said the marble floor wouldn't be laid until after the festival of light, although she supposed they could just be measuring up now.

Noah was behind the reception desk with a woman who had scarlet hair wrapped up in some kind of bun. She was wearing a dress suit and looked effortlessly glamorous and smart at the same time. They were chatting and the woman kept throwing her head back and laughing loudly. As he carried on talking, she reached out and touched his arm.

Aria watched as Noah looked down at where the woman was touching him, as if he didn't know what to do with this sign of affection. He stepped back slowly, almost as if he was trying to be subtle about it rather than just shrugging off her hand. That was what Aria would have preferred him to do, but then he was obviously trying to be professional and not be rude.

Clover was on the phone to someone and caught Aria's eye

as she approached. She very subtly gestured to the woman and rolled her eyes.

'Hey!' Aria said and, as the woman looked round at her, Noah shuffled further away from her. That made Aria smile.

'Aria, this is Zoe, our new receptionist. Zoe, this is Aria, the hotel manager.'

That was a very formal way to introduce her, considering their past, but Aria couldn't fault Noah for his lack of professionalism.

Zoe's eyes cast down Aria and she couldn't help feeling like she was being judged, and certainly not favourably.

'*You're Aria?*' Zoe laughed incredulously and then quickly straightened her face. 'Sorry, Noah has talked about you so often and I thought...'

'Thought what?' Aria said, taking an instant dislike to this woman. It was quite obvious what Zoe was thinking, the relief was written across her face. *I was worried you were going to be beautiful and Noah was going to fall in love with you but now I've seen you I'm not bothered anymore.*

'Oh no, you're just not what I was expecting.' Zoe cleared her throat awkwardly and looked around, obviously trying to change the subject. 'I bet you're glad to have Noah here, this place is a complete mess.'

Aria felt her eyes widen at the bluntness. She knew the hotel wasn't looking its best but to say it was a complete mess felt a bit harsh.

Deciding that talking to Zoe for any longer was going to make her more pissed off, she turned her attention to Noah. She gestured to the men. 'What's going on?'

'They're measuring for the new carpet,' Noah said.

'I thought we were having marble flooring?' Aria said.

'I think Noah probably knows best,' Zoe said. 'He's been doing this job for many years.'

Noah deliberately ignored her. 'I decided you were right, blue carpet would be cosier and more comfortable than the coldness of marble flooring.'

Aria turned round to look at the men. She hadn't seen them before; she didn't think they were part of Noah's crew. And they certainly weren't from the island.

They were from off the island.

'Noah, can I have a word with you?' Aria gestured to her office.

'Oh, sure,' Noah said.

He followed her in and closed the door behind him.

As soon as the door was shut, she was aware of his proximity, his warmth, his delicious tangy scent. He glanced down to her lips. There was so much chemistry between them, fizzing away like a firework about to explode. He wanted to keep things professional between them. She wanted to respect her sisters' wishes and not get involved with him, at least until the hotel was back on its feet, but could they really deny this connection for the next year or more?

He swallowed and cleared his throat. Obviously he was thinking the same.

'What did you want to talk to me about?' Noah said, his voice strained.

She sighed and stepped back away from him, trying to separate work from this wonderful man she was slowly falling more in love with.

'We're having carpet in the lobby?' Aria said.

'That's what you wanted.'

'Well yes, but—'

'And you were right, I was trying to change the hotel into something it wasn't. Blue carpet will be much more welcoming. We want our guests to feel comfortable and at home. Making the people feel that this is an exclusive and luxury hotel is not the atmosphere we want to create. The hotel has character and we don't want to lose that.'

Aria felt heartened that he had listened and taken her words on board.

'But you're not using Nick's carpet shop from the village?'

Noah pulled a face. 'I went down there and he had about twenty rolls of carpet to choose from, most of them various shades of beige.'

'But he could order stuff in.'

'Yes, he said that, and he also said it would take two months.'

'So you're using someone off the island?' Aria said, exasperated.

'These guys are used to fitting carpet in big places like shops and hotels. I've used them before and the quality is very good, plus they can deliver and have it fitted a lot sooner than two months. They have massive warehouses of carpet and they think they might even be able to do it at the beginning of next week, just before the festival. They're going to do the bedrooms too.'

'But you're taking thousands of pounds away from a man who really needs it and giving it to a big company that really doesn't. I talked about this with you. I said I wasn't prepared to get my food supplied by someone from off the island, and I told you how important that was to me, and yet you still went ahead and did this.'

'I figured this was a bit different. You also said how important the festival of light was to you as well, so I was trying to get the lobby completed ready for that. The old carpet is very dated and worn and we don't want that to be the first thing our guests see when they check in. We want them to see it has changed in a positive way and that there are bigger and better changes on the way.'

That took the wind out of her sails. Noah was doing all of this for her. The blue carpet, making sure everything was ready for the festival... and nobody was going to come apart from six bloggers and a load of villagers who were just there for the free food.

This was all her fault. If she hadn't rushed him to get as much finished as possible for the festival, then they could have taken their time to get things right.

'I'm sorry, I hate arguing with you,' Noah said. 'This is why I was worried about starting a relationship with you when we have all this to deal with. What if we were to use Nick for some of the bedroom carpet? I hadn't planned on replacing the carpet in the downstairs rooms until after the festival. There are ten rooms there so a nice sum for Nick.'

'I think that's a nice idea,' Aria said, quietly. 'And listen, about the festival...'

'I think that was a great idea of yours,' Noah said. 'It'll be nice to drum up some interest before the hotel officially reopens in the summer. I think it'll be great to invite those guests back who used to stay here quite regularly and stopped visiting years before so they can see that changes are coming too.'

Her heart sank. No one had replied.

She didn't know whether no one was interested, it was too short notice or whether her dad's friends and loyal customers had changed email addresses. It had been a year since her dad died; people moved on and they forgot. But so far, beyond the six bloggers Noah had organised and the small number of guests who had already booked prior to Noah coming to the hotel, there was no one else. There was Cal and Lottie, the honeymoon couple who would be staying for two weeks, another couple who were coming for just that one night, who she thought were connected to Cal and Lottie in some way, and a twin booked for two friends. Sylvia had said she might extend her stay but hadn't confirmed that yet. That was it. As far as good ideas went, this had to be the worst. Maybe Aria just needed to give those guests a bit more time before writing them off completely. Or maybe she should be honest with Noah now so he didn't feel so much pressure to get everything finished in time for the festival. Although it seemed it was too late for that, the bloggers were already coming.

'And look, I'm sorry about Zoe. She's a pain in the ass sometimes and I forgot that,' Noah said.

'You talked to her about me?' Aria asked, remembering Zoe's first comment to her.

'Hell no. I haven't talked about you with anyone apart from Angel and I certainly haven't given him a running commentary. I guess she's been around when I mentioned you to him. I've known her for several years and I always bring her in to work at a new hotel if we are short-staffed or the staff we have aren't very good. She's really good at her job.'

'I've not seen that from her so far. She's as subtle as a low-flying brick.'

'There seems to be two sides of the coin with her. This… *mask…* where she is professional and polite to customers, and this other side which is just blunt and annoying when the mask comes off. She is very efficient and organised though, I can't fault her for that. But yes, she can be downright rude.'

'If I catch her being as rude to any of the guests as she was to me, she's out.'

'Fair enough. I am sorry she was rude to you. I'll have a word.'

'I don't like her,' Aria said, feeling like a child.

'You don't have to. She'll be here for a month while we advertise and recruit some more staff. And then she'll be gone.

I'm not asking you to be best friends with her, just try not to kill her.'

Aria sighed. 'I suppose I can do that.'

She made a mental note to put an advert in the newspaper for staff and do an online advert on various job sites the very next day. The sooner Zoe was gone the better.

Aria had spent a while the next day trying to find a firework company that would be able to come to the festival of light at such short notice, finally locating one who was happy to do it.

She got up and went through the connecting door into Noah's office to leave a note for him about the firework company. She stopped when she noticed on a notepad on his desk was a handwritten note that said, 'Ring Starburst Heights Hotels'. Why would he need to ring them? Surely this didn't have anything to do with her hotel.

She glanced up and saw Zoe watching her.

She wandered into reception and Zoe quickly went back to her computer. Clover was up the other end of the desk; Aria wondered if her sister had got sick of Zoe already.

She looked around the lobby, spotting Angel busily working away on his laptop. She was surprised to see that Tilly was sitting opposite him reading a book. Aria smiled and wandered over to talk to her.

'Tilly, what are you doing here?'

'I'm not here to work,' Tilly said, defensively. 'I'm a paying guest today and quite frankly the time I've had to wait to be served is disgusting. Where's the manager?'

Aria laughed. 'Angel, how long has she been here?'

'About five minutes,' Angel said, not even looking up from his laptop.

'He's hot,' Tilly whispered a bit too loudly. 'Who's he?'

'Angel Mazzeo,' Angel said. 'And thanks for the compliment.'

'Angel is Noah's assistant. Angel, this is my receptionist, Tilly, who was sacked for being indiscreet.'

Angel laughed.

Tilly shrugged. 'I'm twelve months pregnant, I can get away with anything.' She paused. 'Oh, you're the man from the photo.'

'What photo?' Angel asked.

'We were Googling who Noah's assistant was and we found a photo of Noah, you and a woman. We assumed you were the woman,' Tilly said.

'*You* assumed Angel was the woman,' Aria corrected.

Angel shrugged. 'Happens all the time. If I had a pound for every hotel manager or executive who has been disappointed to meet me after chatting to me on email for several weeks, I'd be a very rich man. They obviously all hoped I'd be a sexy woman. Which photo was this?'

Tilly did a quick search on her phone and then offered it out to him.

'Ah, that's Georgia, Noah's ex-wife. That's a very old photo though. God, I think that was the night he met her. You can almost see the pound signs in her eyes in this photo,' he shook his head. 'I never did like her.'

Aria stared at him in surprise. She didn't really know a lot about Noah's marriage or Georgia, but this was a tiny unexpected glimpse. She glanced at Tilly, who was watching him with wide eyes at the mere sniff of gossip. Aria decided to change the subject.

'Well, Tilly, as you're a paying guest and definitely not here to work...' Aria gave her a meaningful look and Tilly crossed her heart and held up her hand in a Girl Guide salute. 'What can I get you?'

'One of those delicious hot chocolates with cream on the top, a plate of biscuits – don't be stingy – and one of those wonderful apple muffins please.'

Aria smiled. 'Coming right up. Angel, keep an eye on her for me.'

Angel saluted her and Aria laughed as she walked back to the reception desk, thinking about what Angel had just said.

'God, he's such a child,' Zoe said, not even bothering to be quiet. 'I'm not sure why Noah insists on keeping him around.'

Aria turned to see Angel's reaction to that. She watched him give Zoe the finger without even looking up, which made her snort. Angel didn't like Zoe either.

Aria so wanted to say to Zoe she'd been wondering the same thing about her, but she would keep things professional for Noah's sake. Or at least she'd try.

She phoned through to the kitchen and placed Tilly's order with Jeremy, the porter, then put the phone down.

She watched Zoe for a moment as she carried on typing away. Maybe she'd try to be nice.

'So Zoe, how long have you been working with Noah?'

'About eight years.'

Aria felt a little pang of jealousy that he'd known Zoe longer than he'd known her.

'And you've worked with him in hotels around the world?'

'Yes, he always brings me in if the staff in a hotel are crap.'

Aria felt her eyebrows shoot up. She was so blunt, how had Noah put up with this for eight years?

'Well, I can assure you that's not the case here,' Aria said, although she knew that wasn't completely true. She was a crap manager, they hardly had any guests, they were in debt. Had

Noah really brought in Zoe to replace her after his big speech about how the hotel was still Aria's baby?

Zoe smirked as if she thought differently. 'Everyone always thinks that, but Noah and I get a sense of the kind of staff working in a place as soon as we walk through the door and, well… so far I've not been impressed. He'll start phasing you out soon enough.'

'I live here, I own twenty-five percent of the hotel. There will be no phasing out.'

'He'll suggest you take some time off to do the things that make you happy, pursue a hobby,' Zoe said. 'He'll tell you that he's more than happy to take the load.'

Aria stared at her, because Noah had said those exact things to her a few days before.

Zoe saw her face and smiled, smugly. 'Oh, he's already said those things to you. Wow, he must be keen to get rid of you. He normally waits a few weeks at least before he starts sacking the staff.'

Aria refused to believe this. She and Noah had shared too much, a kiss, promises of the future, too many warm glances and affectionate touches for her to believe that this was all part of a manipulative plan to get rid of her. This was just Zoe being a bitch. Zoe didn't know anything about their relationship and how close they were.

She decided to take another approach. If she kept talking to Zoe, then maybe she could get her on side. 'So, apart from sacking the staff, what's his normal way of doing this? Does he just buy the hotel, do it up and sell it on?'

'Normally. He's kept two hotels over the years, I think he uses the profits from them to help fund the renovations of other projects.'

'I did wonder where he'd got the money to decorate this place, there's so much that needs doing.'

And the last thing Aria wanted was for Noah to spend money he didn't have just to help her.

'He's gotten very good at running renovations to a budget and ignoring the demands of managers who just see him as a free ticket to get the hotel of their dreams.'

Aria instantly felt guilty about pushing him to reinstate the swimming pool. They needed to concentrate on the basics first, get more guests through the doors before they moved on to any big changes.

Noah walked into reception then and the look he gave her made almost every doubt fade away. It was as if she made him happy just to see her.

To Aria's surprise he was wearing jeans, a paint-splattered t-shirt and work boots.

'Are you helping the decorators?' she asked, incredulously.

He grinned, a sparkle showing in his eyes. 'Sometimes it's good to get your hands dirty. I'm just doing a bit of painting, but it's very therapeutic, helps to clear the mind.'

Aria wondered why he wanted to clear his mind. Though if he was feeling as frustrated as she was about this temporary hold on their relationship, then perhaps he needed time away from that.

'And if you want to see some of the work we've been doing, most of it is taking place on the second floor right now. I'm in room sixty-three if you want to have a look.'

'I'll pop up shortly.'

He moved away and Aria couldn't help appreciating how neat his bum looked in his jeans and how strong his arms were.

She turned back to see Zoe watching her. Restraining herself from giving Zoe the finger too, she spun on her heel and walked away.

CHAPTER FIFTEEN

Aria found Noah in one of the bedrooms later, knocked on the door and peered round into the room. He was painting one of the walls, singing along to the radio and had evidently not heard her. Already, in such a short amount of time, he had made such a big difference; the dated floral wallpaper had been stripped off, the carpet ripped up, the curtains taken down. All the furniture had been removed and it looked like the ceiling had already received a coat of bright white paint. The room was looking so much better already, although there was still so much to be done.

Noah was painting the walls in a pale blue as he sang, even giving his bum a little wiggle as he danced along with the music.

Aria giggled and Noah turned round, his eyes wide.

'I suppose it's too much to hope that you didn't hear me singing?'

'I'm afraid so. I also enjoyed the dancing.'

'There was no dancing.'

'There was definitely dancing,' Aria laughed and it made

her heart swell when he smirked and gave his bum another little wiggle for good measure.

'What do you think?' Noah gestured to the paint.

'It's looking good. I came to help.'

She had an ulterior motive of course. After talking to Sylvia a few days before, she knew that if things were ever to move forward between her and Noah, she needed to take the time to really get to know him.

He eyed her clothes. She had changed into an old pair of shorts and a worn t-shirt. She had been tempted to get some paint and start doing the hotel up herself so many times but her dad had never let her. Now there was no excuse and it felt good to be contributing in some way, as she wasn't doing it financially.

'Do you have a steady hand?'

'Sure,' Aria said, not really knowing if she did.

He smirked. 'Why not start on the gloss on the skirting boards over there. There's a tin and brush by the window.'

She prised open the lid and gave the paint a good stir, before sitting down on the floor and getting to work.

'I have to say, when you said you were going to oversee the renovations, I never pictured this,' Aria said.

'I used to do a lot of the work myself in the early days, before the hotels got bigger and more exclusive. I haven't done this kind of thing for years,' Noah said, and there was evident pleasure in his voice.

'How did you start in this business anyway, buying and selling hotels?'

He was silent for a while and, when he answered, she got the impression he was being careful about what he said.

'When I was seventeen, I ended up living in a small hotel with Elsie.'

'Oh, I never realised she ran a hotel.'

Aria had never really gotten to know Elsie properly, but she wished she had. Elsie was the reason Noah had first started coming to the island all those years before. Elsie had moved to the island to be closer to her sister but she'd only been there a few years before she'd died.

'More of a guest house really. Ten rooms,' Noah said. 'In return for some light maintenance, she gave me free board and food. Light maintenance turned into a complete restoration over the next few years. I decorated every room, every corridor, taught myself how to plaster with a lot of trial and error. The place looked amazing when I was finished. Then she sold me the hotel for a pound and moved here to Jewel Island to retire. I had no idea how to run a hotel and I wasn't particularly a people person either at that stage, so I didn't want to deal with guests, but I did know how to make something old look good. So I sold the hotel and bought another one. They were smallish hotels at first, but over the next three years I bought, redecorated and sold eleven hotels. I loved it. It kind of felt like I was an artist but working on a giant canvas. I started to get a bit of a name for myself, people started approaching me asking me to take certain projects on. By this time, I had a small team of decorators I took with me. I started my own company, Eden Vision. The hotels started getting bigger, the renovations were on a much larger scale. Things escalated very quickly.'

She wanted to ask him how he came to be living in a hotel with Elsie at the age of seventeen but he deliberately hadn't explained that so she didn't feel like she could.

'It sounds like it was something you were really passionate about.'

'It is. It was. I love doing stuff like this and I love coming up with a plan for the bigger hotels. But I'm not the one implementing it anymore and I miss that. I think it got harder and harder to step away from. I'd never had any money before, and suddenly I had more money than I knew existed. I didn't realise I wasn't enjoying my job anymore until it got too late and I didn't feel like I could walk away. Until, one day, I found something that I was prepared to give it all up for.'

'Your wife?' Aria said.

He was silent and she looked up from her painting.

He was rolling the paint onto the wall, the roller making a strange squelching sound which seemed at odds with the sudden seriousness of the conversation. 'My ex-wife, Georgia, was a whole other story.'

Aria carried on painting, being careful to get an even coverage on the wood. She wondered if Noah was in the mood to tell that story.

'Georgia was a woman I slept with once and got pregnant. She came and told me a few weeks after we'd been together. Of course I'd used protection so it came as something of a surprise. She told me she wasn't sure she wanted to keep it, that the thought of raising a child alone scared her. Looking back now, I think she just wanted the money, so she pretended it was for an abortion.'

Aria frowned in confusion.

'She's American, from New York actually, so she'd have to pay for an abortion. I think she thought I wouldn't want a baby and would just give her the cash,' Noah explained. 'But I really wanted a family of my own. And one thing I knew for sure, if we were going to have a kid, we were going to do it properly. And that child would be loved and adored, at least by me. So we got married, very quickly. And then she lost the baby.'

'Oh, I'm sorry,' Aria said. By the wistful tone of his voice when he'd talked about his child, she knew that must have been painful.

197

He shook his head. 'Honestly, Aria, when I look back on it all now, I don't think Georgia was ever even pregnant. I think she came to me for money knowing that I was a wealthy businessman and thinking I wouldn't want a baby to interfere with my life, and that I would give her money to go away. She underestimated me. When I offered her marriage instead, I think she saw a Cinderella story, an answer to all her financial problems. But I don't think there was a child. I came home from work one day, not long after we'd got married, and she told me she'd had her period so that was the end of that. I urged her to go to the doctor, as I know women can bleed during a pregnancy without actually miscarrying, but she refused, said the baby was gone. And I think I knew then. She didn't care, she wasn't upset. She even went out to a party that night while I sat at home and wondered where we went from there. We'd got married purely because she was pregnant. If there was no child, there didn't seem much point staying together. We certainly didn't love each other; it had been a one-night stand.'

'But you did stay together?'

'Yes, for nearly two years. She came home that night in tears saying we could try for another baby, begged me not to hate her for losing my child, and I couldn't do it, I couldn't walk away.'

He was quiet for a while and Aria sensed there was a lot more to this story.

'I'd never had a family growing up and here I was with a wife and she wanted to try for a baby and... it was everything that I'd ever wanted. It didn't seem to matter that she wasn't who I wanted to do those things with. I was in love with the idea of having a family more than I wanted to be with her. But I was determined to make it work. We had made a commitment to each other and I wanted to see it through. I tried to make a success of it, I really did. I was away with my job a lot but when I was back I tried to be a good husband, brought her gifts, did nice things for her, tried to talk to her – although I quickly learned we had nothing in common.' He shook his head. 'We fought constantly.'

'And she never got pregnant?' Aria asked.

'No, but I found out that she had been taking the pill the whole time we were together.'

'Oh.' This was getting worse. He'd wanted a family so badly and Georgia was never going to give him that.

'She was also having an affair.'

'Oh, Noah.'

'But when I found out, I actually felt relieved. I didn't want to bring a child into a loveless marriage. I mean, if we'd had a baby, I would have loved that child so much but an environment where both parents don't even like each other is no place to bring up a child. And I knew then that I didn't want forever with her. She was not the family I wanted and I was better off alone rather than spending the rest of my life with someone I didn't like, let alone love.'

She stared at him. 'I'm sorry it didn't work out for you, but it sounds like it was the right decision.'

'Yeah,' he said, sadly.

'So why do you feel responsible for the marriage breaking up? You looked after her for two years, you tried to make it work after she conned you into marriage in the first place. She was having an affair, for Christ's sake. You have nothing to feel guilty about.'

He carried on painting for a while, then when he finally spoke he didn't look at her. 'There was someone else for me too.'

'You had an affair?' Aria gasped.

'No, god no, I would never do that. We had our issues but I

was loyal to her until the very end. But there was someone else I wanted that life with. And I often wonder if I hadn't had feelings for this other woman, whether I'd have made more of an effort with Georgia. Maybe I subconsciously sabotaged my marriage because of my feelings. Maybe I sent her into the arms of someone else. Maybe Georgia sought solace from him because there was something she wasn't getting from me.'

'I don't think so. With or without this other woman your marriage would have ended. You need to stop blaming yourself. You did the right thing. What kind of future would you have had with her when you didn't love each other?'

'Yeah, I know you're right, but I can't help feeling a bit guilty about it.'

'You can't help who you have feelings for.'

'I know,' Noah said, softly.

Aria carried on painting and frowned slightly. Who was this other woman?

'So you've been divorced for what, a year and a half, two years? Did you never try to get together with this other woman, after your marriage came to an end?' Aria asked.

'I did, just over a year ago.'

She stared at the paint, not really seeing it, and then turned round to look at him. He was staring right at her.

She stood up because this felt like too important a conversation to have while she was sitting down with a paintbrush in her hand. But once she was standing she had no words at all.

Noah dropped his roller in the tray and moved towards her slightly. 'I think the most frustrating thing about all of this is you.'

She swallowed. 'Me?'

'I've known you for five years and I knew right from the very first time we met that you were somebody wonderful.'

'But you never… we…' Aria was still struggling with this.

She'd been the other woman. All this time, he'd had feelings for her and he'd never acted on it.

'We were friends. I'd not had the best childhood and that led to me having a few trust issues, I guess I was scared of having a relationship. It was hard to really get to know you when I was here for such a short amount of time. I knew you were special but I didn't start having feelings for you until after I'd married Georgia. I should have stayed away, knowing I had those feelings for you and they were getting stronger every time I came. I was a married man, and although I was never unfaithful with my body, I was with my mind. But I couldn't keep away. Every time I needed a break from work, I came here instead of going home.'

Aria didn't know how to react to all of this. She actually felt like crying over all the lost time. They could have been together years ago.

'I think about all that wasted time, of where we could have been now if I'd been brave enough to take a chance with you before I'd met Georgia.'

She moved closer. 'But I'm here now. Forget the past, forget the missed opportunities. You've waited five years and I'm here. Take a chance on me now.'

He shook his head.

'Why the hell not?' she said, her voice raised.

'Because this is too damned important to screw up. I want this to work more than anything and working on the hotel is going to get stressful. I don't want to argue with you all the time. That's not how a relationship should work.'

She shook her head with frustration. 'You are one of the most infuriating men I have ever met but unfortunately that doesn't stop my feelings for you, the feelings I've had for you for the past five years, and I'm not prepared to wait any longer. A very wise man once said to me that I should

201

pursue the things I want. You are everything I've ever wanted.'

She leaned up and kissed him and he immediately kissed her back, wrapping his arms around her and hugging her tightly.

Aria slid her arms round his neck, pressing her body against his. She ran her fingers through his hair at the nape of his neck and he groaned against her mouth. He moved his hands to her waist, his fingers playing at her hips for a second before he slid them under her top and wrapped his hands around her back, holding her close. She gasped against his lips at the feel of his skin against the bare flesh of her back. His hands on her body was the most incredible feeling in the world. The warmth of his body against hers, his tangy, fruity scent enveloping her, the feel of his hands stroking her bare skin, god this was heaven. His mouth was moving slowly against hers, his tongue sliding into her mouth. Holy shit, this was the hottest kiss she'd ever had in her life.

He shuffled her back against the wall, thankfully not one that had been painted, and pinned her to it with his weight as the kiss continued. She hooked a leg around his hips, holding him tight against her. She could feel he wanted this as much as she did. He moved his hand to her waist, ran his finger across the top of her shorts and then slowly started tugging the waistband down.

'Noah...? Shit, sorry.'

Noah snatched his mouth from hers, though he didn't move away, didn't take his eyes from her face.

Aria was vaguely aware there was a man standing in the doorway. She tried to catch her breath, tried to straighten her thoughts. Noah's chest was heaving as if he'd just run a marathon.

'Sorry,' the man said again, trying to look everywhere but

at them. 'There's a problem in room seventy-three, we're not sure how you want to handle it.'

'I'll be there in a minute,' Noah said, although he was still staring at Aria, a thousand emotions playing across his face.

The man left and they continued to stand wrapped around each other, their eyes locked. They had probably been no more than a minute away from the kiss turning into something a hell of a lot more. She reached up and stroked his face and a small frown appeared on his forehead.

'I'm sorry—' Noah started.

'Don't. Don't apologise for that.'

'I—'

She pressed her finger to his lips. 'That kiss was incredible, don't ruin it with apologies and regrets. It doesn't change anything, I know that, but I feel nothing but relief that it happened. The last few days have been driving me mad and I did wonder if what I felt for you was completely one-sided. I'm grateful to know that it isn't.'

'Of course it isn't. It's just—'

'I know,' she sighed. 'I better let you go.' She turned to leave.

'Aria—'

'It's fine, I'll see you later.'

Her heart racing, she turned and walked out the room, with no idea what she should be feeling right now. Part of her wanted to dance on the spot, punch the air and jump for joy over that wonderful kiss, but there was also a huge part of her that felt so frustrated that it wouldn't happen again. They both had feelings for each other but he wasn't willing to take it any further. There was also the fact that she had assured her sisters that things would stay professional between them. She was ashamed to say, they hadn't even entered her mind when he'd been kissing her.

She went back to her room and got changed into her normal smart clothes. She should never have gone up to help in the first place. Being alone with Noah was a recipe for disaster. Except if she hadn't they would never have kissed and she couldn't regret that. She had also learned a lot more about him that she'd never known before, but there was so much more she felt she needed to uncover.

She went back down to reception just as Callum Marlowe and presumably his wife Lottie arrived. Of course Aria knew of him; as a Paralympian gold medallist, pretty much everyone knew who he was. But the Philips Hotel was a professional establishment, and they would treat him respectfully just like any other guest. None of her staff would be starstruck and ask for his autograph or take pictures of him, she was sure. Although Katy's eyes were definitely a little wider as the couple approached the reception desk. Thankfully Zoe wasn't around. Aria hurried over to greet them. Despite the fact that all of their emails about their stay had been signed Cal and Lottie, she decided to address them formally as she would any guest.

'Mr and Mrs Marlowe, I'm Aria Philips, the manager. Welcome to the Philips Hotel.'

'Thank you,' Cal said, looping his arm around Lottie's shoulders, who was beaming massively.

'If there's anything you need during your stay here, please don't hesitate to ask,' Aria said. 'Your room is ready for you and you'll find a welcome gift from the hotel to celebrate your wedding.'

'Thank you, that's very kind,' Lottie said.

'Our daughter Poppy will be arriving with my sister Ruby next weekend,' Cal said.

'Oh, they'll be here for the festival of light,' Aria said.

'Yes, Poppy is really looking forward to that,' Lottie said. 'I believe our room has a separate lounge area to the bedroom?'

'Yes, that's right.'

'Can we have a single bed or Z bed made up for her in the lounge that weekend?'

'Yes, that's no problem.'

The lift doors pinged open and Noah walked towards Aria like he was on a mission. But as he approached, his eyes slid to Cal and Lottie and his whole face lit up.

'Callum Marlowe, bloody hell, what are you doing here?' Noah said.

So much for professionalism.

Cal turned round and suddenly the two were hugging.

Cal pulled back. 'This is my wife Lottie, this is my friend Noah.'

'You two know each other?' Aria said.

'Yes, my company sponsored Cal in the last Paralympics,' Noah said.

'Yeah, I had Eden Vision emblazoned across my chest,' Cal said.

'And we've kind of stayed in contact ever since. Although I never got an invite to the wedding,' Noah teased.

'I sent it to your New York address, did you not get it?' Cal said, seriously.

'Ah, no, I don't live there anymore.'

'Well, the wedding happened very quickly in the end. We didn't want to wait.' Cal pressed a kiss to Lottie's cheek.

'Nice to meet you Noah, I've heard a lot about you,' Lottie said, offering out a hand but Noah hugged her instead.

'Congratulations on your wedding,' Noah said. 'I'm so happy for the two of you.'

Aria couldn't help but smile. It was so nice to see Noah so happy and relaxed, rather than the stressed-out version she'd had for the last few days. Was she making him miserable with all of this?

'If there's anything you need, just let us know,' Noah said. 'If you'd like a tour of the island we can do that, it's such a beautiful place.'

'That sounds lovely and I'm sure we'll be exploring the island once Poppy gets here. For now, though, I think we'd just like to see our room,' Cal said and Lottie giggled.

Noah laughed. 'Of course.'

Katy handed over the key and gave them directions.

'Really good to see you again, Noah,' Cal said. 'Let's have dinner or something while we're here.'

'Sounds good.'

Cal and Lottie moved off to the lift and Noah turned back to face Aria, his smile fading. 'We need to talk,' he gestured to her office.

'There's no need,' she said. There really was no point rehashing old ground.

He eyed Katy who was watching their exchange with keen interest. 'I think there is.'

'I'm sorry about… before. You have my word that it won't happen again.'

He stared at her and she turned and walked away.

CHAPTER SIXTEEN

Aria was walking past Clover's office a while later when she heard whispering coming from inside. She paused and looked through the gap in the door. Clover, Skye, Jesse and Angel were all in there.

'Should we tell Aria?' Skye said.

'It will break her heart,' Clover said.

Aria pushed open the door and four pairs of guilty eyes looked at her.

'What will break my heart?'

They all looked awkward. Skye glanced at Jesse and nodded.

Jesse rubbed the back of his neck. 'I overheard two of the decorators talking. One of them walked in on Noah kissing a woman in one of the rooms they're decorating upstairs. Apparently it was very heated.'

Aria had no words at all. How was she going to explain this? She'd have thought Noah's team would have more discretion than this.

'Are you OK?' Clover asked, gently.

She cleared her throat. 'Do you know who he was kissing?'

Jesse shook his head.

'It's got to be Zoe, right?' Skye said.

'I really don't think it's Zoe,' Angel said, giving Aria a meaningful look. He obviously knew exactly who it was. 'Do you have any idea, Aria?'

'No, why would I know?' Aria said, feeling like she was throwing Noah under the bus. God, this was such a mess.

'He's such a dick,' Skye said.

'Hang on a minute,' Angel said, loyally.

'He's kissing someone behind Aria's back,' Clover said.

'He's not with Aria. He's not with anyone so he's free to kiss whoever he pleases,' Angel said.

'Angel's right, we're not together.' At least she could be honest about that. One kiss did not mean anything had changed between them.

'But you still have feelings for him and he knows that. Talk about rubbing your nose in it,' Clover said.

'I really don't think Noah would be kissing anyone,' Aria tried. 'He's been so strict about keeping things professional, he's hardly going to be upstairs kissing random women. Maybe this builder thought it was Noah and it was someone else. In fact, it could have been Cal, one of our guests who has just checked in with his wife. They kind have the same hair, a similar build. Maybe the builder saw Cal from behind and just assumed it was Noah.'

'I bet that's it,' Angel seized on the pathetic excuse.

Clover, Skye and Jesse seemed less than convinced.

'Look, what Noah and I shared was in the past. If it really was him, which I honestly doubt, that's fine.' Aria pulled off a nonchalant shrug for good measure.

'You're honestly not bothered?' Skye said.

'No, I'm not.'

Just then Noah appeared at the door and looked between them. 'What's going on?'

Oh crap, time to see what his acting skills were like.

'Apparently one of your decorators saw you kissing a woman upstairs and has been telling everyone that it looked very heated. I told them that I very much doubt that it was you, and that the decorator must have been mistaken. So, were you kissing anyone?'

She hoped to god Noah would play along. She hadn't told him that her sisters had specifically asked her not to let anything happen between them.

He didn't say anything for the longest time, clearly trying to decide what to say. All he had to do was laugh it off, say it wasn't him, but he said nothing. In fact, the silence dragged on longer than was comfortable. He was shooting himself in the foot here. The more time he left it, the more guilty he looked.

'Aria suggested it might have been Cal,' Angel suggested helpfully. 'As you both have similar builds and hair.'

'Cal, of course it was. Sorry, I was just trying to think who it might have been. It definitely wasn't me. I've been too busy for those kinds of shenanigans.'

Oh god, he was a terrible liar, and, as Skye folded her arms across her chest, it was clear she didn't believe him for one second.

'There you go, case closed,' Angel said, ushering Noah out of the office before he could do any further damage to his reputation.

Aria was left with her sisters and Jesse.

'Are you sure you're OK?' Clover said gently.

'Do you want me to rough him up for you?' Jesse said, which made Aria laugh. Despite his huge size, he was a gentle giant and certainly not capable of roughing anyone up. Skye on the other hand...

209

'No, thank you. I'm fine. Look, Noah is here in a professional capacity, he's here to save our hotel and at great cost to
him. So far, he's doing a wonderful job so what he does in his
own time doesn't affect me or any of you. So, Skye, take that
look off your face. I love you for being protective over me, but
this thing between me and Noah doesn't concern you, OK?'

Skye nodded begrudgingly.

Aria left the office and quickly headed round the reception
desk, deliberately ignoring Zoe who seemed to be watching
her with wide eyes. She knew something was going on. Aria
marched up to her dad's office, which Noah had started using,
and entered without knocking to see Angel and Noah in there.
She closed the door and walked straight up to Noah, cupping
his lovely face and kissing him on the cheek. 'I'm so sorry.'

'God, no, I'm sorry. I didn't know what was the right thing
to say in there, so I just said nothing. I have no poker face; you
might have guessed.'

'I sort of promised my sisters that nothing would happen
between us – they thought things could get awkward with you
being a partner in the hotel. I suppose they were worried
about it going wrong and you leaving. The hotel needs you.
And I worry about you leaving too because *I* need you. You
said yourself you'd see how the next few months go and you
weren't sure whether it would become a permanent thing. I
don't want to do anything to make you leave and now they
hate you because they think you're kissing random women
behind my back and I kind of hate myself for lying to them
and it's such a mess.'

Noah wrapped his arms around her, stroking her back
soothingly, and Angel looked away as if he had suddenly
found something very interesting to stare at out the window.

'Aria, I'm not going anywhere. The biggest mistake I ever
made was walking away from you before. When I said I didn't

know if it was a permanent thing, I meant I didn't know if you were going to put up with me. I'm here now and I'm not leaving unless you tell me to.'

'Oh.'

'Look, why don't we just tell them it was us kissing?'

'They were worried about that too, that us being together would create an unbalanced dynamic in our equal partnership. They said they didn't want any decisions for the hotel to be made in the bedroom.'

'The last thing I'd want to talk to you about in bed is work.'

'So you two *are* together now?' Angel said

'No,' Aria said.

'Maybe,' Noah said at the same time.

'Maybe?' squeaked Aria.

He smiled and stroked her cheek. 'I'm not sure us *not* being together is working out that well.'

'Hallelujah!' Angel said, dryly. 'Now get upstairs and celebrate, I'll look after everything down here.'

There was a sudden knocking on the door – whatever it was, it seemed to be very urgent.

Noah sighed and stepped away from Aria to answer the door.

Zoe was there.

'Sorry to interrupt.' She gave Aria a filthy look. 'I just wanted to go over some things with you, Noah.'

'Sure, come on in.' He turned back to Aria. 'We can chat about this later,' he said formally, as if they hadn't just been discussing something so vitally important.

'OK,' Aria said, uncertainly, and Angel followed her out.

Zoe closed the door behind them a little too forcefully for Aria's liking.

The reception was practically empty, so her sisters had probably gone to start the 'We Hate Noah Campbell' fan club somewhere else. Tilly was still sitting in the lobby area, though, peering over her book at what was going on, and she had been joined by Sylvia, who had absolutely no scruples when it came to staring at the comings and goings.

Aria turned to Angel and lowered her voice.

'You knew it was me he'd been kissing?'

'I knew one thousand percent it wasn't Zoe. Despite her efforts over the years, Noah has never showed any interest in her.'

'Ah, Zoe likes Noah?'

That explained a lot.

'Yeah, but I shouldn't worry. You're all he's talked about for the last five years. I think that ship has sailed for her.'

Aria smiled then sighed. 'It's never easy is it, this love malarkey.'

'No, but I'm reliably informed, it's worth it in the end.'

Noah was woken by a loud wailing and he sat bolt upright in the darkness as he looked around his room, his heart thundering against his chest at the intrusion from his dreams.

It took him a few seconds to realise it was the fire alarm. He quickly switched on the light next to his bed and looked around. There was no smoke here but that didn't mean anything.

He got out of bed and pulled on some jeans and a t-shirt, then made his way to the door, poking his head outside and having a look around. Again there was no sign of smoke, but he knew staying in his room and presuming everything was OK was probably a mistake. Cal and Lottie emerged from their room further down the corridor. He better go and make sure everything was OK.

He quickly made his way down the stairs and saw the guests mingling in the foyer in their pyjamas and nightclothes, evidently not sure what was going on. Xena was trying to get everyone to go outside but not having much luck. There was no sign of Aria. Clover, Skye and Zoe would be in their cottages in the hotel grounds and probably had no clue that the fire alarm was going off. So it seemed it was down to him to direct operations.

He raised his voice. 'Ladies and gentlemen, I'm sure this is a false alarm but while we investigate the cause of the alarm, can you all follow Xena outside to the assembly point and we will try to get this dealt with as quickly as possible.'

There were murmurs of agreement and discontent as they all started to shuffle towards the door.

'Noah,' Sylvia waved at him, as she dragged Snowflake along behind her. 'I'm sure I saw smoke coming out of the back of the hotel.'

Crap.

'Thank you Sylvia. Please make your way out of the hotel and I'll look into it.'

Where the hell was Aria?

Suddenly he remembered, she wouldn't have heard the fire alarm in her bedroom. *And her room was at the back of the hotel.* He was running up the stairs towards her room before he even knew what he was doing, arriving there in what felt like seconds. He hammered on her bedroom door. There was no response so he banged it again. Still no response.

Not wanting to waste any more time, he slammed his shoulder against the door, which didn't budge. He took a few steps back and threw himself against it and it flew off its hinges and crashed into the floor. He stepped over it and quickly made for her bedroom but there was no sign of her, the covers of the bed thrown back where she had clearly left in a hurry.

'Aria!' he called out, just in case, running into the bathroom and then back into the lounge and into the little kitchen. She definitely wasn't here.

He dashed back out into the corridor and made his way back down the stairs, his heart still racing, and that's when he saw her coming up from one of the rooms downstairs.

She waved at him as he got close and he just wanted to haul her into his arms, thankful that she was alive and unharmed, which was probably a bit of an overreaction.

She switched the alarm off and his ears hummed in the silence for a moment.

'I've checked all the main communal areas and the kitchen and there doesn't seem to be anything wrong,' she said. 'But we need to check every bedroom before we can allow the guests to go back to their rooms. I'll get a few master keys and we can start the search. We might as well let the guests sit in the lounge while they are waiting, it'll be warmer for them and I'm pretty sure everything is fine,' she added, grabbing the master key cards and radioing through to Xena on the walkie-talkie.

Noah took a few deep breaths, forcing himself to calm down. She was OK. And the hotel seemed to be fine too.

'Sylvia said she thought she saw smoke coming from the back of the hotel.'

She smiled. 'I imagine that was steam coming from the boiler vent but we'll check everywhere just to be sure. Why don't you take the ground-floor and the first-floor bedrooms and I'll check the second floor and the top floor,' Aria said, ever efficient, despite the fact that she was wearing pyjamas: a tiny pair of bright blue shorts emblazoned with white stars that showed off her wonderful long legs, and a matching vest top that was cut very low.

'Good idea,' Noah said, clearing his throat.

He went off down the corridor and checked the rooms one by one. There was nothing down here. He went back to the foyer and saw all the guests were being looked after by Xena in the lounge as he made his way up to the first floor.

After carefully checking every room, he decided he'd go and meet Aria upstairs as there were more rooms up there. He called out to her on the second floor but there was no answer so he decided to go on up to his floor where the four suites were.

He actually found her in his room over by the table near the window. He hadn't bothered to put any lights on in the main lounge area before he'd left the room and the only illumination came from the moon that was shining brightly over the sea. It painted her in a silvery glow, making her look ethereal.

'I don't think there are any fires in here, I would have noticed,' Noah said, closing the door behind him. Now she was here and they were alone, he really needed to talk to her.

She turned to look at him, her dark hair tumbling over her shoulders. She was... breathtaking.

'I'm making you miserable,' Aria said.

'What? Why on earth would you think like that?'

'Because I saw how you were today with Cal; unguarded, happy, relaxed. You used to be like that with me. But now, with the hotel to deal with and me pushing you to take the relationship further than you want to, it's making you stressed out and I hate that.'

He stepped towards her. 'Of course I want the hotel to be a success again, and more so than any other hotel I've worked on in the past. Because this is your home, your family's legacy. I want it to be a success for *you*, not for me. But there is nothing more important to me in this world right now than you. I have been so scared of taking that step with you because I have convinced myself that it will fail. And I guess I've been putting obstacles in our way. I've been finding reasons to keep us apart when what I should have been doing is fighting for us to be together, just like you are. Kissing you today made me feel like I was home and I know with all my heart that what we have is right. I have wasted five years and I don't want to waste another second.'

She stared at him like a rabbit in the headlights. 'What are you saying?'

Suddenly her walkie-talkie squawked to life.

'Aria, is everything OK? Can I let the guests go back to their rooms now?'

Aria fumbled with her walkie-talkie. 'Yes Xena, we were just on our way back down. Please apologise to all the guests and reassure them that everything is fine and let them go back to their rooms.'

'OK, will do.'

'And let me know if you need anything else.'

'Great, thanks.'

Noah took the walkie-talkie from her and, hoping to god there were no more interruptions, he tossed it on the sofa.

Aria stared at him, her breath heavy. 'What are you saying?' she said again.

'I'm saying, I'd really like it if you'd spend the night with me.'

CHAPTER SEVENTEEN

Aria stared at him, her heart hammering against her chest.

She stepped forward and suddenly they were kissing, greedy hands touching everywhere they could reach. He pulled her top over her head and, as he kissed her again, his hands explored her breasts, running his thumbs over her nipples and making her moan against his lips. She fumbled with his jeans, pushing them down, and was surprised and turned on to find he wasn't wearing anything underneath.

'I sleep naked,' Noah muttered against her lips, stepping out of his jeans and then yanking his t-shirt over his head. 'Something you might want to try.'

He kissed her again and then knelt down on the floor to peel off her shorts, slowly and agonisingly, inch by inch, his eyes taking in her naked body as if she was the most beautiful woman in the world.

She stepped out of her shorts and he leaned forward and placed the briefest of kisses at the very top of her thighs in that exact spot that made her quiver with need for him.

He stood back up, towering over her, then scooped her up

HOLLY MARTIN

in his arms and carried her into the bedroom. The bedside light was on in here, casting a warm glow over his bed sheets as he laid her down and pinned her to the mattress with his weight, kissing her hard.

He pulled back to look at her.

'God Aria, I want you so much. I've thought of nothing else but making love to you ever since that first kiss.'

'Well, that's a hell of a lot of foreplay, so why don't we skip ahead to the main event,' Aria said, wrapping her legs around his hips.

'Not a chance. I've waited too long for this; I'm going to enjoy every second of it.'

He used his fingers to explore and his mouth to taste every inch of her until she was gasping and whimpering with need for him. He placed kisses up her legs and then right at the top of her thighs until she was grabbing at his hair, shouting out his name, that feeling ripping through her like a firework. He held her still as she trembled against him and, as the feeling started to subside, he shifted up over her and kissed her hard on the mouth.

She was still shaking as she wrapped herself around him.

He reached over to the bedside drawers and grabbed a condom, leaning back slightly so he could put it on.

'Why do you have condoms when you were so adamant that nothing was going to happen between us?' Aria said, stroking his back with gentle hands.

'I kind of thought we'd end up here eventually. I have no control when it comes to you.'

He gathered her close and slid inside of her.

She gasped against his lips and he stilled and pulled back to look at her. She wrapped her arms round his shoulders, caressing the back of his neck. 'This was a long time coming, Noah Campbell.'

'I know, I'm sorry, we should have done this years ago.'

He was so big as he surrounded her with his whole body, his glorious weight on her, inside of her, pinning her down.

He started to move, deep, gentle rolls of his hips, taking her higher with every slow, luxurious movement, and that sensation started spreading through her again, tingling through every part of her. His eyes were locked with hers. God, she needed more, that feeling was there but just beyond her reach. She slid her hands down to his bum, urging him on, and he grinned. He clearly wanted to take his time with this, while she was desperate with need for him.

He nipped at her lips, placed kisses down her throat, that wonderful feeling humming through her body. He caught her hands and pinned them above her head, causing her to arch against him and letting him touch that sweet spot inside of her.

'Noah! Christ,' Aria moaned.

He leaned forward and kissed her as she fell apart around him, that sensation exploding through her, and he caught her gasps on his lips. And suddenly he was right there as well, his body shaking against hers, his groan almost animalistic as he collapsed down on top of her.

Her breath was ragged, his chest heaving against hers as he pulled back to look at her as if seeing her for the first time. 'Jesus Christ, Aria, marry me.'

He kissed her hard and, even though she knew he was only joking, it took every ounce of strength she had not to say yes.

Noah hadn't fallen sleep, how could he when the woman of his dreams was finally lying in his bed. They were wrapped around each other as if they couldn't bear to be apart, her legs entwined with his, her hands stroking his back. She hadn't fallen asleep either and he wondered what was keeping her awake.

They hadn't spoken much; they'd stroked and kissed and cuddled but not really talked.

'You seem tense,' Aria said.

Of course he was tense. He felt like one wrong move and the whole thing would fall apart like a house of cards.

'I'm fine.'

She looked up at him. 'You look worried, what's wrong?'

He sighed and sat up, leaning against the headboard. She sat up next to him and took his hand. That small sign of solidarity filled him with strength.

'I guess I'm scared of messing it all up,' Noah said.

'Why do you think it's going to go wrong?' Aria said. 'You know we have something amazing.'

'I guess because I've screwed up every relationship I've ever had.'

'Are you talking about Georgia? Because it's not really fair to hold yourself responsible for that.'

He paused before he spoke. He wasn't sure he wanted to tell Aria all about his childhood but he guessed he should.

'My parents never really got on, they were always fighting, and I got the impression many of the fights were about me. I had terrible pains in my legs growing up, I used to wake up crying most nights because of the pain. The doctors never really figured out why and I think my parents thought I was faking it. They used to tell me off when I'd wake them in the middle of the night – even my little brother used to get annoyed with me. I soon learned to cry into my pillow rather than call out for them.'

'Oh Noah, I'm so sorry you went through that and your parents weren't more supportive. I presume the pain stopped?'

'It did but not before...' he paused. 'When I was six my dad walked out on me, my mum and my little brother. I distinctly remember him leaving, screaming at my mum, telling her he'd had enough of her and had enough of me. I remember my mum being really sad after that, she would cry all the time and nothing I did could get her to stop. She drank a lot. She was a mess. For a week or two I looked after my little brother, fed him, washed him, until my dad came back and took his son to live with him.'

'His son?' Aria asked in confusion.

'Yes, well that was how I found out that the man who had raised me for the last six years wasn't actually my dad at all. I have no idea who my real dad is. There is a blank space next to my father's name on my birth certificate but as it turned out it wasn't the man who lived with us for six years.'

Aria stared at him in shock. 'Oh god, what a horrible way to find out.'

'Yeah, it wasn't good. Mum was less than sympathetic; she was drunk pretty much all the time. A few weeks after that I woke up one morning and found she was gone too. I didn't know what to do but I didn't tell anyone as I didn't want to get her into trouble. I took myself to school every day, made very bad packed lunches. The teachers soon found out though. No one had any idea where she was. There were fears that she might have taken her own life but they never found a body and I never saw her again. I tried to find her when I was older, but if she's still alive she's certainly going under a different name now.'

'Oh Noah, I'm so sorry. Who did you live with then?'

'Well, that was the thing. No one wanted me. Not my grandparents, not my aunts or uncles. I suppose that says a lot about what kind of child I was.'

'It says more about what kind of scum your family was,'

Aria snapped. 'Your dad sounds like a horrible man, who does that to a six-year-old child? Your mum failed you and, just when the rest of your family should have stepped in, they failed you too.'

'I suppose I have to take some responsibility for it though. I must have been a horrible child if both of my parents walked out on me within a few weeks of each other and no one else wanted me.'

'Noah, you can't take that on your shoulders. It sounds like your parents had their own issues that were nothing to do with you.'

'Anyway, things got a bit complicated after that. I don't think I could be adopted as you need parental permission for that. Not that anyone wanted to, I don't think. So I was placed in foster care.'

'That must have been such a scary and upsetting time for you. And you lost your brother too?'

'Yeah, I missed Charlie like crazy. We're in contact now but I wouldn't say we're close. He was three when his dad took him and we didn't see each other again until I was in my early twenties. We call each other occasionally but he grew up without even knowing I existed.'

'So you didn't stay in touch at all?'

'I don't think the man I thought was my dad cared what happened to me. I never stayed in one place for very long so, even if he had any inclination to keep in touch, it would have been quite hard to find me. I was always moving on to the next foster home and the next. Between the ages of six and seventeen I had over a hundred different foster homes. I'm not sure why I was moved around so much in my younger years; whether I struggled to adjust because I missed my mum, or whether it was something else. I know when I was older I was a little shit. I knew I'd get moved on soon enough so there didn't seem any point trying to fit in. No one wanted me, no one attempted to make any connection with me. I was sullen, rude, angry and was treated like a burden that some families had to endure.'

He stared out over the sea, the sky a dusky grey as it readied itself for the coming day.

'I ran away when I was seventeen. I waited for the appeals to say I was missing, the posters, my picture in the news... But if there were any, I certainly didn't see them. No one cared. That's how I came to live with Elsie. I was rude to her too, expecting her to throw me out but she never did. She didn't take any crap either and we eventually became friends. But I never really had any serious relationships after that – well, apart from Georgia and I can't say I made a success of that. No one wanted me as a child, so why would any woman want me? I had casual relationships of course, but nothing serious. No real friendships either. I didn't trust people easily.'

He looked at her, her eyes filled with concern, and he smiled. 'And then there was you. You were so warm and welcoming, and I know that's part of your job, but this was different. I remember the first time you hugged me – I think it was my third or fourth visit to the hotel. I was there for Elsie's funeral and as soon as I walked in through the door, you came over and hugged me. I held you in my arms and I honestly couldn't remember the last time I had ever been held like that. I felt like... you were my forever. And I know it took me five years to do something about it, but here we are. And yes, I am terrified of cocking it all up and losing you like I've lost everyone else.'

Aria let out a heavy breath. 'I had no idea you grew up like that. You always seemed so happy and relaxed when you were here.'

'I was, I am. This place has always been a haven for me.'

'It breaks my heart that your parents did that to you and for one reason or another you never had a home after that. And the fact that you're still relatively sane after all that is a miracle,' she said, teasing him. He smiled at the word relatively. 'You have worked hard and you've built a life for yourself that you should be incredibly proud of. I don't judge the boy or the man that you were in the past, the man I know now is the most wonderful, amazing man I have ever met. I get that you're scared, but I'm not, not one bit. We've got this.'

He smiled at her confidence, leaning forward to kiss her, and she kissed him back, stroking his face.

God, why was he scared of this? Aria was everything he'd ever wanted and she was here in his bed, wanting him as much as he wanted her.

He shifted her so she was straddling his lap, although frustratingly there was still a sheet between them. He moved his mouth to her neck, savouring the feel of her pulse hammering against his lips. He kissed below her ear and she let out a little moan of need. He slid his hands over her body, wanting to caress and stroke and touch everywhere at once. He ran his thumb over her breast, then slipped her nipple inside his mouth.

'Oh god Noah.'

She leaned over and grabbed a condom, yanking the sheet from between them and rolling the condom on. He moved his hands to her hips, guiding her down as he moved inside her.

She smiled and leaned down and placed a kiss over his heart. He stroked her hair, which slipped like black silk through his fingers, and she sat up and kissed him as he shifted her legs around his back. They moved together perfectly, as if they had known each other for years, as if they had always meant to be together.

He stared at her, this incredible woman, and she was here, in his arms. 'Where have you been all my life Aria Philips?'

'I've been here, waiting for you.'

He suddenly felt a pang for everything they had missed before. She was right, this was where he should have been all along.

He had to forget the past now, he had to stop it holding him back. She was his future and the only thing that mattered.

He kissed her hard, gathered her closer against him. She moaned against his lips. He moved against her harder, faster, holding her tighter and then sensed her fall apart in his arms, her fingers digging into his shoulders, her breath in heavy gasps against his lips, her body trembling in his hands. He felt himself fall over the edge, clinging to her as the most incredible feeling ripped through his body. This was everything all at once and he vowed right then and there, he was never going to let her go.

The sun was just starting to rise over Sapphire Bay as Aria lay on Noah's chest. He was asleep but his arm was wrapped around her back. She looked up at him, bathed in gold as he slept with a smile on his face.

What they had shared the previous night had been incredible. She had never been sentimental about sex before. She'd had some lovely boyfriends and the sex had been great but this had been different. This felt like two halves of a whole reconnecting after too many years apart.

If he was to wake up now and back-pedal, say they shouldn't have done it, redraw the professional line between them, she would be gutted. She didn't know how they would move forward now, but she knew they had to move forward.

He stirred, almost as if he knew she was watching him. Her breath caught in her throat as he blinked a few times, frowned in confusion as if he'd registered she was there and then turned to face her. For a few endless seconds he simply stared at her and then he broke into a huge smile.

He leaned forward and kissed her and she felt nothing but relief.

'Good morning, beautiful.'

Her heart soared. 'Morning.'

He glanced briefly at the view, at the rose-gold waves dancing in the early sun. 'God, what a spectacular way to wake up.'

'The sunrises here are pretty wonderful.'

He turned back to face her. 'I meant waking up with you.'

Oh god, this man.

'So, no regrets about last night?' Aria said.

He ran his fingers down her bare back. 'I regret that we didn't do this sooner, but I don't regret what we shared last night, not for one second.'

'So what happens now?' Aria asked.

He suddenly rolled her, pinning her to the mattress. 'What happens now is that I'm going to make love to you again.' He kissed her throat. 'And then, if there's time, I'm going to make love to you in the shower.'

She giggled. 'I meant what happens between us? Although that partially answers my question. Are we going to do this, properly?'

'Aria, I walked away from you before, after that first kiss, the biggest mistake I've ever made. I'm not walking away from you again. We can figure this out somehow. We have to promise that the hotel won't interfere with what we have, that somehow we can keep this separate. But yes, I'd like to give this a go if you want to too.'

'Yes, I want that.' She paused. 'But we have to keep it a secret.'

He frowned and she hurried on.

'I just don't want my sisters to regret their decision to stay. I want them to feel like they are equal partners in all of this, just like we agreed, and not that things are unfairly skewed or that things are happening behind their back.'

'But if we have a secret relationship we will be carrying on behind their back,' Noah protested.

'I meant decisions about the hotel.'

'I don't think lying about our relationship is a great start,' Noah said.

'Just for a few weeks, until everything settles down. At least until after the festival of light.'

He sighed. 'I suppose it makes things easier to keep it separate. During the day, we'll keep things professional, and at night, we'll be here, together, two separate lives.'

Aria wasn't entirely sure how that would pan out but she wanted this to work between them more than anything so she was willing to give it a shot.

'OK.'

'Now listen, about last night. When the alarm went off, I wasn't sure where you were. I knew you couldn't hear the alarm in your room and Sylvia said she'd seen smoke coming from the back of the hotel... Well, long story short, I sort of kicked your door down.'

Her eyes widened in shock. 'You... kicked my door down?'

'Well, threw my whole body weight against it would be a more accurate way of telling it. But either way, it's currently in around three or four pieces on your bedroom floor.'

She stared at him and then let out an incredulous laugh. 'What did you plan to do, carry me from the burning building in your arms?'

He cleared his throat. 'If necessary.'

She shook her head. 'Noah Campbell, you're an impossible man, but thank you for being my hero, whether I needed it or not.'

He smiled, looking a lot happier this morning than he had the night before. 'Well, I don't think you should sleep in there until the door is fixed.'

She smirked. 'And where do you suggest I sleep?'

'I might have a suggestion.'

'I thought you might, but we are supposed to be keeping this a secret,' Aria said.

'Sleep next door, we have adjoining doors. Makes things very easy.'

She laughed as he kissed her throat but her laughter died when he slipped a hand between her legs, his touch igniting a fire inside her immediately. She was never going to have enough of this man.

CHAPTER EIGHTEEN

Noah put the phone down after talking to someone about solar panels and glanced out of the open office door. There was a young girl waiting at the reception desk who looked absolutely terrified. Zoe finished the call she was on and walked over.

'Hello, how can I help you?' Zoe said, oozing professionalism.

'I... I... was wondering if you have any jobs available,' said the young girl, who looked no older than thirteen or fourteen years old.

Noah watched the moment that the professional mask slipped as Zoe literally laughed. 'I don't think so. We hire only experienced, qualified people here.'

And maybe it was the fact that he'd been that terrified child desperate for a job once, or maybe, as with many decisions he'd made over the last few days, his uppermost thought was what Aria would do in this situation, but he suddenly found himself on his feet. He marched straight out the office and addressed the girl directly.

'Hello, I'm Noah Campbell, I'm a partner in this hotel. Why don't you come into my office and we can have a chat about what kind of work you're looking for.'

The girl nodded with wide, fearful eyes and moved inside the office.

Ignoring the look of incredulity from Zoe, he went back inside the office and sat down behind his desk, leaving the door open.

'Let's start with your name,' Noah said, gently.

'Izzy,' the girl said, quietly. 'Isabelle Quinn.'

'OK, Izzy, how old are you?'

'Sixteen.'

There was no way she was sixteen and the disbelief must have been written on his face.

'Fifteen,' Izzy said, then cleared her throat. 'In three months.'

'OK.'

Fourteen was very young but there was an air of desperation about her.

'There are certain restrictions about how many hours a week someone of your age is allowed to work,' Noah said. He turned to his computer and did a quick search on child employment. 'Twelve hours a week during term time, twenty-five hours a week during school holidays. So you could work a bit this week and next week while you're off school for Easter, but after that we're basically looking at a Saturday job, with a maximum of five hours' work, according to government guidelines.'

He turned back to her to see that this was obviously not the news she wanted to hear.

'Listen, I'm not going to let anything interfere with school, but we might be able to add a few more hours here and there as overtime. And if it's overtime, you'd get double pay of course.'

He smiled to himself. A few days before he had been moaning that Aria was seemingly running a charity and now he was doing it too.

Izzy nodded. 'Are you actually offering me a job?'

'Yes.'

'But… you don't know anything about me, or what I can do.'

'What would you like to do?'

'Whatever you want me to do,' Izzy said. 'Clean, hoover, sweep floors, clean windows, I'll do it.'

He liked that attitude.

'Why don't you tell me what you can do, your strengths, and I'm sure we can find something suitable for you.'

'I'm good with computers, I'm good at drawing too.'

Izzy pulled out her phone and swiped a few things on her screen. 'These are some of the things I've been working on.'

She handed her phone to Noah and he was stunned to see some very detailed drawings of cars, houses and animals. They were amazing.

'You really did all these?'

'Yes, I did. Those were drawn by hand but I can also do similar things on the computer too.'

Suddenly he had an idea.

'Izzy, we're making a lot of changes to the hotel over the next few months and we're inviting people to the festival of light next weekend to see our ideas about the renovations. If I talk through with you our plans, could you come up with some kind of design or drawing that would show off our ideas in a visual way?'

'Yes of course,' Izzy said, excitedly.

'OK, good. I'm going to pair you with Angel, my assistant.

He's been starting to put something together for me but I'm sure he could do with some help.'

Noah stood up and moved to the door. He could see Angel sitting on one of the sofas, typing away at his laptop.

'Angel!'

Angel looked up and Noah gestured for him to come in. Angel closed his laptop and ambled over.

'Angel, I'd like to introduce you to your assistant.'

Noah heard Zoe snigger but as Angel walked through the office door, he didn't bat an eye that he was faced with a four-teen-year-old kid. As the older brother to four much younger sisters, Angel was the perfect person to work with Izzy.

'Hey kid,' Angel said, sticking out his hand for Izzy to shake. She stood up and shook it hard. 'You coming to work for the Sapphire Bay Hotel?'

'She's actually coming to work for you – she's going to help us get the presentation of our renovation plan ready,' Noah said, handing Angel the phone so he could see the drawings himself.

'Wow, these are good,' Angel said. 'You can definitely come and work for me if you can draw like this.'

'She starts tomorrow morning at nine,' Noah said and Izzy's face lit up.

'Thank you, I won't let you down,' she said. 'Neither of you.'

Izzy shook Noah's hand, then Angel's again, before hurrying out.

He turned to Angel. 'You OK with that?'

'Sure, drawing has never been my strong point. She can certainly produce something far better than me. I'll keep an eye on her.'

Noah liked that there were no questions about why he had just hired a child, no issues about Angel now being responsible for her. For his assistant this was perfectly acceptable and just one of the many tasks that he had been given over the years.

Zoe wandered over. 'Babysitting is not part of my job description.'

'No, but being nice is,' Noah said, giving her a meaningful look.

'Was that Isabelle Quinn I just saw?' Aria said, walking over.

'Yes, she wanted a job,' Noah said.

'Oh,' Aria said, softly. Obviously she knew more about Izzy's circumstances than he did. 'What did you tell her?'

'That she starts tomorrow at nine, she's working with Angel.'

He tried to judge from Aria's face whether she thought this was a good or bad thing. He probably should have consulted her about any hirings; she was the hotel manager, after all.

'Noah, can I have a word?' Aria gestured to the office.

'Oh, you're in for it now,' Zoe laughed.

'Aria, I really don't mind,' Angel said, coming to Noah's defence.

'Thanks Angel, that's very kind,' Aria said and walked into the office.

Noah walked in after her and closed the door. 'Look, I will take full responsibility—'

Aria reached up, cupped his face and kissed him. He hesitated for a moment and then wrapped his arms around her and pulled her close.

She leaned back slightly and stroked her fingers across his lips. 'I think I'm falling in love with you.'

She looked up at him and his heart slammed into his chest. 'What?'

She smiled. 'You are a wonderful, kind, amazing man and I'm falling in love with you.'

He had no words at all, nothing with which he could convey what that meant to him. It was the first time in his life he'd ever heard those words and they were from this incredible woman. He swallowed the lump in his throat, gathered her close and kissed her.

Eventually he pulled back and she stroked his face.

He wanted to tell her how much she meant to him too but the words dried in his throat. He couldn't even begin to explain the feelings he had for her. It was too big, too much. He decided to change the subject instead, until he could find the appropriate words.

'I take it you're OK with me hiring Izzy then?' Noah said.

Aria laughed. 'I'm more than OK with it. Did she tell you about her mum?'

Noah shook her head. 'No, I could just tell she was desperate.'

'Her mum is Delilah, the woman I said was going to start work here in a few weeks. She has cancer and has just lost her job. I think Izzy needs this job more than you know.'

'Shit, is her mum OK?'

'I think the doctors are happy with how she is doing, Delilah is a fighter. But losing her job is one more stress she doesn't need.'

'No, I can imagine.'

'I told Izzy that her mum could get a job here when she is feeling better but I think the lack of money is an issue now.'

'Yes, I get that. Well, I'll make sure Izzy is paid a good salary for her work, she's going to help us with our renovation presentation.'

Aria smiled. 'That's perfect for her, thank you.' She leaned forward and placed a kiss right over his heart. 'Have you got time to play hooky for a few hours at lunch? We could take a picnic, go for a walk round the island.'

He absolutely didn't have time for that but, as she trailed a finger suggestively down his chest, he found himself nodding anyway.

'Good. I'll grab some food.'

'I'll grab the condoms.'

She laughed. 'Meet me under the willow tree at twelve o'clock.'

He nodded.

She kissed him on the cheek. 'I'll leave you to it.'

He wanted to tell her how he felt about her, what her words meant to him, but she had already left the office. He watched her cross the lobby, say a few words to Angel and then give him a hug before she walked away.

He realised Zoe was watching him and she didn't look happy. He turned and went back into his office; he had a ton of work to do.

Aria had just finished replying to a complaint letter. They didn't get too many complaints sent directly to the hotel, usually because most of the guests who stayed were loyal regulars who came every year and knew what they were getting. And in this day and age of keyboard warriors, any guest who was that unhappy would often leave a bad review on a review site rather than take the time to contact the hotel directly. This particular guest had been unhappy that the pool had been closed, even though that had been mentioned very clearly on their website. They were also annoyed that the room apparently had been cold, which seemed a bit odd when they were experiencing such a hot spell, and in particular they hadn't liked the sheets, which were apparently grey and threadbare.

Aria sighed. In all the big plans for redecorating and renovating the hotel, they hadn't factored in new bedding – well at least she hadn't. It was just another thing to add to the long list of items to buy.

She stood up to go and talk to Skye about the grocery shopping for the coming week and anything she'd need for the festival. She walked out into the reception area, where Zoe was manning the desk.

In the corner of the lounge, an elderly couple were watching a rugby match on TV and Angel and Noah were sitting on the sofas in the lobby, chatting and laughing with each other. She couldn't help but smile. Angel was definitely good for him. Clover came out of her office and sat down next to Angel, showing him something on her tablet screen. Angel said something that made Clover laugh. He was good for her too.

Noah got up and walked into his office, flashing Aria a small smile as he passed. He closed the door behind him.

'Never going to happen,' Zoe said.

Aria turned her attention to Zoe. 'What?'

'You and Noah. You won't be the first person Noah has worked with to have a silly crush on him and you won't be the last.'

A silly crush? Aria stared at her incredulously. Zoe obviously had no idea what Noah meant to her.

'He never mixes business with pleasure so you don't stand a chance,' Zoe went on as she typed something into the computer.

Aria suppressed a smug smile as she stamped down the desire to give Zoe a blow-by-blow account of the night before.

'He won't be here long anyway. A few months and he'll be moving on, like always,' Zoe went on.

'He said he might retire soon,' Aria said, knowing full well she couldn't say anymore. 'I suppose he could move here.'

'He's not going to retire, he's thirty-three years old.'

'And I don't think he enjoys his job anymore.'

'Shows what you know, he loves his work,' Zoe said. 'Besides, if he was going to move here, why has he just bought a house in London?'

'What?' That had Aria's attention.

'Yes, the sale went through four weeks ago. A big four-bed place, just round the corner from me. Looks like the kind of place you might raise a family.'

That didn't make any sense. That didn't fit in with anything Noah had told her. Why would he buy a place in London if he was planning to move here? Aria's worst fear would be to fall in love with Noah for him to leave again, just like everyone else had.

She watched Zoe smile to herself. Was this even true or was Zoe deliberately trying to cause trouble between her and Noah? Everything was going great right now and there was no way she was going to let Zoe ruin things between them. Aria just had to ignore her for the next few weeks and then she'd be gone. And she now had to ignore the stupid seed of doubt Zoe had planted in her heart too.

Sylvia wandered over then and it was quite clear she had heard what Zoe was saying as she passed her a look of contempt which Zoe failed to notice.

'Well, Noah certainly has a spring in his step this morning,' Sylvia said, with no preamble. 'I wonder what could have happened to make him so cheery.'

'Is he cheery?' Aria asked, vaguely aware Zoe was now looking over in their direction.

'I saw him whistling earlier and he was certainly very smiley while he was having breakfast.'

'Who's smiley?' Skye asked as she wandered out of the kitchen.

'No one,' Aria said.

'Noah,' Sylvia said at the same time.

'Why is Noah so smiley?' Skye said.

'Well that's what I was trying to find out,' Sylvia said, ignoring the pointed glares from Aria.

'Where were you this morning anyway?' Skye asked. 'I came up to see you after Xena told me there had been a fire alarm and your door was all smashed in and there was no sign of you. I was a bit worried for a while, until I remembered this is Jewel Island and the scariest thing that happens here is the local newsagents running out of Rolos. Plus Noah said he'd seen you, so clearly you hadn't been kidnapped in the middle of the night. What happened?'

Aria knew her cheeks were burning. Luckily with her darker complexion it tended to hide most of the redness. Noah had seen her that morning, in his bed!

She cleared her throat.

'Well, when the fire alarm went off, Noah was worried that I wouldn't hear it so he... umm, kicked my door in so he could save me. Sadly I wasn't even in there.'

'He kicked your door down?' Skye was incredulous, and for good reason.

'Oooh, I love a good hero,' Sylvia said. 'I might have to use that. I have to say I'm a bit disappointed that there were no hunky firemen turning up to save us from a burning inferno.'

'No, sadly not. And most of the firemen on the island are not that hunky,' Aria whispered conspiratorially. 'Plus no actual burning inferno either.'

'So did you sleep somewhere else for the rest of the night?' Skye said, evidently not letting this go.

Aria nodded and waved vaguely. 'Yes, one of the bedrooms. It was only for one night. Noah has asked for the workmen to fix my door today so...'

'Which bedroom did you sleep in?' Sylvia said, clearly putting the dots together.

Just then, Mrs Kent, one of the guests, came up to the reception desk and Aria nearly lunged forward to talk to her just so she wouldn't have to deal with Sylvia and Skye.

'Hello, can I help you?' Aria smiled breezily.

'Yes, I'm in room fifty-nine and I wonder if we could change rooms.'

'Yes, of course, is there a problem with your room?' Aria said.

'No, only that...' Mrs Kent cleared her throat awkwardly. 'Last night the couple above us were *very* noisy... in the umm, bedroom... several times.'

Oh god, this couldn't get any worse. Room fifty-nine was in the corner of the second floor and therefore directly under Noah's room.

'Oh, I wonder whose room that was,' Sylvia chortled.

Aria glanced over to Zoe who was staring at her as if pennies were dropping into place.

'I'll move you to room twenty-three,' Aria said hastily, tapping away on her computer. 'It's on the first floor but still has magnificent views over Sapphire Bay.' She handed over a key. 'I'll get one of our porters to give you a hand with your luggage, and please accept my apologies for the disturbance. Skye, could you call through to the kitchen to get Jeremy to give Mrs Kent a hand.'

Mrs Kent walked off towards the stairs and Aria didn't

know who to look at first or whether she could scurry off back to her office and hide in there for the rest of the day.

'So, who are the mystery lovers?' Skye asked, as she got off the phone, apparently not as knowledgeable about the layout of the hotel as Aria was.

'No idea,' Aria said, perhaps a little too quickly.

'Fifty-nine, that's on the second floor, isn't it?' Sylvia said. 'So who's up on the third floor?'

'Oh, didn't you say we have a honeymoon couple?' Skye said, just as Cal was walking past.

Aria closed her eyes for a few seconds, hoping and praying this was all a bad dream.

'That would be me,' Cal said. 'But if you're talking about all the sex that was happening last night, we heard it too. It was quite funny actually. We actually heard the headboard banging against the wall.'

'Who else is in the suites?' Skye asked.

Aria cleared her throat. 'Just Noah, but Angel was saying the other day Noah has terrible insomnia. Maybe he was… exercising.'

Angel looked up at the mention of his name.

'I don't think so,' Cal laughed. 'Not with all the moans and groans that were coming from there.'

Cal walked off and Aria had never felt so embarrassed in all of her life. Had they really been that noisy? She desperately tried to think of something, anything, that she could say that would explain the noises.

Angel and Clover wandered over.

'What's going on?' Angel asked.

'A guest has complained about the sex noises coming from Noah's room last night,' Skye said, giving Zoe the side-eye. 'Aria seems to think he might have been exercising because of his insomnia.'

'He does have insomnia,' Angel said, awkwardly. 'He does lots of things in the night to try to get back to sleep again.'

A small cheer went up on the opposite side of the lounge where the elderly couple were watching the rugby game. A team, possibly the All Blacks, were celebrating on the screen.

Aria suddenly had a light-bulb moment.

'The haka,' Aria said, triumphantly.

'What?' Clover said.

'You know, the thing the New Zealand rugby team do before every game. Well, there are exercise classes in it now, I've heard all about it. Kind of a yoga-type tai chi thing, expel-the-bad-energy type of exercise.'

'Really?' Clover said, doubtfully. 'I've never heard of that.'

Of course she hadn't and how could Aria convince a yoga teacher that haka yoga was even a thing?'

'I'm not sure I know what you mean. How does that go exactly?' Sylvia said sweetly.

For a harmless little old lady she had an evil mischievous streak.

'Well…' Aria said. 'Something like this.'

She started slapping her thighs and arms, grunting and groaning, sticking her tongue out, stamping her feet in what she hoped was a convincing haka, but also trying to make them sound a bit like sex noises too to make it extra convincing. In fact, she continued doing her haka sex yoga demonstration for a while so there could be no doubt that that was what Noah had been doing.

Aria finally straightened. 'Maybe he was doing something like that.'

Angel had a big smirk on his face, Clover clearly wasn't buying any of this, Sylvia was clapping her hands together in glee and Skye was simply staring at her.

'Really?' Skye said. 'That's what Noah was doing?'

'Yeah, I think so. He's quite into his yoga, isn't he Angel?'

'Oh sure, yes,' Angel said. 'He, umm, does lots of different types.'

She glanced over at Zoe who narrowed her eyes at Aria. She obviously wasn't convinced at all. Zoe turned and walked towards Noah's office, knocked on the door and then entered, closing the door behind her.

It looked like the cat was out of the bag, at least where Zoe was concerned.

Noah looked up from his work as Zoe closed the door behind her. He had never known her to be so needy before; she normally just got on with her work without the constant need to check in with him. But he supposed he had encouraged this relationship over the years. Zoe would always report to him about the staff in the hotels he would take over, what the feeling was amongst the staff, if there were any concerns, whether there were any weak links. He hadn't really explained that it wasn't necessary here. This place was different.

'You slept with her?' Zoe spat.

'Excuse me?'

Christ, he hadn't been expecting this.

'One of the guests has just been complaining about the sex noises coming from your floor.'

'Well, we do have a honeymoon couple up there too,' Noah said, feeling bad for putting the blame on Cal yet again.

'Funny that because Cal said he'd heard the sex noises too, headboard banging against the wall, moans and groans. Aria is out in reception doing the haka right now, trying to convince everyone you were doing that instead.'

His heart filled with love with Aria and he couldn't help smiling at that thought.

'Eight years I've known you and I've never known you to sleep with any of the clients or staff before. You've been here five minutes and you're already taking the manager to bed. It's so unprofessional.'

'Zoe, I'm not discussing my private life with you. We have never had that kind of relationship and we're not going to start now. I certainly don't discuss with you who you're sleeping with and don't think I've not noticed the members of staff you've had sex with over the years. So don't talk to me about being unprofessional.'

Zoe's mouth fell open in surprise.

Eventually she spoke. 'I've never seen you like this before. This place is so different to what you normally buy.'

'Why do you think I bought it?' Noah said.

'Because her dad emotionally blackmailed you into it.'

'Now hang on. Thomas was a friend.'

'Who manipulated you into giving him millions of pounds for a complete dump.'

Noah sighed. 'I did it for her.'

'She's not who you think she is,' Zoe said.

'Zoe—'

'No, hear me out. That's part of the reason you bring me into these projects, to suss out the staff, find out what's really going on. She is a gold-digger, just like Georgia.'

'Zoe, that's—'

'She was asking me about your money the other day, how much you had, where it all came from, and I saw her in here, rooting around with all your stuff. She's taking you for a ride and you can't see that.'

Noah shook his head. He didn't believe any of that.

'Georgia was bad for you, I told you that before you'd even

got together and I was right about her. Trust me on this. Aria is everything you don't want in a woman.'

'Thank you Zoe, I'm very busy so if that's everything.'

Zoe paused as if she wanted to say more but then turned and walked back out.

He knew Aria, he knew in his heart that the woman that Zoe had described was not her. But now he had this feeling of doubt in his heart that refused to go away.

CHAPTER NINETEEN

Aria stood under the boughs of the willow tree waiting for Noah to join her. He was already ten minutes late. She had a rucksack filled with sandwiches and snacks she'd stole from the kitchens. Skye hadn't been in there when she'd been raiding the fridges and she only hoped her sister wouldn't notice the missing food.

They were taking a big risk going out for a picnic. Aria hated lying to her sisters and she was making the situation worse by making excuses for her and Noah being seen or heard together. She felt like this new arrangement whereby her sisters had both decided to stay was so tentative and fragile that she didn't want to do anything to damage it. Although she was well aware that by going behind their backs, and not being truthful about her relationship with Noah, she was only making the situation worse.

But what would happen if she told them the truth after they had specifically asked her not to let anything happen with her and Noah? Would they leave? Skye was especially worrying. Jesse was here now and Aria knew he was staying in

Skye's cottage with her. She wouldn't be at all surprised if they had rekindled their friends-with-benefits arrangement. With Skye's beloved shop still thriving in her absence and Jesse over there, there was a good chance that when Jesse left after the festival to go back to Canada she would go with him.

It did seem unfair that Aria's relationship with Noah had been building for five years, her feelings for him deepening every time she saw him, and now, just when they finally had the chance to be together, it had been forbidden. She felt sure that if her sisters knew how much he really meant to her they wouldn't have this issue.

But there was no question she could end things with Noah so for now they just had to keep everything secret. Fortunately Aria knew the perfect place for their picnic, where they were very unlikely to be discovered.

Suddenly she spotted Noah hurrying along the path towards her. He parted the boughs and before the branches had even fallen back into place behind him, he was gathering her in his arms and kissing her. For a few seconds all other thoughts faded away, there was just the two of them and none of that other stuff mattered.

'I've missed you,' Noah said, in between kisses.

She giggled against his lips. 'I've been at the hotel for most of the day.'

'Yes, but I've not been able to hold your hand or touch you or do this whenever I wanted. There is a part of me that wishes I hadn't taken this deal, so I could just be with you and not have to worry about any of this.'

'But you can still be with me, we're together right now.'

'I know, but not in the way I really want.' He kissed her again, a slow, wonderful, lingering kiss. He pulled back. 'Come on, let's go and have our picnic. I hope it's somewhere secluded as I have plans.'

She grinned. 'It is and I like the sound of your plans.'

He took her hand and led her out into the gardens. They were hidden from the hotel this far down the gardens so no one would see them.

'So, I understand people heard us last night.'

Aria blushed. 'I didn't think we were being that noisy.'

'You were quite vocal,' Noah said.

'You roared.'

He laughed.

They were quiet for a moment as they took the gate to leave the gardens and walk over the headland.

'Zoe knows,' Noah said.

'Yes, she didn't believe that you were doing the haka last night in your room.'

He laughed again.

'She's not a fan of yours,' Noah said, casually.

'You know what, I'm not a fan of hers either.'

'She thinks you're only with me for my money.'

'Oh, she can go to hell. She has no idea what we share. Angel says she has a crush on you and has been trying to get with you for years.'

'It did occur to me that her issues with you might be mainly jealousy.'

They stopped to admire the little village, the white houses and the shop windows gleaming in the midday sun. The sea that surrounded the little island was a gorgeous emerald green today. Diamond River and Crystal Stream glittered as they tumbled through the hills and fields.

Aria turned to look at Noah, who was clearly deep in thought.

'You don't believe her, do you? You can't possibly think I'm with you for your money?'

'No, of course I don't think that,' Noah said. 'It's just… she said you were asking about my money.'

Aria stared at him in confusion as she tried to remember what she'd said to Zoe.

'Oh god, that. I was just worried about all the money you're pouring into this place. I feel so bad that I'm not contributing anything and I don't want you to agree to things that you can't afford just because you're thinking with this,' she placed a hand over his heart.

He stared down at her. 'Every decision I've made over the last few days has been led by my heart.'

'That's not a bad way to live. You should always trust in your heart. What does your heart say about whether I'm just with you for your money?'

'It says we share something far deeper than that.'

'Damn right we do. Now, let me show you the Golden Lagoon. It's a bit of a treacherous climb down to the beach but, fortunately, me and my sisters found an alternative route.'

She led him over to the cliff face which was thick with ivy, moss and other plants. She looked down on the floor for the rocks she and her sisters had placed there to mark the opening, reached through the ivy to find the gate and heaved it open.

'What is this?' Noah asked in wonder. 'A secret tunnel?'

'That's exactly what it is. I don't know if it was just a path to the lagoon that got lost over the years or a tunnel used by pirates to smuggle in their goods. It's more likely it was the former as someone took the time to hang a metal gate on it and it's been dug out fairly cleanly, but I like to think it was the latter.'

They stepped inside the cave that sloped down onto the beach and then out onto the golden sands. It was such a tiny little cove with a beach of no more than ten metres at its widest point. The thing that made it special was the large natural pool that was separated from the sea. When the tide was high, it would fill the pool and, when the tidal waters receded, the pool was deep enough to swim in.

Aria took her rucksack off and pulled out a large blanket which Noah helped her spread across the back of the beach. There were other little caves in the cliff face but, although some of them went fairly far back, they didn't lead anywhere.

'This place is amazing,' Noah said.

'I know and I don't think any of the islanders know the gate is there, so we should have it all to ourselves. Me and my sisters were the only ones to use it when we were children, it was kind of our special place.'

'And you're sharing it with me?'

'Well, you're pretty bloody special too,' Aria said.

Noah lay down on the blanket and she cuddled up next to him. He sank his head into the sand and closed his eyes.

'God, I could just go to sleep,' Noah said.

'I thought you had big plans?' Aria said.

'Oh I do.' He gave her a mischievous grin.

She stroked his face. He did look tired.

'Or we can just doze here in the sunshine. I can think of no better way to fall asleep than wrapped in your arms.'

'I'm OK. This project is just wearing me out, trying to get it all done in time for the festival.'

Aria felt a pang of guilt. 'I think we should forget the festival and run away to Bali, lie on a beach in a hammock, drink cocktails and make love under the sun.'

'Now that is very tempting.' Noah looked up at the sky. 'Although we do have the sun here.'

She grinned, catching onto his mood.

He turned his attention back to her and held her face while he kissed her gently. She stroked the hair at the back of his neck. He peeled off the dress she was wearing and flung it across the sand, then his hands caressed and explored her body, his mouth tracing a trail across her skin too. He took off her underwear as she undressed him.

He slipped his hand between her legs as he returned his mouth to her lips. His touch was gentle, but confident, that feeling spreading inside of her so quickly as if it had just been bubbling there under the surface and now he had set it free. It roared through her so fast she felt like she couldn't catch her breath, every nerve ending bursting to life. She moaned his name, her body trembling beneath his.

He kissed her, smiling against her lips, and then leaned over to grab a condom from his trouser pocket. Before her body has stopped shaking, while her breath was still heavy, he slid inside her and started moving against her, his eyes locked on hers.

This man. Sex had never been like this before. She could see in his eyes that he had no idea. God, was this really the norm for him?

She put a hand on his chest. 'Noah, wait.'

He stilled, his eyes clouding with concern. 'You OK?'

'Yes… Of course, yes,' she could barely get her words out. There was a tightness in her chest as if she wanted to cry or laugh or scream for joy all at once. 'Just give me a moment.'

He nodded, and placed soft kisses on her shoulder, stroking her arm gently as she cupped the back of his head.

'God Noah, no one has ever made me feel like this before.'

He pulled back slightly to look at her. 'I think you've probably been with the wrong men if none of them have made you scream during sex before.'

She stroked his face, trailing a thumb across his lips. And that was it in a nutshell. This wasn't just amazing sexual chemistry. It felt so incredible, so different, because she had never felt this way for a man she had slept with before. 'I think I have. Because none of them was you.'

He stared at her.

She blushed. She had already told him she was falling in love with him earlier and he hadn't said it back. She didn't want to put pressure on him if he didn't feel those things.

'Ignore me. I'm just saying you're pretty good at this sex malarkey.'

She wrapped her arms and legs around him and kissed him so he wouldn't have to see her face. He started moving again, kissing her hard as her body responded to his.

It was OK that he didn't feel the same. Although they had known each other for years, this was all so new for them. Why was she jumping ahead to the final page with marriage and babies and the happy ever after? They were just starting chapter one, they had months of getting to know each other in a whole new and wonderful way, and she was going to enjoy every second of it.

Unless he wasn't really intending to stay at all.

Aria pushed that stupid thought away. She knew he cared for her and he'd had feelings for her for years. There was no way he was playing games with her.

He slid his hand round her lower back, holding her closer against him. That feeling started to build inside her again, his eyes locked on hers as he moved against her faster and harder. Sensations exploded through her, she felt him lose control too, and as he collapsed down on top of her, he kissed her.

Her heart was too full of him. How could he not feel this? How could he make love to her like that and not feel the same?

But they had plenty of time. There was no rush.

She stroked his back and closed her eyes, hoping with everything she had that one day he would feel the same as she did.

~

Noah was lying on his side staring at Aria as he stroked her hair, letting the ebony silk run through his fingers. She looked up at him and smiled. His heart was full of her in a way he had never felt before. The sea was lapping onto the golden sands, the midday sun was warming their skin. There was no finer sight in the world than a naked Aria Philips, lying on the beach staring up at him with love in her eyes.

'God, Aria, I want to stay here forever,' he said, running a hand up her ribs.

'Then stay,' Aria said, simply.

'I don't think it's as simple as that.'

Not yet. He still had one hotel in Dubai that he was in the process of selling. Plus there were his two flagship hotels, one in New York, one in London; he was always being called away to deal with business in those. Of course he could sell them too, but that would be a massive upheaval. He needed to make sure the jobs of his hotel staff were safe, that the sales were to reputable companies. But maybe in a year's time he could finally sever all ties and settle here. God, that felt like a big step though. He had romanticised this vision of a future with Aria for the last five years and now it was happening he had to be sure he was doing the right thing for him and for her before he started setting those wheels in motion. Everything was perfect right now but he had rushed into a marriage before and that had been a disaster of epic proportions. He just wanted to take his time to get this right and not put on his rose-tinted glasses and get caught up in the moment.

'You don't need to make this complicated. As long as we're together, that's all that matters,' Aria said.

He was just about to explain what he needed to do so he could move here when they heard laughter and talking.

Judging by the echoing it sounded like it was coming from the tunnel they'd entered through earlier.

The smile fell from her face. 'Oh my god, someone's coming. Shit, that sounds like Skye and Jesse.'

She scrabbled up and looked around desperately, scooping up all their clothes and her bag and hot-footing it into the caves at the back of the beach.

Noah stood up, went to make a run for it, but realised one of his shoes was further down the beach. He ran forward to grab it just as Jesse and Skye appeared out of the tunnel.

They stared at each other, Jesse and Skye holding hands, Noah holding a shoe over his manhood.

'Noah? What are you doing here?' Skye said.

'Sunbathing,' Noah said, glad that he could think of something plausible this time.

'Naked?'

'Well, I didn't think anyone would be coming down here so… yeah.'

'Come on, we should go,' Jesse said, awkwardly.

Skye didn't move.

'And you're alone?' She looked around sceptically.

'Yes, of course.'

Skye spotted the picnic blanket and looked into the caves at the back of the beach.

'So if we were to go and look in those caves, we wouldn't find anyone else?'

'By all means, go and look,' Noah said, hoping his double bluff would be enough to convince them.

Skye narrowed her eyes, studying him. 'I'm not sure what would be worse, you screwing around with my sister after we specifically asked her not to let anything happen between you, or you screwing around with someone else when you know what my sister feels for you.'

'Which begs the question, if *you* know what your sister feels for me, why would you ask her not to do anything with me? I would presume you'd want your sister to be happy.'

'Honestly? Because I don't trust you not to hurt her again. You broke her heart before and I don't want that to happen again.'

Noah sighed. He totally deserved that. He should have come back once her dad had told her he was dying, so he could have supported her through it. He should have made it a condition of the deal that her dad had told her what was happening with the hotel so he didn't have to keep that from her.

He wanted to explain that he would do everything he could never to hurt Aria again but that was kind of giving the game away that they were together. It was also really odd to be standing here having this conversation when he had only a shoe to protect his modesty.

'I understand your protectiveness but we both want Aria to be happy. It just seems that we're coming at it from different angles.'

'She doesn't need you to make her happy. Those dreams of hers you were asking about, she can do all of that without you. Any child would be lucky to have her as a mum and...' Skye trailed off, realising she'd said too much.

Aria's dream was to have children? Well, that explained why she was reluctant to pursue those dreams now.

'Come on,' Jesse said. 'Why don't we leave Noah to his sunbathing?'

Skye hesitated and then nodded, allowing Jesse to lead her off the beach.

Noah could hear their voices echoing through the tunnel as they walked away.

'I don't like him,' Skye said.

'Well you need to get over that because Aria does,' Jesse said.

Their voices drifted away and then there was silence. After a few moments, Aria appeared from the back of one of the caves, fully dressed and looking very apologetic and guilty.

He sighed. As he'd said the night before, lying about their relationship was definitely not the best start.

Aria walked out of her office and headed towards the kitchen. It was getting late and she was tired but Skye had just finished cooking dinner for the guests and she wanted to share a new dessert she had been working on with Aria and Clover.

She hadn't really seen her sister since the disaster at the lagoon earlier, at least not to speak to, but it was clear Skye wasn't happy about what was going on. Noah hadn't been happy about the whole debacle either; he still felt that they had nothing to hide and didn't like all the sneaking around. Aria didn't know what to do.

She walked into the kitchen and Skye and Clover were already waiting for her, with several bowls, tall glasses and a few bottles laid out in front of them.

'Hey,' Aria said, sitting down next to Clover and eyeing the bowls. 'What have we got here?'

'I haven't got a name for it yet but it's roasted strawberry and raspberry ice cream and—'

'Wait, roasted strawberries?'

Skye grinned. 'Yes, it's like roasted vegetables but with fruit instead. So the berries have been roasted and then used to make strawberry and raspberry ice cream. You two can help me assemble this dessert. So take two scoops each and put them in the tall glass.'

Aria and Clover did as they were told as Skye opened the bottles.

'Now pour this over the top,' Skye said.

Aria looked at the bottle. 'Rose lemonade. We're having ice cream floats?'

Skye nodded.

'Oh my god, we used to have these when we were kids. Mum made the best floats, Coke ones, Fanta, Lilt floats were always my favourites,' Aria said.

'Don't forget the fizzy Vimto ones,' Clover said, eagerly pouring the rose lemonade over the top of her ice cream.

Aria followed suit. 'Dad loved the Cherry Coke floats.'

The lemonade fizzed and bubbled over the frozen ice cream. Skye shook a can of squirty cream and sprayed it over the top of each of their glasses, then added white chocolate sauce and sprinkles. She gestured for them to try it.

Aria eagerly tucked in, taking a spoonful of the ice cream but making sure to get some of the rose lemonade on her spoon too. 'Oh god, this tastes like heaven,' she said. 'The roasted berries are so intense.'

'It is good, isn't it,' Skye said proudly.

They were silent for a few minutes as they ate, every mouthful like a little party on Aria's tongue.

'OK, something positive,' Clover said. 'As this is a family meeting, after all.'

'Well, my something positive is creating this,' Skye said. 'Also, Jesse has been working hard down in the shack and, although we are still a long way off it being finished, we have progress and it's starting to feel a bit real. Basia is absolutely amazing in the kitchen. I really feel happy about leaving her in charge of cooking in the hotel so I can get on with developing the shack. So three positives really. Clover, what's yours?'

Clover paused as she studiously licked her spoon. 'My

positive is that for the first time in three years, I actually have feelings for a man.'

'Oh my god, Clover, I'm so happy for you,' Skye said, hugging her sister.

After her last relationship with Marcus had ended so horribly three years before, Clover hadn't wanted another boyfriend since. The thought of sex even turned her off. So for her to be thinking about a man in that way again was huge progress.

'This is amazing news,' Aria said. 'Is it Angel?'

Clover blushed and nodded. 'I have no idea if anything will ever happen between us, or whether he even sees me that way, and that's OK. I honestly don't even know if I'm ready for a relationship yet, but the fact that I fancy the arse off this man, the fact that I'm thinking what it would be like to kiss or make love to him is just… I was starting to believe that part of me had died. And for now, and maybe for the foreseeable future, I'm happy just talking and laughing with him, flirting with him and just enjoying having these wonderful feelings again. I don't need more than that right now.'

Aria grinned and gave her a big hug. 'I'm happy for you. He seems like a lovely man.'

'It's not a big deal and please don't go warning him off before we've even kissed,' Clover said to Skye. 'Because it's quite likely it will never get that far. So let me just go at this at my own speed and enjoy it for what it is.'

Skye held her hands up. 'You won't hear a word from me.'

'Me neither,' Aria said.

'Well let's change the subject before I embarrass myself even more,' Clover said. 'Aria, what's your positive?'

Aria thought about it for a moment. She and Skye had naturally been so happy for Clover and this change in her life.

Wouldn't her sisters be happy for her and Noah too? It had to come out sooner or later.

She took a deep breath. 'Noah and I have been seeing each other.'

Skye and Clover stared at her. There was no happiness and joy as there had been when they'd been talking about Clover moments before.

'I knew it,' Skye said, dropping her spoon into her glass. 'The kiss the decorator saw, the sex noises last night, today at the beach, it was all you?'

Aria nodded. 'I'm sorry.'

'I thought we agreed that nothing would happen between you,' Clover said.

'I know but… I love him, I have done for several years. I want forever with this man and he is the only one I've ever felt that about.'

Clover's face softened immediately. 'Oh Aria, I had no idea.'

Skye clearly wavered over what she should be feeling with this news, but settled on the side of anger. 'I'm relieved that he isn't screwing around with another woman behind your back, because the last thing I'd want is for you to get hurt again, but I can't believe you lied to us. We have always, always been honest with each other, no matter what, and now you've lied to us. I just don't know how to deal with that right now.'

This was all so spectacularly unfair. 'What would you have done if I'd asked you not to see Jesse anymore?' Aria asked.

Skye's mouth pulled into a thin line. 'I'd have been honest that I couldn't have done that.'

'But when you asked me not to do anything with Noah, I had no idea that we were going to get together. There was too much hurt from me and he wanted to keep things professional.'

258

'But you should have told us when things did change. You kissed him and lied about it. You stood in reception doing the bloody haka and humiliating yourself rather than tell us the truth.'

'I'm sorry, I really am. I was scared you'd leave.'

'What?' Skye said.

'I thought you'd change your mind about staying.'

'Because my sister fell in love?' she said, incredulously.

'Because I did the one thing you asked me not to do.'

Skye sighed. 'Yes, that's pretty crappy, but as Noah quite rightly pointed out it was pretty crappy for us to ask you to do that when we both knew you had feelings for him. I didn't know you loved him, but we knew those feelings ran deep. You should have been honest with us. I'm happy that you're happy but I hate that you lied.' She rubbed her head. 'I'm tired and I'm going to bed.'

Without another word she walked out.

'I'll talk to her,' Clover said. She gave Aria's hand a squeeze and then ran out after her sister.

Aria stared at the unfinished ice creams. She couldn't eat another bite now, she felt sick and it was nothing to do with the delicious flavours.

She tidied everything away and then went upstairs to bed. As Noah wasn't in the best mood with her either, she decided to sleep alone, hoping that somehow the next day would be better.

CHAPTER TWENTY

The next day, Aria watched Izzy as she sat on the sofas in the lobby with Angel, Skye and Jesse and they discussed the plans for the hotel and the ice cream shack. Izzy was busily making rough sketches as they spoke to try to visualise what Skye wanted, and Jesse was coming up with different suggestions too, which Izzy was sketching out. This job couldn't have been more perfect for her.

Izzy was so engrossed that she didn't notice her mum walking into the reception behind her. Delilah stood and watched her daughter for a few minutes, a huge smile on her face, before she walked over to the reception desk to talk to Aria.

'Thank you so much for this,' Delilah said, gesturing to Izzy, who couldn't have looked happier. 'When Izzy first told me about the job, I was horrified at the thought that my daughter would be financially supporting me, but I think this has given her something to focus on rather than cancer, chemotherapy, radiotherapy and me being sick. Look at her, she's loving every minute of this.'

'She's exactly what we were looking for,' Aria said. 'Although I can't take the credit for giving her a job, Noah did that. But I'm glad we can help.'

Delilah tugged on the end of her headscarf, nervously. 'Is the offer of a job for me still available?'

'Of course. We need a new receptionist,' Aria said and she noticed Zoe look up from her work. 'Zoe here is kindly standing in but she'll only be here for a few weeks so we need someone more permanent.'

'I'll be here as long as Noah needs me,' Zoe snapped.

Aria decided to ignore her. 'Whenever you're ready, you can start.'

'My last radiotherapy session is tomorrow morning so I could start tomorrow afternoon.'

Aria paused before answering. 'Don't you need to get some rest for a few days first? I know how tiring this has been for you.'

'I'd like to start tomorrow,' Delilah said. 'Get back into a routine.'

Finances were obviously tighter than Aria had realised. She wanted to do something for Delilah but she couldn't offer any money; the hotel didn't have any and all the funds for the renovations were coming from Noah.

'Anytime you're ready – maybe you might want to just work part time, a few hours a day to start with, so you don't wear yourself out.'

'Well we'll see how I feel,' Delilah said, her mouth set in a determined line.

Aria got the feeling that she would work full-time hours regardless of how she felt.

Delilah's shoulders sagged a little and, looking around to see if Izzy was far enough away, she leaned forward. 'There's a chance we might lose our house,' she whispered. 'I couldn't afford to pay the mortgage last month as I'm only getting paid statutory sick pay and now I've lost my job, I won't be able to pay this month either. I'm getting demands from them and utility companies every day and I don't know what to do. I need this job, Aria.'

'And it's yours, whenever you're ready. We'll pay you daily too if that will help.'

'Thank you.'

Aria saw Izzy looking over and she smiled brightly so Izzy wouldn't realise what they were talking about.

'She's looking over here, isn't she?' Delilah muttered.

Aria nodded. 'OK. Let me take your photo. We're updating our website with photos of all the staff so I can put you on there too.'

Delilah tugged on her headscarf and plastered on a big smile while Aria took her photo.

Zoe walked over. 'By the way, Izzy had breakfast here this morning, so that's eight pounds fifty please.'

Aria stared at her in horror.

Delilah's face fell and she pulled out her purse with shaky hands. Aria put a hand over Delilah's to stall her.

'Delilah, I'm sorry, Zoe has just started here, she obviously doesn't realise that all staff can eat for free while they are on shift. Zoe also had breakfast here this morning and I wouldn't dream of charging her either.'

'Because I'm staying here, there's a big difference,' Zoe said.

'It's OK, I can pay,' Delilah said, pulling open her purse to reveal no more than a few coins.

'No you won't.'

'I don't need charity,' Delilah said.

'It's not charity, this is company policy,' Aria said. 'Staff do not pay for meals while they are on shift, that goes for everyone.'

'I'll have to talk to Noah about this,' Zoe said.

'You do that,' Aria snapped.

Zoe walked off, apparently not bothered by Aria's tone. Aria turned her attention back to Delilah, who was still rooting around inside her purse, trying to find some money that she clearly didn't have.

'Delilah, you do not need to pay for Izzy's breakfast. I assure you; this is not something I'm offering Izzy because I know you're short of cash. You ask any of the people who work here – the cleaners, the gardener – everyone eats here for free. It has been that way as far back as I can remember, even when my mum was still alive, and it will always be that way. I would not expect anyone to pay for the food they eat while they are on shift or even just before or just after a shift. And when you start working here, you will have the same benefits as everyone else. Please pay no attention to Zoe.' Aria looked around but Zoe was nowhere to be seen. She lowered her voice anyway. 'The girl is a complete bitch trog and the sooner you can come and work for us the better.'

Delilah paused, a small smile on her face. 'I don't want you to get in any trouble.'

'I won't get in any trouble. This is my hotel and I make the rules and one of the rules is we look after our staff.'

Delilah sighed in relief. 'OK, thanks.'

'And you be sure to let Izzy know she can come for breakfast tomorrow too. She needs to have a full stomach if she's going to be working here.'

'Thank you, I will. I better go. I've got to get over to the mainland for my radiotherapy. If I'm feeling OK I may see you tomorrow afternoon.'

'OK, but only if you're feeling up to it.'

'I will be. Besides, I can't leave you alone with the trog.'

Aria smiled. 'No, you can't.'

Delilah left, giving a little wave to Izzy on her way out.

Zoe returned at that point and Aria went back into her office because she simply didn't want to be around her. Why on earth would Noah bring someone like Zoe to the hotel? She was an awful woman.

Aria was starting to upload Delilah and Izzy's photos onto the website when Angel walked in.

'I just need to print something off,' Angel said.

'Sure, do you need to plug into the printer?'

'I should be able to do it wirelessly once I know which printer you have. It won't take a few minutes.'

Angel sat down and started typing away at his laptop.

'How's Izzy doing?'

Angel smiled. 'She's doing great. We're going to have something wonderful for the festival; I think your guests are going to be very impressed.'

Aria couldn't help letting out a small groan, which had Angel looking up from the laptop. 'What's up?'

'Oh Angel, I've been lying to Noah and now I don't know what to do.'

The smile fell from Angel's face and he leaned back and pushed the office door closed.

'Firstly, I wouldn't trust Zoe as far as I could throw her, so don't go saying things like that with her around. Secondly, I really like you, Aria, I think you're perfect for Noah. But he is my boss and my friend and my loyalty will always be to him, so before you bring me into your confidence, you need to remember that.'

'It's not something bad, well I suppose it is. Angel, no one is coming to the festival of light. Noah has some bloggers coming, and all the villagers will be here to take advantage of the free food and drink, but I have no other takers and I haven't told Noah. I assured him that I'd get lots of guests but

I haven't got one single person yet and we have less than a week to go.'

Angel sighed with relief. 'Christ Aria, I thought you were going to tell me there was another man, some rugged handyman called Xander who's good with his hammer.'

Aria burst out laughing. 'Oh yeah, me and Xander have been going at it like rabbits with all the free time I have. I barely have enough time to make a go of things with Noah, let alone have an affair behind his back. Besides, I'm pretty sure I'm in love with your boss so... there's that too.'

A smile spread across Angel's face. 'Well that's definitely something you should tell him.'

'I did... but... well it's very early days for us.'

He frowned. 'He didn't say it back?'

'No but... he's only been here a week. I'm jumping ahead and I just need to be patient with him.'

'I think patience is a great quality to have when starting a relationship with Noah,' Angel said, carefully. 'Give him time.'

Aria nodded and then decided to change the subject as talking about this with Angel didn't exactly seem fair, to him or to Noah. 'In the meantime, what are we going to do about the festival?'

'You have no guests at all?' Angel said.

'No. I have three bedrooms already occupied by guests, but no one new, and I know that we'll be spending a lot of money on food and drink and getting nothing back. Our first event and we were going to showcase all the changes and no one will be there and no money will be coming into the hotel either.'

'OK, we can fix this. We can run a Facebook advertising campaign, maybe even run some Google ads too,' Angel said, as he started typing away on his laptop.

'We can? Won't that be expensive?'

'It doesn't have to be. We could run a few different ones fairly cheaply and just for a few days, considering how soon the festival is. Leave it with me, I'm sure I can get a few more guests through our doors. But I wouldn't worry too much, the bloggers and journalists will be the ones that Noah will be keen to impress and it will be good for the villagers to see the plans too. Anyone else is just a bonus.'

'Thank you. I should have come to you sooner.'

'It's not a problem, it won't take me long to do,' Angel said. 'And at least we've tried everything.'

He continued to type away at his laptop and Aria felt nothing but relief that they would at least be doing something to get more guests through the door.

She returned her attention to the website, making sure Delilah's photo was in the right place. Aria wanted to do something for her; she should be at home resting, looking after herself and not having to worry about money, at least for the next few weeks. Giving her a job didn't seem like it would be enough right now either, they needed to do something else.

'Of course, if you're that worried about money,' Angel said. 'You could charge the villagers an entrance fee to come to our party. Five pounds a head to cover the food and drink sounds like a good deal to me.'

Aria stared at him and then back at the photo of Delilah.

'That sounds like a very good idea,' Aria said.

Aria hurried down the road towards the village hall. For the first time in all her years living on the island, she had called an emergency village meeting. There was an unwritten code amongst the islanders that if an emergency meeting was called, everyone had to attend, and normally they all did. Thankfully Delilah wouldn't be there as she was having her radiotherapy but hopefully everyone else would show up. She wasn't sure if what she was about to say counted as an emergency but she knew it couldn't wait until the next village meeting in a week or two.

Seamus greeted her at the entrance to the village hall as crowds of people filed through the doors. Aria walked straight up to the front, her heart slamming against her chest.

Kendra was one of the last to arrive and she gave Aria an encouraging smile as she stood at the side, despite not knowing what this was about. Seamus held up his hand and everyone fell silent.

'Thank you all for coming at such short notice,' Seamus said. 'I'll hand you straight over to Aria.'

Hundreds of eyes swivelled in her direction. Her mouth was dry and she only hoped that Delilah would understand what she was about to do.

Aria cleared her throat, just as Noah slipped into the back of the room. She didn't know if she should be more nervous now he was here or whether to feel bolstered by his support. He probably wouldn't appreciate what she was going to do.

'Thank you for coming. I won't keep you long as I know some of you are very busy. I want you to know that the party at the hotel for the festival of light will now be a ticketed event. Five pounds a head, which will include food and drinks.'

There was uproar in the room and Aria winced that she hadn't led with the reason why she was going to be charging the villagers for the first time ever. She had never been any good at public speaking, she should have at least practised what she was going to say before she stood up in front of hundreds of people. People were shouting, Madge looked very red in the face, even Seamus didn't look happy – and nothing rattled him.

Aria held up her hand to quieten them down and with some help from Seamus the room fell silent once more.

'I'm sorry, it wasn't my intention to upset you. If you give me a moment, let me explain. As I'm sure many of you are aware, our Delilah Quinn has recently lost her job due to having so much time off to have her surgery and then chemotherapy and radiotherapy. What you might not know is that she is now at risk of losing her home as well. The situation has gotten so bad, her fourteen-year-old daughter came to the hotel yesterday looking for work. At a time when Izzy should be having fun with her friends, not only has she had to shoulder the burden of her mum having cancer, but also now she has the worry of them having no money too.

'I have offered Delilah a job at the hotel but at this time she needs to be focusing on resting and recovering from the effects of the chemotherapy and radiotherapy. I'm sure many of you in this room have been touched by cancer, either directly or with a loved one, and I'm sure I don't have to explain how exhausting it can be, mentally and physically. It is my intention to charge the villagers to come to the party and give every penny to Delilah so she can pay off her debts. That way she can rest and recover without the stress and worry of losing her home and then come to work at the hotel when she is ready. I've been telling Noah that we are a family here and we all look out for one another. Delilah needs our help now and I thought this would be the quickest and easiest way to do that. I'm sure the party will be brilliant as it always is, especially as the town council have donated the cost of the fireworks, and I don't think five pounds is a bad price to pay considering what you'll be getting and what the money will actually be used for.'

People started murmuring between themselves.

Aria raised her voice. 'I'd like everyone to buy their tickets in advance, mainly because the sooner we can give Delilah the money the better, but also so we can get a better idea of numbers up at the hotel. So if you'd like to come down to the front and buy your ticket now that would be great, or you can come up to the hotel over the next few days and buy your ticket from there. Equally, if you want to tell me what a terrible idea this is, you can come and do that too, although maybe we can have a separate queue for that.'

Some people laughed and she felt slightly encouraged by that.

She moved to the stage and took out her notebook and pen so she could record the names of those who were buying the tickets. To her surprise, Noah came and sat next to her.

'Let me help,' Noah said, quietly. 'I'll take the money; you can write down the names.'

For a moment no one seemed in any rush to come forward, too busy talking between themselves, but then Seamus moved towards them, taking out his wallet.

'I'll have two tickets, please,' he said loudly, and Aria smirked at his lead-by-example attitude.

She wrote his name down and assured him the tickets would be delivered before the festival of light.

'This is a wonderful idea. I was just talking about poor Delilah this morning and how we needed to do something to help. I thought about a cake sale or something similar but I didn't think we would raise enough money. I think lots of people will be willing to contribute in this way,' he said, loudly and meaningfully.

But it was unnecessary. Lots of people were already

making their way down to the front and, judging by the way they were pulling out their wallets and purses, it didn't look like anyone was coming to complain. In fact, so many people wanted to pay, Seamus had to collect a bucket for the money and he and Kathy spent an hour helping to collect the money and write down all the names. Other people came and said that although they didn't have any money on them at the time, they would be up to the hotel later to buy their tickets then.

Madge was one of the last ones to come up and Aria braced herself for a barrage of complaints.

Madge cleared her throat. 'I may not agree with some of the things you're doing up at the hotel, but this… this I do agree with. Toby and I will be there.'

She offered out ten pounds and Aria took it. 'Thank you.'

Madge nodded and left.

As the last few stragglers paid for their tickets, Seamus took Aria to one side.

'This is a lovely thing you're doing,' Seamus said.

'I've just felt so helpless over the last few days and beyond offering both Delilah and Izzy a job there was very little I felt I could do. This felt like a good way to do it. Everyone wants to come to the party so I figured if they wanted it badly enough they'd pay the entrance fee. I think people were a bit upset when they thought the money would be going to the hotel but, even though the hotel will be running at a loss for the party, it was never my intention to charge people.'

Seamus cocked his head. 'The hotel will be running at a loss for the party?'

'Well, yes. There are no guests coming to stay, and no money coming in to pay for the food, desserts and drinks. I feel bad for Noah, he's putting so much money into renovating the hotel and now he's having to pay out for the party too. I kind of hoped we would have enough guests to break even on the costs of the party but it doesn't look like anyone's coming.'

'Oh Aria, I didn't realise... stupid of me really...'

'It's fine. It's not like I'm at risk of losing the roof over my head like Delilah is. And I know many people on the island are feeling the pinch lately. I've been lucky, I've been thrown a lifeline in the shape of Noah and others don't have that. Besides, it's my own fault. I wanted to prove I was a valuable member of this community just like my dad was. But Dad's generosity got him into debt and I need to get better at saying no. Hopefully next year we'll be in a much better position financially, the hotel will be a success and we won't be counting every penny. But still, paying out for food and drink for a party where no money is coming into the hotel doesn't make good financial sense and I think we will have to consider very carefully whether we do it next year, regardless what the villagers think.'

'Aria, of course you're a valuable member of this community. You grew up here, you're one of us. And you do so much for all of us, you always shop local for all the hotel needs, you give jobs to people on the island, you've helped Stephen by giving him a job after his stroke, you've helped Neil with his donkey and so much more than that. You have nothing to prove. And if you'd told us that you couldn't afford to have the party, we would have understood. I do feel bad that you've felt pressured into this. What can we do to help?'

'Nothing, it's fine,' Aria said.

Seamus looked thoughtful for a moment. 'Me and Kathy were actually thinking of staying in the hotel the night of the festival. It's a long walk from one end of the island to the other, and neither of us is getting any younger. After a few drinks, I won't be in a fit state to make the walk back so it makes sense to stay over. Plus I get a lovely cooked breakfast the next day.'

Aria smiled. 'Thank you, but you don't have to do that.'

'I want to. I had breakfast there last summer, when my son stayed for the weekend. Skye's breakfasts are amazing, so it will make a nice treat for us. And maybe some of the other islanders might do the same.'

'You mean after you've persuaded them to,' Aria laughed.

He shrugged. 'Maybe. But I think quite a few might want to make a proper night of it. Enjoy the celebrations to the full.'

'Well, thank you. That would mean a lot.'

Seamus smiled. 'Consider it done.'

It would be nice if the villagers gave something back to the hotel for a change, but at least they were more than happy to be generous when it came to Delilah and that was all that mattered. Aria glanced over at Noah who was collecting the last of the money and taking down names. He looked up and smiled at her. She was sure he would be rolling his eyes at her ploy to help Delilah. He always said that she wanted to make everyone happy, but instead of walking away from a village meeting thinking she had been taken advantage of yet again, for once in her life, this felt really bloody good.

Kendra walked out the hall with Aria a while later. Noah was still inside talking to Seamus.

'Thanks for taking that,' Aria said, gesturing to the bucket of money that Kendra was holding. Kendra was going to deliver it to Delilah later as she lived next door to her. Aria also thought Kendra might be better able to persuade Delilah to take the money than Aria; her godmother had that way about her that would present the money as a done deal rather than a choice.

'No problem. I think this is a lovely idea and a great way to help Delilah. I think the villagers should pay, rather than just expecting free food and drink, but it's nice the money is going to a good cause.'

Noah came hurrying out and snagged Aria's hand. 'I've got to dash; I have a Skype meeting in ten minutes. I'll see you later.'

He squeezed her hand and ran off. Aria supposed now that her sisters knew, they could share their relationship with everyone, although something was holding her back from announcing it.

She turned back to Kendra who was watching her with wide eyes. 'Are you two together now?'

'I think so. I mean yes.'

'What does that mean?'

'Oh god, I don't know. Intimately, yes. He says he wants to move here but then yesterday we were on the beach and he said he wanted to stay but that it wasn't as simple as that. He's also just bought a house in London, so that's not exactly positive either. I'm just not sure where we're at. With his words and his actions, it seems like we're going to be forever, but...'

'You don't know if you can trust him after what happened last year.'

Aria sighed and shook her head. 'I want this to work so much, but... he has spent his whole life moving from one place to another. Even as a child he didn't really have a steady home. I think his job of travelling around the world has suited him, never having to put down roots. Even when he was married, he spent more time away from his wife than he did at home. I know part of that is because they didn't love each other but maybe another part of it was that fear of staying in one place.'

'Maybe you need to talk to him about all of this,' Kendra said. 'If you really are to move forward, you need to be honest with each other about your worries and doubts.'

Aria nodded. She knew her godmother was right but telling Noah that she didn't trust him didn't feel like the best start to a relationship.

CHAPTER TWENTY-ONE

Noah was sitting in his office a while later, working on costing an ever-growing list of all the renovations, when Aria walked in. He'd had visions of working alongside her in the connecting office next door but she was so rarely in there, she always seemed to be on the go.

'Here's a list of all the wines we currently sell in the restaurant, in case you want to order something different for the party,' Aria said.

'Thanks. I've sorted out a bar manager for the night of the party, I'll be in touch with him to see what kinds of things he would like. We can get Skye to liaise with him too.'

Aria pulled a face.

'Is she speaking to you yet?' Noah asked. He knew that Aria had finally told her sisters the night before and it hadn't gone down well.

'Not really, a few words here and there when it's necessary, but we've not really addressed what we talked about last night. I'm sure she'll come round,' Aria said. 'Oh by the way, thank you for coming to the meeting this afternoon. I wasn't expecting you to drop everything and come.'

'I signed up for notifications from the island forum. When I saw there was an emergency meeting called by you, I thought I should find out what was going on. If it's important to you, then it's important to me.'

She smiled. 'I bet you think I'm a right fool for going to all that trouble for Delilah.'

His eyes widened. 'Aria, I don't think that at all. I think you're the most wonderful woman I've ever met. I feel like I'm really getting to know you over the last few days and I like what I see very much. My only regret is that all of this…' he gestured to his desk, 'is preventing me from spending proper time with you.'

'I know. There's so much to do before the party and I feel terrible about that.'

'I think it was a good idea for the bloggers and travel journalists. I think it will help in the long run.'

'I hope so,' Aria said.

He stared at her across his desk, she was so utterly lovely. 'How about we go away for a few days after the party? Angel can oversee things here and my team know what they are doing in terms of the renovations. We can spend some quality time together.'

'I'd really like that.'

'Good.'

He reached out to take her hand just as Zoe walked into the room. He quickly moved his hand to a piece of paper and picked it up instead.

'Can I have a word with you?' Zoe said to Noah.

'Of course.'

'Alone.' Zoe gave Aria a pointed look.

Aria muttered something under her breath he didn't quite

catch and got up and walked out. Zoe closed the door behind her.

'Look, I know you and Aria are having some kind of fling but...'

Noah held up a hand. 'What is going on between me and Aria is completely my business, not yours. If you're here to talk to me about hotel business then go ahead. If not then I'm not interested.'

'I just don't think you're going to get what you want out of it. She's seeing someone else.'

'What?'

'Someone called Xander. I heard her and Angel laughing about it.'

Noah frowned. Somehow, he just didn't believe this. Aria was not that sort of person. Maybe it was naïve considering his past, but he trusted her. And if there was one person he could count on for loyalty, it would be Angel. There was no way his assistant would be laughing about Aria having an affair behind his back. It was no secret that Zoe and Angel didn't get on so he wasn't sure if this was an attempt to get one over on Angel or Aria or, he supposed, maybe Zoe had just misheard.

He decided to give her the benefit of the doubt. 'I think you probably misunderstood what they were saying. Aria is not having an affair.'

'Why don't you ask her about Xander, see what her reaction is? Ask them both.'

Noah cleared his throat. 'Is that all Zoe, because I have a lot of work to do.'

'She's lying to you about the festival of light too, I heard her say that to Angel as well.'

'What about the festival of light?'

'I don't know, but I think you need to prepare yourself for a big disaster.'

He had no idea what Zoe was talking about, but if there was a problem with the festival of light, he needed to know about it.

'OK, thank you.'

She hesitated and walked out.

Noah stared at his list for a moment but he couldn't concentrate. He got up and went to the door. Angel was sitting on the sofa in the lobby, where he'd been all day, tapping away on his laptop as if he was typing out his memoir.

'Angel.'

Angel looked up and, at Noah's nod towards the office, stood up and ambled over.

Noah waited until Angel was inside the office before he closed the door.

'Is there a problem with the festival that I don't know about?' Noah said, sitting back down.

'Not that I know of,' Angel said, in confusion.

'Something that you discussed with Aria?'

Angel still seemed to be confused and then his face cleared. 'Oh that. It's nothing.'

'Zoe said it was something Aria was lying about.'

'Good lord, was she listening with her ear pressed up against the door?'

'Something like that. She also told me that Aria was having an affair with someone called Xander and that you know about it.'

His eyes widened. 'Holy shit. She really is poison. You can't see it and I have no idea why, but she is an absolute cow. She's deliberately trying to ruin things between you and Aria.'

'Yes, I got that sense too. Who is Xander?'

'He doesn't exist. He was a joke. Aria is not having an affair behind your back.'

'I know that.'

'And the issue with the festival is tiny and completely under control. You don't need to worry about it. And Aria didn't lie to you, she just didn't tell you when she realised it was a problem as she didn't want to worry you. I'm in the process of sorting it out. But if you want any more details than that, you need to ask her, because I feel like I'm stuck in the middle here.'

'You're employed by me,' Noah said. He knew he sounded like a complete arse but he didn't like that there was stuff going on behind his back.

'And she's the best thing that ever happened to you, so excuse me if I don't want to hang her out to dry. My advice is that you let this go. You're making this into a much bigger thing than it is.'

Noah stared at Angel, wondering whether to push it.

'In my opinion, you should be focussing on why Zoe is trying to destroy what you have with Aria,' Angel said.

He had a point. 'OK, thanks. But if there are any more problems with the festival, I want to know about it.'

'You will.'

Angel stood up and left.

Noah didn't like this. He had spent his working life knowing about every little wrinkle so he could ensure they were ironed out. However, he trusted Angel and he trusted Aria too, so for now he would just let it go.

Aria was outside, having just finished talking to Stephen about the lights he was putting up in the gardens for the festival, when Angel came outside. He spotted her and walked over.

'I need a word.'

Aria nodded her thanks to Stephen and fell in at Angel's side.

'You need to watch your back, Zoe has it in for you,' Angel said, without any preamble.

'What? What's happened?'

'I've never liked her but I've always respected whoever Noah chooses to employ. She does seem to be efficient; I'll give her that, but I think she's sunk to a new low.'

'What did she do?'

'She obviously listened in to our conversation earlier – she told Noah that you were having an affair with Xander.'

'What? There is no Xander, we were joking and she would have known that. Christ, does Noah believe her?'

'No, he doesn't. He's more worried about what you've been lying to him about regarding the festival. Something else Zoe picked up from our conversation.'

'What the hell? What's wrong with her?'

'I don't know.'

'I need to talk to him.' Aria stopped. 'No I don't, I need to talk to her.'

Aria turned and stormed back to the hotel.

'Wait, Aria—' Angel called after her but she carried on.

Aria marched straight back into reception and was gratified to see that only Sylvia was sitting in the reception area and there would be no other witnesses. Sylvia could probably use this as inspiration for her book.

'Zoe, you can get your things and go,' Aria said as she walked up to the reception desk. Angel was hot on her heels.

Zoe looked up. 'What?'

'You're fired.'

'Oh crap,' Angel muttered.

Zoe stared at her for a moment and then burst out laughing. 'You can't fire me.'

'I think you'll find I just did.'

'I was brought here by Noah; I work for him.'

'And this is my hotel and you're not welcome here,' Aria said, feeling her anger rise.

Noah appeared out of his office and looked around in confusion at the raised voices. 'What's going on?'

'I've just fired Zoe,' Aria said, folding her arms over her chest.

Noah's eyebrows shot up into his hair. 'What?'

'I'm not having that woman working here for one more second.'

Zoe scoffed. 'And I told her I work for you, not for her. You're the only one who can ask me to leave.'

Noah looked between Zoe and Aria, clearly trying to decide what to do. Finally he spoke. 'I'm sorry Zoe, but I think this is for the best.'

'What?' Zoe said, incredulously.

'I don't know what game you were trying to play back there when you came to see me, but it didn't sit well with me. You can go back to The Pennington.'

'Are you kidding?' Zoe said, still not moving.

'No I'm not. Thank you for coming but your services are no longer needed,' Noah said, calmly.

Zoe stared at him for a moment and then started gathering some of her things.

'Aria, a word,' Noah said, gesturing to the office.

Aria followed him into the office and he shut the door.

'What the hell was that?' Noah said.

'She told you I was having an affair; she's trying to split us up. I'm not putting up with that crap in my own hotel.'

'I didn't believe it.'

'That's not the point. Why would she do that? She's an awful woman. She's been rude to me, you told me she was rude to Izzy, and earlier today when Delilah was standing there telling me she was at risk of losing her house, Zoe marched over and tried to charge her for Izzy's breakfast.'

'She's used to running a business, not a charity,' Noah said.

'I'm sorry I'm not more like her,' Aria snapped.

'I don't want you to be like her, I love you just the way you are.'

'And why the hell are you apologising to her? This is all her fault.'

She noticed a flicker of hurt cross his face and she didn't know why. Then it was gone.

'Because she came all the way down here to work for me and we're sending her packing after just a few days. Plus I still have to work with her in my other hotel so it would be good to keep things professional between us, even if you prefer the more childish approach of sacking her because she did something you didn't like.'

'Like telling lies about me and trying to ruin what we have before it's barely started.'

Noah sighed and rubbed his head. 'And what are we going to do now? We have no receptionist to work here, other than two part-time teenagers, who by all accounts will be off the island the first chance they get, and a woman who won't be starting work for several weeks who has zero experience as a receptionist.'

'Those *teenagers* are efficient, friendly to guests and bloody hard workers. And I'd rather have them than have to fear getting stabbed in the back every time I walk away from Zoe. I can't believe you brought her here, how could you possibly think she would be a good fit?'

'You were short of staff; I was just trying to help you. Everything I've done is to help you.'

'She lied to you.'

'Maybe she just misunderstood what she heard. And if you want to talk about lying, what is it you're keeping from me about the festival of light party?'

Aria groaned. 'There are no guests coming. Are you happy now? I thought I could get all of Dad's old friends and regulars to come but not one of them has replied to my emails. No one cares anymore. They would have come for him but not for me.'

His face softened. 'I'm sorry, Aria.'

'And then I felt awful that you had gone to so much trouble for me, to get so much finished and ready in time for the party, and I didn't want to tell you that I'd let you down.'

'You haven't let me down. I'm disappointed for you but not in you.'

They were quiet for a minute and Aria just wanted to step forward and hug him.

'I hate arguing with you,' Noah said. 'It's not a good start for a relationship, is it?'

'You've said that before. Couples argue, Noah, you're deluding yourself if you think they don't.'

'Georgia and I used to fight all the time and our relationship failed spectacularly.'

'Your relationship failed because you didn't even like each other, let alone love each other. The arguing was a by-product of that, not the cause.'

'You think this is healthy?' Noah asked.

'I think it's normal.'

'I'd rather be spending my time talking with you, or walking on the beach with you, which is what I imagined I'd

283

be doing when I retired here. I hate that all this stupid hotel business is getting in our way.'

'You keep saying that too. We're supposed to be a team, in our relationship and in the hotel. You said if this place was going to be a success everyone involved had to be passionate about it, that you didn't want people sticking around out of loyalty. That includes you. How do we have any kind of future together if you're not happy here?'

'I am happy here, why do you not believe that I am?'

'Because I don't trust that you're going to stay,' Aria said, blurting out what was in her heart. 'You want to know why I didn't want to tell my sisters about us? Because part of me thought that it wouldn't last. That you'd leave just like last time.'

He stared at her in shock.

'I left last time because I made a promise to your dad.'

'You also made a promise to me too, so where does that leave us? You broke your promise to me to keep your promise to my dad. And there is a part of me that doesn't trust you not to do it again. You even said that you weren't sure if this was a permanent thing. When we were talking yesterday down on the beach, you said you didn't think it was simple to move here, as if it wasn't going to happen. You've even bought a house in London – that hardly shows commitment, does it? You have a back-up plan for when it all goes wrong.'

'How would you know I've bought a house in London? Zoe said you'd been going through my stuff, and I didn't believe it but how else would you know that?'

'Because *she* told me,' Aria said in exasperation. 'But *you* didn't, did you?'

'That house has nothing to do with you or us.'

'Of course it does. You didn't think you'd be staying here either.'

Noah spun away to look out the window, pushing his hands through his hair. He turned back to face her. 'If you don't trust me, then what the hell are we doing? Why are we even trying?'

'I don't know.' Aria shook her head. 'I thought because I loved you that was all that mattered, but maybe it's not enough.'

There was a knock on the door and Angel poked his head in. 'Sorry to disturb you two, but Noah, Chloe from Starburst Heights is here to see you.'

'Thanks Angel, I'll be right out.'

Angel closed the door and Aria rounded on Noah. 'Starburst Heights? Why are you meeting with them? You explicitly said that you had no intention of selling the hotel to them.'

'Aria—'

'Is this what you've been planning all along?' God, Starburst Heights. She couldn't think of anything worse. 'We're not on the same page about this hotel at all, are we, we never have been.'

'I'm not selling the hotel to Starburst Heights. How could I when I only own twenty-five percent? But there's a part of me that bloody wishes I could.'

Aria stared at him. He didn't want this. He didn't want to be a part of the hotel. And if he wasn't happy here, he'd leave soon enough.

She marched next door to her office, grabbed the cheque Kendra had given her from her desk drawer and then stormed back into his office.

'Here.' She thrust the cheque towards him.

He took it. 'What's this?'

'A cheque for half a million pounds in return for your share of the hotel.'

He stared at it and then stared at her, his eyes wide and full of pain. 'This is what you want?' he asked, quietly.

She wanted to protect herself against getting hurt again, because watching her sisters and her friends grow up and leave the island had hurt, but losing him the year before had been the hardest thing of all and she couldn't go through that again.

'Yes.'

He stared at the cheque again and then placed it on his desk.

'OK. Well, I have this meeting to deal with so if you wouldn't mind.' He gestured to the door, his voice stiff and formal just as it was when he'd first arrived.

Aria hesitated, feeling like she'd just made a terrible mistake. He was everything she ever wanted and she was pushing him away. She had a huge lump of emotion sitting in her chest, she couldn't breathe.

She walked out on shaky legs and Noah followed her out into the lobby to greet his guest.

'Chloe, thank you for coming,' Noah said, shaking the woman's hand. His voice was broken and he cleared his throat.

'No problem at all.'

'Please, come into my office.'

Noah escorted the woman inside without another look in Aria's direction.

God, what had she done?

She turned around and saw Zoe watching her with a smug smile. It was quite clear she had heard at least some of her conversation with Noah.

Aria glanced over to the side of the reception where Skye, Clover, Jesse and Angel were staring at her in shock.

She couldn't stay here, not now. She turned and walked out of the hotel.

Aria hurried down to Kendra's bakery, her heart aching, her mind a swirl of emotion and confusion. By the time she reached there, tears were coursing down her cheeks.

Luckily no one was in there and Kendra was out the back baking. She looked up as she heard the shop door open, a big smile filling her face and then immediately falling off again as she saw Aria was crying.

Kendra opened her arms to her. 'Oh Aria, what happened?'

'Me and Noah just broke up.'

Her godmother enveloped her in a big hug and Aria leaned her head against her, feeling the warmth of someone who loved her unconditionally.

After a while Kendra guided her to a seat at the table, thrust a cup of tea into her hands and sat down opposite her. 'Tell me everything.'

Aria gave her a rundown of her horrible row with Noah.

'Oh Aria,' Kendra said.

'I know, I'm such an idiot.'

'You're not an idiot.'

'He is everything I've ever wanted; I've been in love with this man for years and I've just pushed him away because I didn't trust him to stay.'

'He let you down last year.'

'He was put in an impossible situation.'

'Then you need to learn to forgive him for it, otherwise you're never going to be able to move on.'

'I think my trust issues go a lot further back than last year.

I think being abandoned as a baby led to a lot of issues in my life.'

'I think…' Kendra said carefully. 'You have to rewrite your life experiences to see the good, not the bad. Being abandoned as a baby led to you being raised by two amazing parents, to having two brilliant sisters, and to Jewel Island where you found a home. It led to you working in a hotel and that in turn has helped lots of people: Stephen, Neil, Delilah, Izzy and so many more people on the island. These are all good things that would not have happened had you grown up in a different family, perhaps even in a different country. Working here at the hotel led you to the man of your dreams, maybe you were meant to be here. Noah leaving last year led to you having quality time with your dad and sisters before your dad died. That time would have been very different had Noah been there. That time led your sisters to choose to stay here a bit longer because they enjoyed being here with you, and ultimately they decided to stay here permanently. Maybe that would have been very different had Noah been there throughout all of that. We can't regret the things in our past because they help to define our future.'

Aria remembered Noah saying a very similar thing about his life. *The experiences of my life shaped me into the man I am today. The path I took has led me to here and I don't regret that.*

'Embrace the life you've had, because it has led you to being one of the most amazing, kind and generous people I have ever met.'

Aria smiled slightly.

'Trust has to be earned, it does not appear overnight,' Kendra went on. 'But I think if you move forward being completely honest with each other about everything then you can gain each other's trust again.'

Tears welled in Aria's eyes because of course she had hurt

Noah in this stupid row, she had pushed him away just like everyone else in his life. Would he ever be able to forgive her for that?

'I need to talk to him,' Aria said.

'And I'm sorry for giving you that cheque. I honestly think he's the best thing that has ever happened to you and the hotel.'

'I do too and I need to go and tell him that.'

She stood up, kissed Kendra on the cheek and ran out the bakery.

Noah threw some clothes in his suitcase and looked around the room. His chest ached as he replayed the stupid row he'd had with Aria, trying to pinpoint where it had all gone wrong. He had hurt her spectacularly the year before and if he could do it all again, he would never have left. He'd thought he was doing the right thing at the time but he'd just proven that he couldn't be trusted.

'Are you really going?'

He turned at the voice from the door and saw Skye watching him.

'Isn't this what you want too?'

'Do I want to see my sister heartbroken again? Do I want to see the only man my sister has ever loved walk away from her? Do I want to see her belief in herself that she isn't good enough confirmed? Of course not.'

Noah sighed as he turned back to his suitcase, throwing the last few belongings inside 'This is what she wants. She gave me the cheque to buy me out of the hotel – she doesn't want me here.'

He hated the way his voice broke as he said that.

'Of course she doesn't want that. She got scared that this didn't mean as much to you as it did for her and decided to push you away before you left and she got hurt all over again. She was trying to protect herself, that's all.'

Noah zipped up his case. 'She doesn't trust me, and quite rightly so after what I did last year. But if there's no trust, how do we ever move on from that?'

'By proving to her, every day, every week, that you're here for the long haul. By not running away at the first hurdle.'

Zoe arrived at the doorway. 'The taxi's here.'

Noah nodded and, picking up his suitcase, he walked out the room. He'd asked Angel to book two train tickets for him and Zoe to take them both back to London on the next available train, which was leaving in about thirty minutes.

Skye turned to Zoe. 'I bet you're feeling really proud of yourself right now.'

Zoe shrugged. 'I think this is the best decision Noah has made over the last few days.'

How could this be the best decision? He loved Aria with everything he had. But then men like him didn't get happy endings. His parents hadn't wanted him, neither had any of his foster parents. Why had he ever hoped that Aria would be different?

'What is this, did she hurt your pride when she asked you to go?' Skye said, following him down the stairs. 'Is that what this is?'

Angel was waiting for him at the bottom of the stairs. 'Are you really doing this?'

'Are you happy to stay here and oversee all the renovations for the next few months?' Noah asked.

'Of course but—'

'Just give her whatever she wants,' Noah said as he walked towards the door.

'Running away isn't going to solve this,' Angel said. 'You left her last time without explaining, you need to stay and talk to her, calmly.'

'Give her this.' Noah handed him the cheque. 'We'll sort out some kind of profit share once the hotel is up and running again.'

'Noah, she loves you, and you love her, this doesn't make any sense,' Angel said.

'She needs you,' Skye said.

He walked past Sylvia who was watching the whole thing unfold with wide eyes. God, his chest hurt so much, his throat felt raw. He just needed to get out of here.

He reached the door and then turned back to Angel and Skye. 'And tell her I'm sorry I wasn't enough.'

With that he stepped outside.

CHAPTER TWENTY-TWO

Aria hurried back to the hotel, desperately needing to see Noah to sort all of this out. She ran in through the entrance, nearly tripping over a pale blue suitcase just outside the doors.

Clover was behind reception on the phone and she waved Aria over. But Aria needed to talk to Noah before she did anything else.

His office door was open but she was surprised when she walked in to find Angel sitting behind the desk.

'Oh. Is Noah around?'

Angel stood up. 'Aria, he left.'

'What do you mean, left?'

'I tried to call you, Clover did too.'

'I didn't have my phone with me,' Aria said, in confusion. 'What do you mean, he's left? Where has he gone?'

'Back to London with Zoe.'

'What?' Aria looked around frantically for him as if he might still be here.

'He said you didn't want him here anymore,' Angel said.

'No, no, no, that was a stupid row.'

'You gave him a cheque to buy him out,' Angel said.

'Yes but...' her voice choked. 'I can't believe he left.'

Angel pushed his hand through his hair. 'I told him he needed to stay and talk this through with you.'

'God, I need to talk to him. What's his number?'

Angel grabbed his mobile, found Noah's number and then handed her the phone. She pressed call.

It rang and rang but there was no answer. 'He's not answering.'

'Leave a message,' Angel urged.

It rang a bit longer and anger bubbled up inside of her. How could he have left? Every single abandonment scar was suddenly ripped open. Her biological parents dumping her as a baby, the children of guests she had played with and the guests she had dated when she'd been much younger had all left, most of her childhood friends had grown up and moved away. Her sisters had left as soon as they were old enough. Her mum had died, her dad had too, and although neither of them had left her by choice, it was tantamount to the same thing: she was alone. Finally, it clicked over to the answerphone.

'I can't believe you left,' Aria said. 'We had a stupid fight and I got scared and I'm sorry but you left? Is this what you do in a relationship when the going gets tough? You leave? Why would you not stay and fight instead of calmly walking out the bloody door? We were supposed to be forever and you just gave up on us at the very first hurdle. Even sodding Georgia got more than that and she lied and cheated on you. All your life you've moved around so much that you never knew what it was like to have a home or to be loved. You had that here and you just walked away from it. God, I should have seen this coming. Zoe said you would never stay, that you'd just bought a house in London, but I convinced myself we had something special, that you would stay here for me. But you were just biding your time until you could leave.'

Aria fought back a sob.

'I love you. How could you hold me in your arms and make love to me the way that you did and not feel that too? I know you're scared but running away when things get tough is not the answer. Now you get your arse back here right now and deal with this like a man, not a coward.'

She hung up and, as she passed the phone back to Angel, he nodded towards the door behind her.

Clover, Skye and Jesse were standing in the doorway.

'I'm sorry,' Aria said. 'For all this. I should have consulted you first before giving him the cheque. The hotel is as much yours as it is mine and I've ruined everything.'

'Oh shush,' Skye said. 'The hotel will be fine. We're more concerned about you.'

'I'm sorry I lied.'

'We never should have asked you not to see him,' Clover said. 'That was a crappy thing for us to do.'

'Never mind that now, you need to go after him,' Skye said.

She did. Nothing was going to be resolved by unanswered answerphone messages. She had caused this, she had upset him so much he had left, she needed to fix it.

She turned back to face Angel. 'Where is he now?'

Angel consulted his mobile phone. 'You have just over ten minutes before he catches the train to London.'

'I can take you on my bike,' Jesse said. 'It'll be quicker.'

Aria nodded. 'Let's go.'

They hurried out of the hotel, nearly tripping over the blue suitcase again, and Jesse passed her a helmet. He climbed on his bike and she scrambled on behind him. She looked at her watch; the tide was coming in and the bridge to the island would be closed soon, if it wasn't already.

'Jesse, you need to be quick,' Aria said.

The engine roared into life and Aria wrapped herself around him as the bike shot off. They reached the bridge in less than a minute – the blockade to close the road had already been put across but water was just licking the edges. Jesse didn't even pause as he negotiated around the blockade and tore across the bridge.

Aria shouted out directions to him. The station wasn't too far away but it was far enough for her liking and when they got stuck behind some roadwork traffic lights, she wanted to scream in frustration.

They pulled into the station car park a few minutes later and Aria scrambled down, yanking the helmet off and passing it to Jesse before running into the station. It was small enough that there wouldn't be anyone manning it after five o'clock but the side gate was open so people could get on and off the platforms. She could see the train and could hear it was getting ready to go. She ran onto the platform and ran up the length of the train, trying to see Noah through any of the windows, but there was no sign of him. The train started pulling out and that's when she saw Zoe. Zoe blinked in surprise for a moment at seeing Aria and then flipped her the finger as the train pulled away. Aria didn't even have time to return the gesture, but one thing she was sure of was there had been no sign of Noah sitting next to her.

What was going on? Where was he?

Jesse came running into the station, holding out his phone. 'It's Angel.'

Aria took the phone.

'Aria, he's still here,' Angel said.

'What?'

'His suitcase is still here and Sylvia has just come up to

reception and said she asked Noah to take Snowflake for a walk and he did.'

'He's still there?'

'Yes. I haven't seen him but yes.'

Aria wanted to cry in relief. He hadn't left.

She quickly hung up. 'Jesse—'

'I heard, come on.'

They ran out the station, clambered onto the bike, and were roaring down the road a few moments later.

They arrived back at the bridge but it was completely underwater this time.

'Shit,' Aria said, climbing off the bike after they'd come to a stop. She looked at the bridge, still visible under the clear waves.

'I'm going to go for it,' she said, taking off her shoes.

'I don't think that's a good idea,' Jesse said. 'We just need to wait.'

Aria shook her head. 'It's still two hours to high tide and then we'll have to wait at least another two hours until the water has receded. I can wade and, if necessary, I'm a good swimmer.'

'Look, if you can't get on the island, then Noah can't leave either.'

'But that's four hours that Noah will be thinking I don't want him. I can't not see him for that long, I need to explain.' She tied her dress up in a knot so it hopefully wouldn't get too wet. 'I'll see you in a few hours.'

Jesse smiled. 'Good luck.'

She started wading out as she walked along the bridge. At first the water came only halfway up her calves but the further along the bridge she went, the higher the water level was until it was over her knees and slowly inching up over her thighs. It wasn't exactly flat calm either; the waves weren't too big, but they threatened to knock her over on more than one occasion.

She noticed Clover and Skye on the other side, cheering her on. Clearly, Jesse had phoned through to tell them what was happening and they had come down to meet her. She doggedly made for them.

Finally she reached the other side and Clover wrapped her in a towel. Aria hopped around, putting her shoes back on, gave a wave to Jesse on the other side, then her sisters ushered her to the waiting golf buggy.

'I don't know where he is,' Skye said. 'He hasn't come back to the hotel. Maybe he might be down on Sapphire Bay, or you could try the Golden Lagoon.'

Clover negotiated the buggy back towards the hotel and Aria smiled to herself.

'I know exactly where he is.'

They pulled up outside the entrance and Aria climbed out and hurried off through the gardens, following the paths that were illuminated with the rose gold of the setting sun. Some of the trees were already lit up for the festival of light and up ahead the willow tree was strewn with fairy lights.

She pushed the boughs aside and, sure enough, Noah was standing there, a bored Snowflake lying by his feet. Noah was staring out at the sea through a gap in the branches.

'Noah!' Aria nearly sagged with relief. He was here. He'd never left.

He turned to look at her, a myriad of emotions playing across his face.

'I thought you'd left.'

He shook his head. 'I know that's what you wanted but I couldn't do it. I—'

'I didn't want you to leave, that was the very last thing I wanted. I panicked. What with the house in London, and Zoe saying you'd never stay, and she's known you longer than me. Then when you said you wished you could sell the hotel I got scared I was going to lose you again. It was a pre-emptive strike. I'm so sorry.'

He stared at her. 'You don't want me to go?'

'No.'

He let out a heavy breath. 'I thought it was happening all over again. My mum and dad didn't want me, I was moved on from every foster home I was placed in. I'm used to rejection and I thought...' he shook his head. 'I thought you'd had enough of me too.'

'A lifetime with you would never be enough.'

He smiled and then opened his arms. She stepped up to his chest and he wrapped her in a big hug. Oh god, they were going to be OK. Tears welled in her eyes. He tilted her chin so she was looking up at him.

'Aria, when I said I wished I could sell my part of the hotel, I purely meant because I just wanted to be with you with none of the interruptions and stress. And the house in London is for my brother, Charlie. I'm in a fortunate enough position that I can help him, so I bought a house for him and his family.'

'Oh god Noah, Zoe made it sound like the house was for you.'

'I think she manipulated us both. But you should have talked to me about this.'

'Well, I did,' Aria said, although the middle of an argument had perhaps not been the ideal time to discuss her concerns. 'I probably should have done it under calmer circumstances.'

Noah nodded. 'If this is going to work, we have to be honest with each other.'

'I know, I'm sorry.'

'I'm the one who should be sorry. I betrayed your trust last year and you have no reason to believe in me. But if you let me I will spend every damned day for the rest of my life trying to prove to you that I'm in this for good, that you are my forever.'

'And I believe you. You did a wonderful thing for my dad and for all of us, I can't hate you for that.'

'For you, Aria, I did it for you.'

She leaned up and kissed him, smiling against his lips.

She pulled back. 'Why didn't you leave?'

'Because Sylvia grabbed me and asked me to walk Snowflake,' Noah said and Aria laughed. 'And because Skye and Angel both told me I was being a complete idiot. But most importantly because I love you.'

Aria gasped as tears welled up in her eyes.

'I told you back there, in my office, but you were too busy shouting at me to hear it.'

'You did not, I would have noticed that.'

'Are we going to argue about that too? I said, I love you just the way you are.'

'Oh my god.' He had said that.

He stroked her face. 'I love you, Aria Philips. I think I always have.'

'I love you too. God, Noah, you are everything to me.'

He smiled and kissed her, and she let out a sigh of relief against his lips as he gathered her close against him.

She eventually pulled back. 'So what happens now?'

'A number of things. I'm not going to take that cheque; you can tell Kendra thanks but no thanks. As you pointed out back there, we're a team, through all the highs and lows.'

Aria nodded. 'I know sometimes we'll fight, but you show me one relationship where a couple never fights. It's because we both care that we do fight. The important thing is that we don't let it come between us.'

'Agreed. There will never be a perfect time to have a relationship, it will never be smooth sailing. But I'd sail the wildest seas for you.'

She smiled. 'I like that.'

'Secondly, we're going to fulfil your dreams together, because your dreams are my dreams and I want to help you achieve them. I know you want to have children and I can't wait to raise a family with you,' he said, resting a hand on her belly.

She smiled. 'I love the thought of carrying your baby, but my dream was always that one day I would adopt a child, give a loving home to someone who needs it, just like my parents did for me. I always thought I would adopt a baby but, after talking to you, I know now I want to adopt a child. Babies will always find a home. But it's the older children who need it more and I'd like to adopt one of them, show them what it means to be truly loved.'

Noah stared at her. 'Jesus, Aria, I didn't think it was possible to love you more than I did but I think you just topped that.'

She smiled and leaned up and kissed him. 'Doesn't mean we can't have children of our own too. I always wanted a big family. Sisters are important.'

'They are, every child needs a big sister to protect them. But brothers are important too.'

She nodded. 'We'll have two or three of each. Is there a thirdly?'

'Yes, we're going to find out how good make-up sex is.'

He kissed her and shuffled her back against the tree.

She laughed. 'Here? It's not very professional.'

'I don't care.'

And as he kissed her, she found that neither did she.

EPILOGUE

Aria looked around the reception area as the staff bustled about doing last-minute preparations for the festival of light party in a few hours. The blue carpet had finished being laid the day before and it looked smart but cosy and welcoming at the same time. The whole of the lobby area looked amazing. Mira the florist had been working there right up until that morning, pinning swathes of chiffon and satin across the ceilings and walls. Lights twinkled amongst the folds and blooms of hundreds of different flowers that she'd displayed in arrangements or garlands across the room. It was so magical; Aria was tempted to keep it this way all the time. She wondered what Noah would say about that.

He was standing near the display boards with Angel, putting the last finishing touches to the renovation plan for the guests and the villagers to look at. Aria smiled as they bickered over where to put a photo.

Noah had been a lot more relaxed in the last week; there hadn't been the mad panic to get everything finished as there had been before. It also felt like Aria had more of a say with regards to the changes – Noah would suggest things and they would discuss them together, the four of them. It had definitely felt more like an equal partnership rather than Noah being their boss, which Skye had said it'd felt like before.

Noah and Aria's relationship had also blossomed. Now there was no need to hide it, they could relax and just be together. Of course, they weren't kissing each other in front of guests, but there was no sneaking around anymore, which was a big relief.

Skye and Clover had taken their relationship surprisingly well, especially considering they had banned her from getting together with him only two weeks before. Skye had said they'd had no right to tell her who she could and couldn't date, and Clover was just pleased to see Aria so loved-up and happy. She had even started talking about their wedding being the first in the hotel. It seemed very early for that kind of talk but, at the same time, Aria knew what she and Noah had was forever.

She walked over to the board and slipped her hand into Noah's. He turned to look at her, his face breaking into a huge smile as he bent down and gave her a brief kiss.

'This looks great,' Aria said, admiring the display. Izzy had done a wonderful job with her drawings and, coupled with the photos Noah had taken of all the newly decorated rooms, it was a great demonstration of what was to come. Noah's team had managed to complete eight bedrooms with brand-new bathrooms, and a further fifteen bedrooms that still needed to have their bathrooms replaced. There was still a ton of work to do but already the hotel was starting to shine, as if emerging from a long sleep.

Thanks to Angel's advertising, they had secured twelve bookings for that weekend, coupled with the six bloggers and journalists that Noah had organised and four rooms that had been booked by the villagers who wanted to support the hotel. It was a great start and Aria was hopeful that some of the guests might rebook for the grand opening in the summer. The bloggers seemed impressed with what they had seen so far when they had arrived earlier that day so she was confident that the coverage in newspapers and social media was going to be good.

'I think we're nearly done,' Noah said, scanning the boards.

'But Angel is right, that photo looks better there,' Aria said.

Noah's smile fell from his face as Angel let out a bark of laughter. Noah begrudgingly handed the photo to Angel to place on the board. Angel winked at Aria as she turned and walked away.

She made her way into the dining room to check that Skye had everything ready for her dessert station. The drinks and nibbles were going to be in the lobby area to encourage people to look at the display boards, but after the fireworks the desserts were going to be served in the dining room. They had discussed having it in the ice cream shack but, despite Jesse and a few others working their arses off, it wasn't quite finished yet and Skye had decided she would prefer people to see it when it was completely finished.

There were several different-flavoured soft whip ice cream machines along one table, with festival-of-light-themed flavours, such as Sunshine, which was banana and pineapple; Moonlight, which was blueberry and marshmallow; and Firework Fancy which seemed to be a celebration of a whole cacophony of flavours. There were bowls of every possible topping, from chocolate buttons, to Smarties, to tiny jelly bears, and Aria knew that chilling in the fridges in the kitchen were a load of other wild and wacky desserts. There were lights strewn from the ceiling in here too and out on the terrace where everyone would be watching the fireworks.

Aria moved over to the kitchen to talk to Skye, who was undoubtedly doing last-minute preparations too, but through the windows of the kitchen door she spotted Skye and Jesse kissing. She smiled. She knew Jesse was due to go home in the next few days so they were no doubt making the most of the time they had left. She decided to leave them to it. She was confident that her sister had everything under control.

She walked back into the reception area just as a young couple with a little girl arrived at the reception desk. Xena was busy helping Jeremy shift one of the sofas so Aria moved over to check the couple in just as Noah did the same.

'Checking in?' Aria said, looking behind the desk to find their check-in card.

'Yes we are, just for one night,' said the man.

'OK, lovely, you've come for the festival of light?'

'Yes we have. This one is beyond excited,' the woman said, gesturing to the girl with them.

Aria smiled at the little girl and then turned her attention back to the couple. The festival was going to start shortly and they would need to leave soon to go and watch it. 'What name is your booking under?'

'Is it under yours or mine?' the woman asked the man.

'Mine, Mr and Mrs Jacob Harrington.'

The woman laughed. 'We're not married yet.'

'But we will be soon. It was easier to put it under one name and I kind of liked the sound of it,' Jacob said.

The woman smiled. 'I'm Ruby Marlowe, Cal's sister. This is Lottie's daughter, Poppy. She will be staying with them for the rest of their honeymoon.'

'Ah, let me ring up to their suite and let them know you're here,' Noah said, picking up the phone, while Aria found their check-in card and handed it over to them to sign.

'This place is beautiful,' Ruby said, while Jacob filled the card in. 'I love what you've done with the lights and flowers. We could get married here.'

'We could if you would actually pick a bloody date,' Jacob said, signing the card with a flourish.

'Well, it has to be Christmas time.'

'Obviously.'

'But not so it will interfere with my shop, December is the busiest month. Maybe Christmas Eve, so I could wake up married to you on Christmas Day.'

'That sounds good,' Jacob smiled. 'Now let's book it before you change your mind.'

Ruby laughed.

Clover had arrived at reception at that point. 'We will be offering weddings here later on in the year. If you want to come and find me tomorrow, I could show you around and talk through with you the kind of things we could offer. No pressure, but it might just give you a few ideas.'

Ruby and Jacob exchanged glances and they both nodded. 'That would be lovely, thank you,' Ruby said.

Noah put the phone down. 'Cal and Lottie are on their way down. I'm not sure where you intend to watch the parade but my assistant Angel could give you a lift to the start and then you can follow the procession back to the hotel where we will be having drinks, nibbles and a fabulous dessert station and a firework display too. Or you can join a few of us who will be watching the parade as it enters the hotel grounds near Emerald Cove – not so much walking and hills to climb.'

'Let me see what Poppy wants to do,' Jacob said, kneeling down and then signing to her.

Aria watched the conversation the two of them were having, the little girl's hands flying at a hundred miles an hour.

Jacob stood back up. 'Yeah, a lift to the start would be great, Poppy's keen to be a part of the procession.'

'Well, if you want to drop your stuff in your room, you'll need to leave shortly. Come back here when you're ready and Angel can take you down,' Aria said.

Noah knelt down and Aria watched as he very carefully signed something to Poppy. Her face lit up as she started signing back. Aria's heart filled with love for Noah. He was an incredible man.

He stood back up.

'Thank you,' Jacob said. 'It always means a lot to her when strangers communicate with her in sign language too.'

'My pleasure,' Noah said.

Jacob, Ruby and Poppy moved off towards the lift and, when the doors opened, there was much hugging and kissing from Cal and Lottie as they were reunited with their daughter and their family.

'You can sign?' Aria said.

'A little, I picked up a few things over the years.'

She smiled and hugged him. 'I'm completely and utterly in love with you, Noah Campbell.'

'I love you too.'

She leaned her head against his chest as she glanced over at Angel and Clover talking. Angel swept a lock of hair from Clover's face and Clover smiled up at him.

'Those two are getting close,' Noah said.

'Yes, I've noticed that over the last week or so too.'

'Want me to beat him up for you?'

Aria laughed. 'I don't think that's necessary. Angel seems like a decent bloke.'

'He is.'

'Besides, despite the little looks between them and the flirting, I don't think anything will happen. Clover was hurt badly by her last boyfriend and she hasn't let anyone get close to her ever since.'

'Did he break her heart?' Noah asked.

'No, much worse than that. But it's safe to say she has trust issues when it comes to men. It's nice to see her relaxed enough to flirt and laugh with Angel but I think it will take a special kind of man to break down her walls.'

'Maybe Angel could be that man for her.'

'Maybe. I hope so. She needs someone nice for a change,' Aria said.

'Right, I better go and check in with the fireworks display team, make sure everything is OK. I'll meet you near Emerald Cove in a while.'

'OK.' She reached up and gave him a brief kiss and he hurried off.

She looked around. Everything was ready. Now all she had to do was get changed into her favourite dress.

~

Aria walked through the gardens towards Emerald Cove, the lights on the trees illuminating the path through the flowers and bushes. Stephen had done a wonderful job – it looked spectacular and the perfect place to end the parade.

Up ahead, on the headland, she could see Noah waiting for her. There were lanterns lit with candles forging a path across the headland and she walked between them towards the man she loved.

He turned and smiled as she approached and held out his arms for her. She stepped straight up and leaned her head against his chest as he wrapped his arms around her.

'The parade has started,' Noah said, gesturing to a trail of lights as it snaked its way across the island towards them. They were too far away to see the details of the lanterns yet but it didn't look any less magical.

'It looks beautiful,' Aria said.

He stared down at her. 'So do you. You're wearing my favourite dress,' Noah said.

'If you're good later, I'll let you wear it.'

Noah laughed. 'Kissing you in this dress was the start of something spectacular.'

'Our new beginning starts here. The Sapphire Bay Hotel, us, our children, our happy ever after.'

'I like the sound of that. I rushed into my last marriage for all the wrong reasons and I don't want to rush this, but I know I'll be asking you to marry me soon.'

'And I'll say yes. When you're ready.'

He smiled and then nodded behind her. She turned and saw some of the other hotel staff and a few guests coming out to watch the parade. Skye was with Jesse, Clover and Angel were talking together, Sylvia, Delilah, Izzy, Xena, Katy and Jeremy, Tilly and her husband Ben and a few others followed closely behind. They all came to stand next to her and Noah as the parade drew nearer. Aria could pick out the silhouettes of people now and the lanterns were starting to take shape.

Sylvia came and stood next to her. 'This looks amazing, I've never been here for this before. I'll be going home tomorrow, but I'm glad I stayed to see the parade.'

'Well we look forward to welcoming you back again soon. Did you get everything you came for?'

Sylvia smirked at the two of them still holding each other. 'I certainly did. Don't worry, all names will be changed to protect your identity.'

Aria laughed. She glanced over at Delilah and Izzy standing close together, their eyes lit up with the lanterns that were almost upon them. She eased out of Noah's arms and went over to talk to them.

Delilah smiled at her as she approached and gave her a hug.

'How are you feeling?' Aria asked.

'Good, thanks. Rested. The money you gave us paid off all our debts and has given us some breathing space until I come back to work. And there was a bit left over for me and Izzy to go on a short spa break tomorrow, just for two nights, but there will be massages and lots of rest and relaxation.'

'Sounds perfect,' Aria said.

'And then maybe next week, I could do a few hours here, ease myself in gently?'

'Whenever you feel ready. We'd be happy to have you here, even if it's only one day a week to start with.'

'Thank you.'

'And thank you for loaning me your daughter. The renovation presentation is looking spectacular, Izzy. You've worked so hard on it and it will really help us to show off the Sapphire Bay Hotel and all the changes that are coming.'

'I really enjoyed doing it,' Izzy said. 'Angel said he might get me to paint some murals in the pool room when it's ready and Skye has said there's some pictures she'd like painted in her dessert café.'

'Seems like we'll have lots to keep you busy,' Aria said.

Just then the first lantern appeared over the crest of the hill. A huge whale carried by maybe ten people, all made from some kind of waxed paper stretched over a wire frame with lights inside. It looked spectacular. A load of schoolchildren followed the whale with little fish lanterns they were each carrying. Aria watched an elephant go past, followed by a huge pirate ship with sails and an octopus with its eight legs dancing in time to the music. It really was a wonderful sight to see. As a large teapot floated serenely past with what looked like steam coming out the spout, Skye and Clover came to stand either side of her.

She looped her arms around them and they leaned into her.

'I'm so glad you two stayed,' Aria said.

'We're glad too,' Skye said. 'It's wonderful to be working together as a family again.'

They were quiet for a while as they watched the lanterns drift past.

'What's your something positive, Skye?' Clover asked.

'I'm excited about the desserts I've created for tonight, I think they'll be a big hit with all our guests. And the shack is really coming along, I can't wait for it to be finished.'

A large owl with eyes that moved floated past them.

'And Clover, what's yours?'

'Well the dance studio is nearly finished too and I think just being here with you guys, it's all worked out perfectly.'

'And do you have another positive?' Skye said, her eyebrows waggling mischievously.

Even in the darkness, Aria could see Clover blush.

'Angel's nice,' Clover said, carefully.

'You two do seem to have got a lot closer in the last week,' Aria said.

'He asked me out on a date earlier,' Clover said.

'Oh my god, that's—' Aria started.

'I said no,' Clover said. 'I told him I was very tempted because he was just so lovely but that I wasn't ready for a relationship yet.'

'What did he say?' Skye asked.

Clover's smile stretched across her face. 'He said to let him know when I was ready. He said he wasn't in any rush and that I was the sort of woman that was definitely worth waiting for. And then we hugged and it was just... perfect.'

'Well, that sounds like a really big positive if you ask me,' Skye said.

Aria smiled. Angel really was one of the good guys.

'What's your positive, Aria?' Clover asked.

Aria glanced over to Noah who was busily chatting with Angel. Almost as if he could feel her eyes on him, Noah looked up and smiled at her.

'Him. I don't think I have ever been so utterly happy in my life as I am right now. He's my missing piece.'

If you enjoyed *Sunrise over Sapphire Bay*, you'll love my next gorgeously romantic story, *Autumn Skies over Ruby Falls*, out in September.

STAY IN TOUCH...

To keep up to date with the latest news on my releases, just go to the link below to sign up for a newsletter. You'll also get two FREE short stories, get sneak peeks, booky news and be able to take part in exclusive giveaways. Your email will never be shared with anyone else and you can unsubscribe at any time
https://www.subscribepage.com/hollymartinsignup

Website: https://hollymartin-author.com/
Email: holly@hollymartin-author.com
Twitter: @HollyMAuthor

ALSO BY HOLLY MARTIN

Sunrise over Sapphire Bay
The Summer of Chasing Dreams

The Happiness Series
The Little Village of Happiness
The Gift of Happiness

Sandcastle Bay Series
The Holiday Cottage by the Sea
The Cottage on Sunshine Beach
Coming Home to Maple Cottage

Hope Island Series
Spring at Blueberry Bay
Summer at Buttercup Beach
Christmas at Mistletoe Cove

Juniper Island Series
Christmas Under a Cranberry Sky

A Town Called Christmas

≈

White Cliff Bay Series
Christmas at Lilac Cottage
Snowflakes on Silver Cove
Summer at Rose Island

≈

Standalone Stories
Fairytale Beginnings
Tied Up With Love
A Home on Bramble Hill
One Hundred Christmas Proposals
One Hundred Proposals
The Guestbook at Willow Cottage

≈

For Young Adults
The Sentinel Series
The Sentinel (Book 1 of the Sentinel Series)
The Prophecies (Book 2 of the Sentinel Series)
The Revenge (Book 3 of the Sentinel Series)
The Reckoning (Book 4 of the Sentinel Series)

A LETTER FROM HOLLY

Thank you so much for reading *Sunrise over Sapphire Bay*, I had so much fun creating this story and the beautiful Jewel Island. I hope you enjoyed reading it as much as I enjoyed writing it.

One of the best parts of writing comes from seeing the reaction from readers. Did it make you smile or laugh, did it make you cry, hopefully happy tears? Did you fall in love with Aria and Noah as much as I did? Did you like the gorgeous little Jewel Island? If you enjoyed the story, I would absolutely love it if you could leave a short review on Amazon. Getting feedback from readers is amazing and it also helps to persuade other readers to pick up one of my books for the first time.

My next book, out in September, is called *Autumn Skies over Ruby Falls.* It's the second book in the Jewel Island Series.

Thank you for reading.

Love Holly xx

ACKNOWLEDGEMENTS

To my family, my mom, my biggest fan, who reads every word I've written a hundred times over and loves it every single time, my dad, my brother Lee and my sister-in-law Julie, for your support, love, encouragement and endless excitement for my stories.

For my twinnie, the gorgeous Aven Ellis for just being my wonderful friend, for your endless support, for cheering me on, for reading my stories and telling me what works and what doesn't and for keeping me entertained with wonderful stories. I love you dearly.

To my lovely friends Julie, Natalie, Jac, Verity and Jodie, thanks for all the support.

To the Devon contingent, Paw and Order, Belinda, Lisa, Phil, Bodie, Kodi and Skipper. Thanks for keeping me entertained and always being there.

For Sharon Sant for just being there always and your wonderful friendship.

To everyone at Bookcamp, you gorgeous, fabulous bunch, thank you for your wonderful support on this venture.

Thanks to the brilliant Emma Rogers for the gorgeous cover design.

Thanks to my fabulous editors, Celine Kelly and Rhian McKay.

To all the wonderful bloggers for your tweets, retweets, facebook posts, tireless promotions, support, encouragement and endless enthusiasm. You guys are amazing and I couldn't do this journey without you.

To anyone who has read my book and taken the time to tell me you've enjoyed it or wrote a review, thank you so much.

Thank you, I love you all.

ISBN 978-1-913616-04-5

Cover design by Emma Rogers

Printed in Great Britain
by Amazon